A

Whisper Away

A Novel

By

Mike Axsom

D1519922

This book is a work of fiction. Names, characters, places, and incidents are either products of the author's imagination or are used factiously. Any resemblances to actual events are locales or persons, living or dead are entirely coincidental.

The scanning, uploading, and distribution of this book via the internet or via any other means without the permission of the publisher is illegal and punishable by law. Please purchase only authorized electronic editions, and do not participate in or encourage piracy of copyrighted materials. Your support of the author's rights is appreciated.

Inquires about bulk orders or to book appearances/ book signings by the author please contact the author himself at _____ or email mike.axsom@yahoo.com

This novel is dedicated to my mother, Sadie,

my sister, Linda,

and my niece, Kelsey Corns

Introduction

Just two weeks after marrying her childhood sweetheart, Ellen Mackay received a mysterious letter from her husband alluding to a secret Army mission. When he doesn't return, Ellen spends the next decade holding out hope for his safe return and taking care of her young son. At the same time, Logan Mackay is trying to recover from injuries sustained from the mission, including memory loss, as he looks to rebuild his life under an adoptive name. Ellen's passion for finding Logan is the embodiment of love and faithfulness. Over her lengthy quest to find her soulmate, she clings to what Logan wrote in the letter he sent her years before. "Wherever you go, and wherever you may be, I will only be a whisper away."

Chapter 1

It was a misty early morning in the mountains of North Vietnam in 1966 as Logan lay in the wet grass that loomed about a foot high above his head. As the dense fog began to lift he realized that he was at a small opening near a field, but was otherwise confused about his surroundings. He could hear a whirring sound in the distance. The treetops began to swirl from the high winds created by a green Red Cross helicopter that seemingly appeared out of nowhere.

The helicopter initially hovered over the small opening, lingering about 30 yards from Logan's location before landing. Two young men reached out, grabbed him by the arms and rushed him towards the helicopter. The soldiers pulled him inside. As the helicopter began to lift, Logan heard a flurry of gunfire. The helicopter churned in its pursuit of a safe zone. Logan took a look around at the soldiers who had helped him into the helicopter, each with a look of astonishment that he would never forget.

Logan then looked down at himself. All he had on was some type of coarse cloth wrapped around his waist, working its way to his backside before coming up between his legs where it was tucked in front of his stomach. Logan could not tell his own nationality; he looked like someone who had been swimming in a mud hole.

His beard touched the top of his chest. His hair rested on his shoulders with entanglements akin to someone who had never bathed. As he looked down at himself he could count the ribs running down each side of his chest. Logan could only view the left side of his nose, realizing that he could not see out of his right eye. He looked back at the soldiers, noticing that one of them was staring at his left hand. He started to feel faint as he glanced down. His hand was resting on his knees as he sat in a squatting position. The thumb was missing, with a portion of skin still clinging. It had turned brown. It had obviously been that way for a long time. A portion of his index finger was missing down to the first joint.

As he gazed back at the soldiers, Logan could see that one of the men had begun to tear up. The soldier crawled over and sat down beside Logan, putting his arm around his shoulders.

"Don't worry soldier," the savior said. "We're taking you home."

The next thing Logan remembered was a woman's soft voice. "Soldier, soldier, soldier. Can you hear me?"

Logan managed to open his left eye to look at her.

"Can you hear me and understand what I'm saying?" the woman asked. "If you can, just blink your eye."

Logan responded.

"Well, it's about time soldier," she said. "I am glad to see you finally come around. I'm going to get Dr. Stillman. He'll be glad that you have finally woken up. Don't go back to sleep. I'll be back in a few minutes."

As the nurse left the room, Logan began to look round. Without moving his head, Logan knew he was in a hospital, but he had no idea how long he had been there. The last thing he remembered was being pulled into the helicopter and the two soldiers looking at him with puzzled looks on their faces. All else was a blur.

The nurse returned to the room, accompanied by Dr. Stillman. The doctor was tall and slender with a thin mustache. He held a clipboard as he approached the bed before sliding a small stool over to make sure Logan could hear him.

"Well, young man, just to let you know you're at Walter Reed Hospital," the doctor said in a calm, assuring voice. "I'm glad to see you're awake – not that you didn't need sleep. You look a lot better today than you did four days ago. Of course, the haircut, shave and bath helped tremendously."

The doctor smiled as he introduced himself.

"I'll be your physician as long as you're here," Stillman said. "Do you understand what I'm saying?"

Logan quietly responded with a nod.

"Let me give you an update on what has taken place with you the last few days," the physician continued. "Your right eye was half out of the socket when you arrived. I had to perform some slight surgery to put it back in place. The cornea – the clear front part of the eyeball – has some damage. When you're feeling better, I'll go over it with you in greater detail."

Logan took a deep breath, processing the information.

"I also had to work on your left hand," the doctor said. "Right now, I just want you to get your rest and do what Nurse Noble asks of you."

Silently, Logan mouthed his appreciation.

"You're welcome, soldier," Stillman replied. "I'll check on you as I make my rounds this morning. As you get to feeling better – in a week or two – we'll have more discussions. I have a lot of questions that need answers, and I'm sure you have a lot for me as well. For now, just listen to the nurse. I'll see you later."

Dr. Stillman made a few notations in his clipboard as he stood up, handing the chart to the nurse before leaving the room. Nurse Noble walked over and examined the needles in Logan's arms, making sure they were secure while checking the fluid levels.

She walked closer to Logan, putting her hand on his shoulder.

"I think you have one of the best doctors in this hospital caring for you," she declared. "As far as I'm concerned, he's the best. So get your rest and I'll be back to check on you within an hour."

Logan appreciated Nurse Noble's professional manner. She was distinguished looking and poised, and seemed to be in her mid-50s.

Logan burrowed his head into the pillow, though that lasted only a few seconds before he sat straight up in bed. He ran his hand over his head.

What hair he had was wet, as if he had been under a shower. About that time, a nurse turned the light on and ran to his side.

"Are you okay soldier?" a lady's voice said.

Logan put both hands over his eyes as though they were pained by the light. The nurse rushed to turn the switch off. He kept his eyes covered as she returned to his side.

"It's okay now," she assured, gently putting her hands over his. "It's okay, you're in the hospital, remember? You're at Walter Reed Hospital."

She convinced Logan to lower his hands. As he opened his left eye, Logan could make out the outline of a young woman kneeling in front of him, still holding his hands. "Did you have a bad dream soldier?"

He simply nodded as he tried to focus his sight on the nurse attending to him. "Would you like a glass of cold water?"

"Yes, that ... that would be fine," Logan managed to stammer, uttering his first words since being admitted to the hospital. "Thank you."

The nurse acted surprised. She had been working the third shift since Logan had arrived, mostly witnessing the soldier sleep during his stay.

As Logan took a sip of the cool water, the nurse walked over and turned on a small lamp that was sitting in a corner of the room.

She looked back to see that Logan had turned sideways with his legs hanging off the side of the bed.

"You must have had a bad dream," she said.

"I've been having this dream for a long time," Logan said. "I just can't figure it out." "Well, I assure you that you're not the only soldier here that has bad dreams," the nurse replied in a calming tone.

"God only knows what some of these soldiers have been through. Would you like to tell me about it? No, not right now? If it's a little weird, then maybe some other time. I'll be here when you are ready to talk about it. People tell me I'm a good listener."

The nurse paused.

"By the way, my name is Terry Warner," she added. "You can call me Ms. Warner, or nurse, either one is fine with me. I work the night shift and I'll be checking in on you from time to time. If you need anything just press that button and I will be here in minutes."

She took the clipboard from the foot of the bed.

"The chart says you're a John Doe," she said, waiting for a reaction.

Logan looked at her with a puzzled look. He opened his mouth, but hesitated as though he wanted to say something, but was unsure what it might be. "I ... I ..." he stammered again, this time with a shocked look on his face. "I can't remember."

"You can't remember your name?" the nurse asked.

"Not right now," he said. "But when it comes to me I will give it to you."

"Can you tell me what branch of service you were in?" Nurse Warner persisted. "Army? Navy? Air Force?"

Logan looked at her again without saying a word. "I can't remember being in any branch of service," he said.

"Do you know where you have been for the last year or so?"

"The only thing I can really remember right now is running toward the helicopter, and seeing the look on those soldiers face when they first looked at me," Logan said.

"Well, I'm sure it will all come back to you," the nurse said. "It's just going to take some time, but for right now our job is to make sure you get some meat on your bones and to see to it that your hand and eye heal properly. Just lie back down and get some rest."

As Logan returned to his pillow, Nurse Warner noticed something on the side of his leg.

"That's an interesting tattoo you have on your leg, soldier."

Logan looked down to see a perfectly shaped four leaf clover on his right calf. He strained to take a closer look. It wasn't a tattoo. Rather, it was a birthmark shaped like a shamrock.

"Isn't that interesting?" the nurse remarked. "Kind of like having a free tattoo. Go ahead and try to get some sleep. I'll leave the lamp on just in case you wake up again and need some light."

She left the room.

Two days later, Logan was already up and had eaten breakfast when Dr. Stillman walked in.

"Well, good morning soldier," the doctor said. "I see you're up and ready to go."

"I'd like to, Doc, but I don't know where I would be going," Logan said.

"I understand you only remember getting on that helicopter. Is that right?"

"For now, Doc."

"And you don't remember anything before then," Dr. Stillman inquired.

"That's all I can remember," Logan said. "It's like I have it right on the tip of my tongue, but it just won't come to me. It's frustrating as hell."

"I'm sure it is associated with your injuries," said the doctor. "Lord knows what other trauma you must've gone through. We'll work on getting your memory back, though it's going to take some time. For now, we're going to see what we can do about your eye and hand, and we'll get some weight back on you"

Dr. Stillman turned his attention to Logan's eye.

"We need to talk about your eye for a minute," the doctor said, pointing above the socket. "There are glands under the eyelid that produce tears and keep your eyes lubricated. There's a drainage channel that lets the tears flow out of the eye into the nasal passages. Unfortunately, yours have long-term damage.

Dr. Stillwell paused so Logan could take it in.

"Your eye isn't producing the lubrication it needs. Until we can fix it, you'll need to wear an eyepatch, and your eye must be lubricated at least three times a day, or it could get infected."

The doctor reached for Logan's left hand.

"The good news is that your hand is doing fine," Dr. Stillwell said. "I think by the time we finish, and it heals completely, that you'll be able to make a fist for gripping. I also put some padding in the palm of your hand to help you hold certain things after it heals. Our next order of business will involve working on your memory bank, but for now just eat well and listen to the nurses. I'll be back to check on you in the next couple of days. Do you have any questions?"

"Not at this time Doc," Logan said, attempting to process all he had been told. "Thank you for all you've done for me."

"No, let me thank you for all you've done for this country," the doctor said as he was leaving. "Just hang in there."

Nurse Noble walked over and handed Logan a couple of pills and a glass of water.

"Take these," the nurse said. "They will help you relax and get some sleep."

It was nearly 11 in the morning when Nurse Warner walked into Logan's room. She always arrived in an upbeat, friendly mood, wearing a big smile. She was petite; maybe a shade over five feet tall, with light sandy colored hair that ran halfway down her back.

Logan was sitting up on the side of the bed.

"Did you have another nightmare," Nurse Warner asked as she reviewed Logan's chart.

"No ma'am. I was just sitting here wondering if there's a family out there looking for me," the patient said. "I'm curious about how long have I been gone, and why I can't think of my name. If I could just remember who I am, maybe this could all come to an end."

Logan paused.

"Maybe I could get on with my life."

"I'm sure it will all come to you," Nurse Warner said, walking over to his side. "You're just going to have to give it time."

As she looked up from the chart, the nurse could see Logan's pain and frustration as he tried in vain to figure it all out.

"John, you need to relax." Before she could finish her words, Logan turned and gave her a puzzled looked. "I'm sorry, but your chart has John Doe. I wasn't thinking."

"That's okay, John is fine, until I think of my own name."

"Your chart says your eye and hand are about 90% healed up and that you've put on about 13 pounds. That's good, and you've started to get a little color in your face. The doctor wants to start your therapy this week, which will give you an opportunity to get out of this room and start walking around some. It's time you got out of here, John."

"Well, I'm ready to start," Logan said, pausing for a moment. "I need to find out who I am before it drives me crazy."

"I know it will all come back to you, so don't worry about it," the nurse said as she walked over to take Logan's temperature. "Let's get you well first, and then we can concentrate on who you are. Would you like to take something that will make you rest?"

"No, I think I'm just going to sit here for a while. I've been in bed too long."

"That's fine," Nurse Warner replied. "I'll be coming around about every 45 minutes to check on you. Is there anything I can get you?"

"No, I'm okay for now, Ms. Warner," the patient said.

As Nurse Warner walked out of the room, she looked back at Logan. He had his back turned to her with his shoulders slumped down as he looked down at the floor. She knew he was suffering from a pain that she could not relieve.

Chapter 2

"Hi sweetie. I only have time for a few lines because I have been assigned a top secret mission. I will be leaving in a few minutes and I can't say how long it will take. All I know is it's a one-man show, and I'm the man. For security reasons, do not show this letter to anyone. Just know that I will be back as soon as possible, and I love you with all my heart. And remember wherever you go, and wherever you may be, I will only be a whisper away. And I'll be thinking of you with every breath I take. Tell mom I said hello and that I love her.

P.S. Ellen, just know I will be back, trust me.

Logan

Ellen carefully folded the letter and placed it back into the envelope that had been taped up many times along the creases; necessary repairs after it had been folded and unfolded so many times. She looked up at Debra after reading the letter as tears ran down her face.

"You are the first person that I have ever read this letter to," Ellen told her friend between sobs. "I read it every night before going to bed because it makes me feel close to him. I know he'll be back someday, and I'm going to be waiting until he does."

Debra, a tall and striking woman with long dark hair, placed her hand on Ellen's shoulder.

"I know it's got to be hard on you," Debra said. "By God, you've been with him since the first grade…"

"If it wasn't for Little Logan," Ellen interrupted. "I don't think I could make it. That little guy seems to be the only thing keeping me together. He looks more like his father the older he gets. I don't know what I would do without him and college."

"How are you doing with your studies?" Debra asked.

"Growing up helping dad at the drugstore has helped a lot with my grades," Ellen replied. "You always said you were going be a pharmacist," Debra said. "I think you're going to make a good one.

"Little Logan and pharmaceutical school are helping me keep my head straight."

"When do classes start again?"

"I have another week and a half," Ellen said with a sigh. "Mom and dad are going to drive me back up to Boston."

"I've got one more week before I head back to Carolina," Debra said. "You let me know when you come back home, and we'll spend some more time together."

At that time, the door opened and Alice Garrison, Ellen's mother, entered the room holding Little Logan.

"He is an arm full," Ms. Garrison said, walking over to hand the infant to Debra.

"Let me hold him just for a little bit before I leave," Debra said as she gazed at the child.

Little Logan had on short pants that revealed a curious mark on his tiny left calve.

"Look at that," Debra remarked. "He has a little birth mark on his leg, just like his daddy. Can you believe that?"

Ellen burst out laughing. "I told you he was just like his daddy."

"Yes, but you didn't say the resemblance went right down to that birthmark," Debra said. "That's amazing."

Ellen had a big smile on her face as Debra handed Little Logan over to her, though you could detect a hint of sadness in her blue eyes. Ellen took her blonde hair and brushed back over her shoulder as she gazed into Little Logan's eyes. There was love and the joy in her face, but something else was missing.

"I think I'm going to go home, Ellen," Debra said. "Call me sometime, even if it's just to talk about the good old days."

"You can count on that. Sometimes I just need to talk to someone."

"I know," Debra said with a friendly smile. "I'm here for you. Call me anytime you like."

"Thanks, Deb. I'll do that."

Ellen, still holding her boy, opened the door and bid farewell to her friend.

Ms. Garrison returned to the room, looking humble but stern.

"Ellen, your father and I have been talking, and we don't want you trying to go to college and looking after Logan at the same time, you're going to need some help with Logan while you're at school I would like to go back with you and help with him."

"Mom, I can't ask you to do that," Ellen said, astonished at the proposition. "What would Daddy do without you?"

"We've already talked it over," Ms. Garrison repeated.

"He is fine with it, and I can fly back sometimes on weekends, just to make sure he's doing okay. It will give you more time to study, and I will get to spend more time with my grandson. It makes perfectly good sense to me."

Mrs. Garrison paused. "Besides, your dad can come home and read without being interrupted by me trying to talk to him."

Ellen took turns looking at her mother and her son as she processed the offer. "Well, if you want to do that, and it is okay with dad, we can try it. Just to see how it works out."

After a month back at college, with her mother helping care for Little Logan, things were working out fine for Ellen. She was able to spend more time studying, feeling confident about the situation.

Fall had arrived, and the colorful leaves were wafting down from the big oaks trees that lined the sidewalk along her walk.

A cool breeze stirred the leaves, scattering them across the campus grounds as Ellen looked on, thinking of the times that she and Logan would hold hands on their way to school. They were each seven years old, and the other boys gave Logan a hard time. He would just grin and keep walking. Even then, they knew how they felt about each other, although they could never say it out loud. As Ellen approached the apartment, her mother met her at the door.

"Honey, you may want to sit down for this," her mother cautioned.

"What is it, mom?"

"I got a call from a Major McConnell from Dover, Delaware, and he left me a phone number and a message for you to call him as soon as you got in."

"Well, I guess they have a body they think is Logan," Ellen sighed. "This is the third time I've gotten call from him to come down to identify the body."

"You don't seem to be too upset, Ellen."

"That's because I know it's not him, mom."

"But how could you know that?"

Ellen raised her right hand and placed it over her heart.

"Because I would have felt it here if something would've happened to him," Ellen said. "I know that sounds crazy, mom, but he's that much a part of me."

"Well, give them a call any way," her mother responded. "I'm going to check on Little Logan to see if he is still asleep."

Ellen sat at the end of the sofa as she picked the phone up and began dialing. In just a few minutes, a voice answered on the other end.

"Major, this is Ellen Mackay."

"Mrs. Mackay, I hate to call you to inform you that we think we have your husband's body here," Major McConnell said. "I realize this has been the third time we have asked you to come down to identify the body. We have no identification, but he fits the description. Six feet, two inches, with light sandy hair and blue eyes."

"The description sounds right, but I'm going to ask you to do one thing for me," Ellen said. "It could save me a lot of trouble driving down to Dover, if you don't mind."

"What's that Mrs. Mackay?"

"Are you where you can view the body now, Major?"

"I can be in about three minutes."

"Well go down and check his right leg," she continued. "Specifically, the back of the calf, and tell me what you see."

"What am I supposed to be looking for Ms. Mackey?"

"Just tell me what you see."

A few minutes later, Major McConnell returned to the phone.

"I can't see anything on his leg, specifically on the calf."

"If it was Logan, Major, he would have a birthmark shaped like a four leaf clover on the back of his calf."

"Well this body doesn't have anything like that," Major McConnell said.

"You just saved me a trip to Dover, Major," Ellen said. "Thank you very much."

"Sorry to have inconvenienced you."

"That's fine, Major," Ellen said serenely. "Give me a call anytime you think you've found him."

Ellen's mom walked in as she hung up the phone

"Ellen, for the life of me I don't see how you can hold up and be so calm," her mother said. "Under these circumstances, a call like that would scare me to death."

"I knew it wasn't him." Ellen replied. "If something happened to him, mom, I would know it. He's out there somewhere, and I'm going to see him again someday. Come hell or high water, I'm never going to give up."

Chapter 3

Three weeks had passed, and Logan was up and slowly walking up and down the hospital's halls, wearing a black patch over his right eye. He preferred to keep his left hand concealed in his pocket even though it had fully healed.

Logan's weight was up to 160 pounds, and physical therapy was helping him regain his strength. On this afternoon, however, the walk was getting the better of him. A bit wearied, Logan was heading back to his room when he heard a voice behind him.

"Hold on, John, I'll walk with you. I'm headed to your room anyway."

Logan turned around to see Nurse Warner approaching.

"Hey, Ms. Warner, how are you today?"

"I'm fine," the nurse responded jovially. "The big question is how you're doing, John."

"I'm still slow at this, but I'm getting there," he said.

"You seem to be picking up your pace," Nurse Warner said, patting Logan lightly on the shoulder. "That's very good. At the rate you're going, to be out of here in no time. And I was just getting used to having you a round."

As they walked side by side, Logan was getting increasingly weary. Without thinking, he placed his hand on the nurse's shoulder. She placed her hand over Logan's hand, putting her left arm around his waist to provide support.

Logan felt a warm sensation rippling across his body. It was the first time he could recall the tenderness of a woman. While he did not know what that meant, he knew it felt good.

As they entered his room, Nurse Warner led Logan to his bed. As he sat down on the side of the bed, Logan looked up at the nurse. Their eyes met and, briefly, time stood still.

"I guess I need to finish my rounds," Nurse Warner said as the moment passed. "I will see you around dinner time."

Logan looked up with a slightly puzzled look on his face that still managed a smile.

"What the hell was that all about," he said aloud to himself as he watched her leave. He thought about putting his hand on her shoulder and the feeling he had experienced. "This was something new. Or was it? All I know is that it felt good."

Nurse Warner returned to Logan's room around the time he had finished his dinner. He was sitting up on the side of the bed.

"How was dinner?" the nurse asked as she opened a medicine bottle.

"It was okay," Logan responded, watching her take out a dropper of clear fluid. "At least I ate all of it."

"I'd like to remove that patch to add some eye drops," Nurse Warner said.

Logan noticed that the nurse was standing between his legs as she reached over to pull the eyepatch back. She placed her hand under his chin and raised his head backwards, holding his eyelid open to administer the drops. Again, their eyes met, as drops started running down the side of his face.

"I'm sorry," Nurse Warner said nervously as she grabbed several tissues from the end table and began wiping Logan's cheeks. "My goodness!"

They both burst out laughing.

She ran her fingers through a few strands of his hair that had fallen down across his forehead.

"I have to make my rounds now," the nurse said as she headed toward the door. She looked back over her shoulder, wearing a grin on her face. "Maybe we can take another walk tomorrow afternoon."

"I would like that, Ms. Warner," Logan said.

Logan closed his eyes to hear her footsteps go down the hall.

"That's one fine looking woman, and she knows it," he thought, rolling over to go to sleep.

Logan woke up early the next morning. He was fully dressed, and enjoying a cup of coffee, when Dr. Stillman walked into the room holding his clipboard. He stopped Logan from standing up.

"No, no, keep your seat," the doctor said. "There are a few things we need to talk about. I found a few things that I think are very interesting."

"What are they, Doc?"

"Your bloodwork turned up high levels of opium," Doctor Stillman remarked, taking a look at the chart. "I've been wondering how you were dealing with all that pain. Now it makes sense. The opiates could also have something to do with your memory loss. Have you been having any kind of strange dreams? Or have you seen anything that didn't look normal to you?"

"I haven't seen anything unusual since I've been here," Logan said. "And I have only been having one dream."

"Would you like to tell me about it?" the doctor queried.

"Well, it's when I was in the jungle…" Logan stopped abruptly. "Doc, can I tell you about it later? I just don't feel like discussing it now."

"Was it like a nightmare, soldier?" Dr. Stillman pressed.

"No, it wasn't a nightmare," Logan replied. "It was just a little strange, that's all."

"As the drug leaves your system, it won't surprise me if you have some type of withdrawals," Dr. Stillman said, making a few notations in his chart.

"You've had that stuff in your system for a long, long, time," he continued. "And it's going to take some time to for it to clear up. No wonder you can't remember where you've been. But at least we have an idea on how to treat you. Hopefully you'll get your memory back, but we have a ways to go before that happens."

The doctor paused as he headed toward the hallway.

"We're going to set you up with two hours a week to meet with Dr. Elkins, our psychiatrist," the doctor said. "If anybody can help you, he can. For now, just keep exercising and drink plenty of fluids. I'll inform the nurses about what we have found in your bloodstream. I'm also going to prescribe a new medicine for you. I think we're on the right track."

"That's good news," Logan thought, relieved to know something about his addled state. "I feel better already. In fact, I think I'll take my walk around the hospital. And maybe I can find my new walking buddy."

It was almost six the next afternoon when Nurse Noble came to the room to discuss Logan's first meeting with Dr. Elkins.

"Your appointment is set for 10 o'clock," she said, handing him a sheet of paper. "You should give this to his receptionist. The doctor already has your records and will be expecting you. He is located in the administration building. You should have no problem finding him. It's all on that piece of paper."

"I think I can do that, ma'am," Logan said anxiously.

Nurse Warner walked in just as Nurse Noble was leaving. "How is our patient today, Ms. Noble?"

"He's coming along fine," Nurse Noble said. "Just as soon as I clock out, I'm going to be fine, too," she added with a laugh.

"Have a good night," Nurse Warner said as her co-worker left the room.

Nurse Warner assessed Logan's condition for herself. "I see you are dressed like you're going somewhere," she said.

"I was just going to walk around a little bit," he said.

"Well, I was just getting ready to go out and have a smoke," Nurse Warner remarked, pausing for a second. "Would you like to walk with me?"

Logan accepted the invitation. As they started down the hall, Logan was a few steps slower. Ms. Warner put her left-hand under Logan's right arm to steady him.

"It's not far John, just around the corner," Nurse Warner said, pointing ahead to their destination. "It's where everybody goes to smoke. It also gets us out of that hospital for some fresh air."

A pair of glass doors opened out to a cement patio with concrete tables and benches. Several people were already out there smoking. Some were talking, while others were just staring out over the well-maintained lawn. As they walked over to the edge of the patio, Nurse Warner reached into her side pocket and pulled out a pack of Chesterfield cigarettes.

"Do you smoke, John?"

"I don't know, but I will try one, he said sheepishly.

Nurse Warner put a cigarette in her mouth before handing one to the patient. Logan examined it with curiosity, looking at it as though he had never seen one before. She lit her cigarette, and then did the same for Logan.

Logan was watching the nurse as she took a deep puff. He tried to mimic her actions, but ended up bent over and coughing. He struggled for a few minutes to catch his breath. Tears streamed down his face as he recovered. He handed the smoke back to Nurse Warner.

"I guess that answers the question," he said with a laugh. "I suppose I'm a non-smoker."

"Indeed," Nurse Warner said. "I'm sorry, John. I should have told you to go slow, just in case. Are you okay now?"

"Yes, I'm fine."

Logan looked around to see if anyone had noticed. At that point, he realized the state of many of the people on the patio. There were soldiers in wheelchairs and crutches, some with half a leg missing, other with no arms. "I'm not as bad off as I thought I was," he thought.

"Let's go back in," Nurse Warner said as she crushed her cigarette into a metal ashtray. "It's time for my rounds."

As they walked across the patio, Logan saw a bearded soldier in a wheelchair with an army blanket draped over his legs. He wore an army field jacket and long hair pulled back into a ponytail. Though the field jacket lacked an insignia; Logan could see where the sergeant's stripes had been taken off, leaving small holes where the thread had held them on. His name had even been removed. As Logan passed by, the soldier looked up at him and nodded his head with a grin. Logan did the same to acknowledge him.

Logan and Nurse Warner said very little as they walked from the glass doors back to his hospital room.

"Thanks for the walk, John," the nurse finally said as they reached the door. "I'll check on you later."

She briefly hesitated. "By the way, John, don't smoke any more cigarettes," she said with a chuckle.

"You can count on that," Logan said.

They shared a smile as she left, leaving Logan to pour himself a cup of water to cool his throat down from the cigarette smoke. He sank into the bed, thinking about the soldier with the pony tail and field jacket.

"Is there a chance he knew me or had seen me before?" Logan thought, reflecting on the look he had received from the mystery soldier. "Something about him just didn't seem right. Maybe I'm supposed to know him. Maybe I should just go up to him and introduce myself as John Doe. Who knows?"

Logan's mind ran through a variety of scenarios. Maybe they had met. Or perhaps it was just a case of mistaken identity.

"Maybe he'll be out there again tomorrow at the same time," Logan mused. "For now, I should get some rest and get ready for my appointment with Dr. Elkins. Things could be coming around for me. I need to know who I am."

The next morning, precisely at ten, Logan walked into the psychiatrist's office to see an older gentleman in his early 50s talking to the receptionist. The man looked like an Army drill sergeant, with an average build. He stood around 6 feet tall and weighed roughly 180 pounds. He had a clean haircut marked with pronounced gray that contrasted with his dark eyebrows. He turned and looked at Logan.

"You must be John Doe, right on time," Dr. Elkins said, inviting Logan to enter his office. "I like a man that appreciates another man's time. Come on in."

He motioned to Logan to take a seat in a chair in front of his desk. He quickly looked at Logan, then at his chart.

"I see here you're going by the name of John Doe."

"Yes sir."

"I'm going to try to fix that for you, young man," Dr. Elkins said confidently. "Believe me, you're not the only one who has come in here in this condition. There are some things we can do to help. Even for the ones that we can't help, we can help them return out in a society and to become productive citizens."

The doctor glanced at Logan's chart.

"I see here that Dr. Stillman has been trying to get those unwanted drugs out of your system. He says here that, besides your memory, you're not having any other symptoms from the drugs."

Logan nodded.

"So there's no type of withdrawal? Stomach cramps, shaking? Nothing like that?"

"No sir, as far as I know I feel fine."

"That's amazing," Dr. Elkins said. "The brain has different ways of reacting to various drugs. You've been here a little over three months. If you were going to have any kind of reaction, I would think you'd be having it by now."

The doctor laid the chart down on his desk. "Then again, only time will tell…"

While Logan didn't say much, Dr. Elkins managed to detect an accent from the limited conversation.

"One thing is clear, young man, you're not from New Jersey," Dr. Elkins said with a smile.

"I've met a lot of soldiers, and heard my fair share of accents," the doctor continued. "You are definitely from the south, so that's something to keep in mind as we narrow down where you're from. Your accent isn't pronounced enough to be from the Deep South, either. I'd wager that you're from somewhere between South Carolina and southern Virginia."

Dr. Elkins reached for a piece of paper.

"Let's set up another appointment. We'll meet this Friday, at the same time, and we'll discuss some options. You may not like them all, but I'm going to do my best to fix you."

Dr. Elkins stood up from behind his desk, reaching out to shake Logan's hand while placing his left hand on the soldier's shoulder.

"I know this is hard on you, John," the psychiatrist said as he led Logan out of the office. "It's not going in be a quick fix. It will take time. Right now, all you have is time, so hang in there. We'll talk again on Friday."

Chapter 4

"And that's the way it is, Monday, February 5th, 1966. This is Walter Cronkite saying goodnight."

Ellen got up and turned the TV off before picking up the phone to call Debra. Her friend answered after several rings. "Hey Deb, this is Ellen."

"Hey Ellen," Debra said. "I was just headed back to my dorm room. I almost didn't answer. It's usually for one of the other girls. How are you?"

"I'm fine, but I need a favor."

"Sure, what is it?"

"I was just watching the news," Ellen said. "They were showing pictures of soldiers that have been captured. Of course Logan wasn't one of them. It got me thinking. Maybe he's in a veteran's hospital somewhere, like the one in Durham, or Walter Reed."

Ellen paused.

"Mom and I are going in to fly home tomorrow and spend Thursday with dad," she said. "But I'd like to drive down to the veterans' hospital on Friday morning, you know, just to look around. And if he's not there, I want to drive to Walter Reed to check it out, too. Sitting around and doing absolutely nothing is driving me crazy. Would you be willing to drive to Washington? It would only be one night. We can come back Saturday afternoon."

"Ellen, do you think there's a chance he will be one of those hospitals?"

"I don't know," Ellen admitted. "But least I would be doing something, and just checking would make me feel better. I know it's a longshot, but something is telling me to give it a shot. Will you ride with me?"

"Of course I will," Debra said.

"I'll call you when I leave home," Ellen said.

"I can meet you at the front entrance of the hospital," Debra said.

Tom Garrison, a tall, slender man with graying at the temples, picked up his wife and daughter at the Greensboro airport. He greeted the women and helped them put their luggage in the family's green Buick Riviera.

"Well dad, how did you manage to get away from the drug store?" Ellen asked.

"I left Hillary in charge."

"That makes sense," Ellen said. "She's been there since I was a little girl."

"How was the flight?"

"It was great," Ellen said, looking down at her son. "Little Logan did not cry at all."

"Tom, did you miss me at all?" Mrs. Garrison asked, playfully slapping her husband with her purse.

"You have no idea, honey," Mr. Garrison said. "I'm tired of cooking and cleaning."

Mrs. Garrison laughed.

"By the way, Mrs. Dubois was in the drugstore this morning to pick up her blood pressure medicine and she asked me to tell you to stop by," Mr. Garrison said. "She would love to see you."

"That's nice of her. I'll try to visit her before we go home."

"How is she doing since Mr. Dubois died?" Ellen asked.

"I guess you could say she's doing okay," Mrs. Garrison said. "She still has her housekeeper, maid and yard man to keep her company,

"I don't think I've been in that house since Logan and I were kids," Ellen said. "Logan used to peddle his bicycle all the way up that long driveway to deliver the newspaper so Mr. Dubois wouldn't have to walk out and picked it up."

"That's a good quarter of a mile," Mr. Garrison observed.

"Every Christmas, Mr. Dubois would give Logan a $10 tip and a fruit basket," Ellen recalled. "We went to a lot of movies with that money. Mr. Dubois was such a nice man."

Ellen reached over to adjust Little Logan's pacifier.

"By the way, dad, have you seen Mrs. Mackay?" she said.

"She came to the drug store the other day to get her prescription filled," Mr. Garrison said with a sigh. "To tell you the truth, she didn't look well, paler and thinner."

"I'm going by to see her while I'm in town," Ellen said. "I'll take Little Logan. I know she could use the company."

"I'm sure she would love that," Mr. Garrison said. "That lady has seen some hard times."

They made the turn onto Fieldcrest Road, entering the town limits of Draper, North Carolina.

Draper, at that time, was a typical small Southern town, with a movie theater, a five-and-dime, a pool room and a soda shop were all the kids went after school. Like the bank and local YMCA, Mr. Garrison's drugstore was in the center of town, and the nearby Baptist church was by far the biggest structure in town. Most of the town's 3,822 residents either knew each other or were related in some way. When someone passed away, most of the town showed up to pay their respects.

The town was flourished when Marshall Field's, a Chicago department store, built a textile plant there to make blankets, along with housing for its employees. By 1947, the plant was part of Fieldcrest Mills.

On this hot summer day, the Garrisons could see people sitting on their front porches, hoping for a cooling breeze. Everyone knew Mr. Garrison's car, waving as the family passed. Ellen noticed that some kids were playing sandlot baseball in a small field, seemingly oblivious to the sweltering heat.

"Here we are," Mr. Garrison said. "Y'all come on in and see everybody before you go home. I'm sure all the guys are setting around the table at the pharmacy, having their morning coffee and shooting the bull to see who can tell the biggest lie. They'd love to see y'all."

"They've been coming to the store since I was a little girl," Ellen said.

"Yep, they're not just regular customers," Mr. Garrison said. "I guess you could say they're just part of the family."

The family entered the store, with Mr. Garrison holding the glass doors open for Ellen and Little Logan. As expected, the men were sitting around the table drinking their coffee. They met Ellen before she could get to their table, and one of the men reached out in hopes of holding Little Logan. Ellen handed the boy to Moonlight, a gentle giant who was several inches taller than rest and must have weighed at least 300 pounds.

Moonlight, or Moon for short, owned the local taxi service. He always had a wide cigar in his mouth that was never lit. As often as Ellen remembered Moon chomping on the cigar, she had never seen him actually fire one up. Moonlight earned his nickname for selling illegal whiskey out of the trunk of his cab. No one ever arrested him because he used much of his profits to replace the worn out shoes of the town's small children.

One of the other men was Hal Johnson, though the locals knew him as Flick. He ran the local pool hall. His left arm was shorter than his right, and he could not fully use it. Still, Flick could tell the funniest stories that made everybody laugh. The last member of the group was Bullet, known around Draper as the man who had been shot during a card game several years earlier. He never went to the doctor and to this day carries lead in his shoulder.

A lot of folks in Draper seemed to have nicknames, and Ellen could not help but smile as she talked to the extended "family" gathered at the pharmacy.

"Look at that little fella," Moon said. "He looks just like Logan when he was that size."

"And look at the shoulders on the little guy," Bullet added. "I bet he'll be able to hit a baseball like Logan could, too."

"He even has is paw's white hair, like corn silk," Flick said.

Ellen chatted with the men for a few more minutes before excusing herself. Little Logan was getting tired from a long day and needed a nap.

As the Garrisons got closer to their home, Ellen saw a familiar white fence in the distance. She remembered how she and Logan would walk along the fence line on their way to school. The fence led to the Dubois' home. The two-story rock home sat high atop a hill and, with large windows on both floors, it looked like a castle from a distance. The structure had an unusual red tile roof that Mr. Dubois had supposedly ordered from France. No other house in Draper could compare to its size or beauty.

"I'm going to visit Mrs. Dubois for a little while," said Ellen as her mother got out of the car in the drive way of their home. "Then I'm going to stop by and see Mrs. Mackay. I should be home sometime this afternoon. I'll let Logan take a nap at Mrs. MacKay's house while we catch up."

"You be careful, and I will see you this afternoon," Mrs. Garrison said.

Ellen drove up the long drive, following the white fence that meandered up the hill. She walked across the cobblestone walkway and up the stairs to Mrs. Dubois' porch, adorned with large rock columns, each with a brass lamp attached to them. She turned to essay the property. It was a beautiful piece of land, with its rolling hills and grazing horses visible on the horizon. The walkway featured a six-foot granite statue of a lady holding a jug of water. Embossed on the side of the jug was a sign that read: Meadows of Dan. The whole panorama was a stunning sight that brought back scores of old memories.

As she approached the porch, the front door opened. Mrs. Dubois was already standing there with her arms open to help Ellen with Little Logan. Mrs. Dubois was a petite lady who might have reached five feet with heels on. With her graying black hair, the woman looked very elegant and stunning for someone in her mid-60s.

"I'm so glad that you stopped by," the lady said. "I have often thought about you and Logan and how you've been doing with this little guy. Your dad keeps telling me that you're doing fine. That's just wonderful ."

About that time, another woman entered the room, wearing a black uniform and a white apron.

"Doris, this is Ellen," Mrs. Dubois said, introducing her guest. "This is the girl I've been talking to you about."

"Oh yes, how are you Mrs. Mackay?" Doris asked.

"I'm doing fine," Ellen said. "Mrs. Dubois speaks of you often."

"Would you mind getting us a glass of sweet tea?" Mrs. Dubois said.

"Yes ma'am," Doris said as she turned and returned to the kitchen.

"Sit down, dear," Mrs. Dubois said. "Let's talk a little while. How is your mom?"

"She's doing well," Ellen said. "Of course she loves spending more time with Logan, and without her there's no way I could go to school."

"Have you heard anything about Logan?"

"No, Mrs. Dubois, but I'm hopeful every day."

"I know you are, my child, and I'm so sorry. He is such a fine boy – and a good-looking one, too."

Mrs. Dubois paused in front of one of the home's large windows, gazing out upon the hillside vista.

"Jean Paul and I would watch you two walk along that fence holding hands," Mrs. Dubois recalled. "Nancy, that old palomino, would follow you all the way down to the road. As we watched you two kids holding hands, Jean Paul would always say, 'There goes those two cotton heads. They look like twins.' He always got a good laugh from that."

"We love that horse," Ellen recalled. "Logan liked to call him Trigger, after Roy Roger's horse. Boy will he be surprised when he finds out Trigger is a girl."

The women shared a riotous laugh until both had tears in their eyes.

"Yes, Nancy getting some age on her," Ms. Dubois said. "She's about 23 now. When Jean Paul died, we buried him up on that hill overlooking the Dan River. Would you believe that old Nancy to this day trots up there and stands at the fence, looking at where his tombstone is located? She does it every day, late in afternoon, around sunset. Sometimes I wonder what she's thinking as she looks at that monument. I guess I'll never know."

Mrs. Dubois' voice trailed as a sad expression overtook her face. A different type of tear seemed to build up in her eyes.

Ellen, seeking to change the subject, glanced around the room and pointed to a painting hung over the mantel. It showed the Dan River, slightly muddied, weaving its way through a secluded pasture.

"What a lovely painting," Ellen exclaimed. "In fact, you have such a beautiful home."

"Yes, I love it here," Mrs. Dubois said. "We built this house with big aspirations. We started out with 500 acres, and then Jean Paul bought more land, nearly tripling its size. Would you believe that this land now goes all the way to the Virginia state line? Jean Paul loved this place. Always said it was just right for growing grapes. He wanted to turn it into a winery. This house would have been the tasting room and we were going to live on the second floor."

Mrs. Dubois explained that the home had been built with rocks that had been embedded in the rolling hills. It was intended to look like a French château. Jean Paul planned to name the winery Meadows of Dan after the river that traversed the property. Jean Paul, whose whole family had been in the winery business, owned half of the business when he came over here from France.

"He loved it so much," Mrs. Dubois reminisced. "His dream was to stay here in the U.S. and build his own winery brand. It would have happened, had it not been for the cancer that hit him so hard. It was a tough recovery. So he decided to raise horses so the land wouldn't go to waste. And he appreciated the beauty of Palominos."

Mrs. Dubois walked over to the large window facing the front lawn and gestured toward a big stone structure in the distance. "That building over there was going to house the wine press, but turned it into the stables. I bet they are the best and most-expensive stables anywhere around."

The lady laughed slightly to herself. "Mr. Ross looks after the farm these days. Feeds the horses and maintains the property. I don't know what I would do without him. He has really become part of this family."

Mrs. Dubois went on to detail how Jean Paul had found Mr. Ross, a World War II veteran who was reluctant to share much about his time overseas. Jean Paul, who had heard about Mr. Ross through some horse breeders, drove to Roanoke, Virginia, to meet him, and they immediately hit it off. Jean Paul returned to the estate and converted the entire second floor of the barn into living quarters for the horse trainer. Mr. Ross settled in quickly, taking over management of the entire farm.

"He has been a real asset to this farm," Mrs. Dubois added.

"It has really been nice talking to you, Mrs. Dubois," Ellen said, running her hand gracefully across the back of one of the upholstered chairs. "Seeing your beautiful home stirs up so many memories. When Logan and I would pass by the house on the way to school, he would often vow to buy it for us. I knew it was just a dream, but I'd always humor him, and we'd just keep walking."

Little Logan had fallen asleep, and Ellen transferred him over to her right shoulder.

"I'm so glad you stopped by," Mrs. Dubois said. "Please be sure to stop by anytime you're back home."

"Oh, I will," Ellen responded excitedly as she turned the brass doorknob to leave. "Thank you for inviting me."

Mrs. Dubois accompanied Ellen to the columned porch, and waved to the young woman as she walked down to the driveway. Ellen stopped as she approached the columns that served as bookends to the driveway. Nancy the Palomino was there, with her head over the fence, staring at them. Ellen hesitated for a moment. The horse was moving her head up and down as to say goodbye, her mane blowing in the slight breeze that whispered across the pasture.

Ellen stopped short of her car, and instead walked up to the fence as she held her baby in her left arm. "Come on, Little Logan. I'm going to introduce you to an old friend."

"Hey, Trigger, remember me?" Ellen said to the aging Palomino, stroking Nancy's mane with a gentle touch. The horse moved slowly towards Little Logan, pressing her nose to his forehead. "Little Logan, I'd like to introduce you to Trigger. At least that's what your daddy called him. He will always be Trigger to us!"

Ellen ran her free hand along Nancy's strong jaw down to her chin. "We've got to go, girl, but I'm sure we'll see you another time."

The young mother put Little Logan in his seat and started the car. As she eased down the driveway, Ellen could see Trigger trotting along the side of the fence, keeping pace with them. She could not help but smile, though some sorrow lingered in her heart.

"We've got one more stop before we go home, little man," Ellen said, looking back at her child as he cooed. "We're going to see Nana. Your mama has a big day planned for tomorrow. I'm going to see if I can find your daddy."

As Ellen completed the last turn into the housing development, one home stood out. It was the only one flying an American flag. She knew it very well. She pulled Little Logan out of the car and slowly approached the MacKay's home.

The door swung open before Ellen had even knocked. Mrs. Mackay was a slender woman with silky dark hair that rested comfortably on her shoulders. She wore a blue pastel apron and a surprised look on her face as she instinctively reached for Little Logan.

"He looks so much like his daddy," Mrs. Mackay said, showing slight creases as she managed a smile. "Come on in and let me show you something."

Mrs. Mackay led Ellen through the foyer into the living room, motioning to a picture of Logan carefully placed on the mantle that graced a modest fireplace. The elder Logan was five years old in the picture, which had been taken at Alderman's Studio. Beside it stood another picture in a simple oak frame that showed Logan's father, Ben, decked out in his fireman's uniform. Father and son bore a striking resemblance, made uncanny with the toddler's presence in the room for full comparison.

Ben Mackay had blonde hair like his son and grandson, along with broad shoulders and penetrating blue eyes. The picture had been taken just before his death in a fire accident at the old Draper schoolhouse. He was still remembered in town as a hero, after he stayed in the school until all the children had been rescued. The building caved in and collapsed before he could join the children to safety.

Logan was a few days past five when the tragedy happened, but his father's insurance policy provided much-needed support for the child and his mother. The paid firemen on the otherwise volunteer squad also took the child in, giving him role models as he grew up.

"I must say, had it not been for those boys down at the station, I don't know what Logan and I would have done," Mrs. Mackay wistfully recalled as she offered Ellen a chair. "It seems as though all those boys became Logan's surrogate father. They looked after him as if he was their own, and they still come by to check on me, and they still fix things around here. They definitely look after their own."

She told Ellen about the countless times the firemen had offered her rides home when she finished up work at the five and dime store.

"It sure has been a blessing to me," Mrs. Mackay added, handing the child back to Ellen. The woman took her apron off, using a corner of it to dust off her husband's picture before returning it to the mantle.

"I know my boy is somewhere out there, waiting to be found," Mrs. Mackay said, her voice cracking as tears welled in her reddening eyes. "I just don't know where, but he's out there. I know the good Lord would not take both of my guys away from me. He's out there somewhere, and I know he will be home someday. The good Lord will see to that, Ellen."

"I think you're right, and I'm never going to stop looking for him," Ellen assured her mother-in-law. "You can be sure of that."

"That little guy is absolutely adorable," Ms. Mackey said, reaching over to stroke her grandson's cheek. "I know my son would be so proud."

After some time, the women went back to the kitchen. Ellen wished to change the subject. She found her opened as the subtle scent of pinto beans wafted through the room.

"Boy, those beans smell good," Ellen said.

"They'll be ready in about 30 more minutes," Ms. Mackey responded. "Please stay on and have a bowl full with me."

"I would like to, but I must get home," Ellen said with a friendly grin. "I have a full day tomorrow, and I've got to put Little Logan down. It's well past his bedtime."

"I understand, dear," the woman said with a nod.

As they started down the hall the front door, Ellen couldn't help but notice a door to her left. It was slightly ajar, allowing a narrow beam of sunlight to streak across the wooden floorboards.

"That's Logan's room, isn't it?" Ellen said.

"Yes, it is," Mrs. Mackay said with mixed emotion. "Would you like to go in?"

Ellen silently accepted the overture, and Mrs. Mackay swung the door open. Ellen stopped in the middle of the room, adorned with a simple bed and dresser. An oval rug was spread across the floor. Her heart beat fast and her breathing accelerated as she surveyed the room before her eyes set upon an end table beside the bed. The small piece of furniture served as a resting place for two pictures. The first showed Logan's parents standing in front of the home. The other featured Ellen, several years younger and sitting on the front steps of the MacKay's house.

"I remember when that picture was taken," Ellen mused.

Two baseball bats were propped up against the end table, and a trophy rested on the dresser as a reminder of the state championship Logan had helped win as his high school's second baseman. On the wall, over the bed's headboard, was a large poster of Billy Martin with the New York Yankees. The fiery infielder was Logan's favorite player. Whenever he talked about baseball, Logan had to mention Billy Martin, whether it involved his hustle or the occasional scuffle he got into on the field.

"That's just grit," Logan would say with a sheepish grin.

"He did love Billy Martin," Mrs. MacKay said, looking down at her son's oxblood-colored penny loafers. They were sitting at the edge of the bed, slightly askew as though Logan had just stepped out of them.

Ellen handed Little Logan over to Mrs. Mackay. She felt suddenly lightheaded as she sat down on the bed. It was as if her soulmate had never left the room. She could feel his presence, sensing that she could all but wrap her arms around him in that instant. Ellen had no desire to leave the bedroom, realizing that she felt as close to him now as she did the day he left in 1963. Little Logan's crying interrupted the moment, and Ellen slowly stood up.

"This room…" Ellen paused. "It looks just like it did the day he left."

"And it is going to stay that way until he comes home," Mrs. Mackay said with undeniable certitude.

Ellen made her way over to her mother-in-law and gave her a heartfelt embrace and a kiss on the cheek. Tears started to run down each of their faces as Mrs. Mackay handed the youngster back to his mother.

"Yes, please leave this room just like it is," Ellen said, sniffling slightly. "I don't know how long it will take, but I'm going to see to it that he comes back to this room, sooner or later. I will never stop looking for him until he's home again."

"You take care of yourself, dear," Ellen said, slowly making her way to the bedroom door and into the hallway. "I want you in good shape when I bring Logan home."

As Ellen pulled up into her family's driveway, she sat there for few minutes, aiming to compose herself. She could not get over seeing her husband's bedroom. It was hard to accept that so much time had passed since he was last there. She could still smell his scent and envision his blue eyes staring into hers. With amazing realism, she could visualize the dimples in his cheeks as he smiled. To her it was just if she had just left him, not two years ago, at the Greensboro train station.

Chapter 5

"I think I'll stop by the patio and see if that soldier in the wheelchair is out there," Logan thought as he left Dr. Elkins' office.

As he stepped outside, Logan saw the sunlight reflect off the wheelchair, nestled in the far corner of the patio. "There he is, just like when I saw him yesterday," Logan observed.

Logan stuck out his hand to greet the soldier, but there was no reciprocation. The man simply gazed up at Logan with a solemn look.

"How are you today, soldier?" the man said.

"Not entirely sure," Logan responded, gradually lowering his hand. "I'm John Doe."

"John Doe, John Doe," the man said, repeating himself. "Well, John, I guess that means you don't have a clue who you are with a name like that."

The comment took Logan by surprise.

"I suppose you're right," Logan said after the initial shock had worn off. "I don't know who I am, but I'm working awfully hard trying to find out. The doc says it may take some time, but I feel like it will come to me sooner or later."

"How long is later, John," the soldier replied, staring blankly at Logan with no discernable expression on his face. "Six months, a year ... or the rest of your life?"

Logan was taken aback by the soldier's sharpness. "How can someone have so little empathy?" he wondered to himself.

"Well, the doctor said it'll take time," Logan stammered. "He can't put a timeframe on it, but he sounds confident that he can help me."

"Well, I guess you could say that you're a newborn, in a way," the soldier said, leaving Logan with a puzzled look.

"That's right, a newborn," the soldier continued. "See, you don't know who you are, you certainly don't know your name, or where you're from. You have no idea where you're going or what you want to do. It's as if you just come into this world, like a newborn."

Logan had never considered his circumstances in such a way.

"Well, I guess you're right," Logan said.

"So, I guess you're just going to walk around," the man in the wheelchair said. "My advice? Take every day that life gives you, and let it go at that."

"I haven't decided what I'm going to do yet," Logan responded. "I'm just trying to give myself some time to figure it all out."

"Would you like for me to give you a head start on that, John?"

Logan raising his eyebrows, and his eyes widened as they looked straight at the soldier. "Of course, if you have any ideas or any suggestions I would like to hear them."

"If you want to know where you're from, who you are, and were you're going," the solider paused and adjusted himself in his wheelchair. "I have one solution."

"What's that?" Logan said.

"When you return to your room, open the drawer by your nightstand," the soldier advised. "Pull out that black book lying in that drawer. It's called the Bible, John. Start reading it. It will give you all the answers you need."

Logan had no idea what to say. He just stood there looking into the soldier's eyes before turning slightly to walk away.

"Hey John," the soldier called out. Logan stopped, but did not turn around. "You can just call me Sarge. That's what I prefer to be called."

"Okay, Sarge, see you later," Logan said as he hurriedly walked over to the glass doors to reenter the hospital.

As Logan walked down the hallway, he reflected on what had been one hell of a conversation. Shortly after returning to his room, he looked over at the nightstand beside the bed. He hesitated for moment before reaching over to open the drawer. Sure enough, there was the Bible with black leather binding and golden English lettering. For some reason Logan quickly closed the drawer and laid down on his bed, passing over every word of his conversation with Sarge.

"He acted as though he knew me and what I had been thinking," Logan thought. "But I had never been able to talk with anybody about it. And boy, he didn't pull any punches. Damn he sure gave me a lot to think about."

There was a light tap on the door as Nurse Warner quietly entered the room.

"Is it time for you already?" Logan asked.

"Yes it is, John," the nurse stated. "Are you not as glad to see me as I am to see you?"

"I'm happy to see you, Ms. Warner, I just have a lot on my mind right now," Logan said.

"Would you like to talk with me about it, John?"

"Maybe some other time, just not today."

"Okay then, let's pull that patch up so I can put some drops in that eye," the nurse said as she approached the bed.

Logan sat up and pulled the patch up to his forehead. The nurse placed her right hand against the back of Logan's head.

"Let's lean back just a little bit, sweetie," she said.

Nurse Warner squeezed a few drops into the eye, taking time to dab his temple and cheek with a soft pad to remove any excess liquid.

"That should do it," she said.

Logan pulled the patch back down over his eye.

"Are you having a rough day, John?"

"Just have a lot on my mind," Logan mumbled. "That's all."

"I think I know what you need John," the nurse said, as a sly grin came upon her face.

"What's that?"

"We need to get you out of here for a little bit," she said.

"I already went out on the patio this morning," he replied.

"No, I mean, you need to get out of this hospital for a while."

"That would be nice, but I don't see how that can happen," Logan said with an air of despondence.

"Well, I'm going to think about it for a spell," Nurse Warner said. "When I come back around supper time, we'll discuss it some more. I have an idea that just might work."

"That sounds good to me," Logan said as curiosity overtook his short-lived sadness.

"For now, you just get your rest and don't worry," the nurse said. "I'll come up with something."

As she walked out, Ms. Warner turned and looked at Logan with a smile and a quick wink.

"Oh man," Logan thought. "I wonder what she's going to cook up. It has got to be good since I can see it in her eyes. That woman is up to something."

Logan reached over and reopened the drawer of his side table.

"Well, this can't hurt," he thought as he reached for the Bible. "Sarge said the answers are in here, so I'd better get to reading. It's a thick book with a lot of thin pages."

It was about half past seven that evening when Nurse Warner returned with a tray of food. She sat the tray down, and hurried back to close the door. "Are you ready for this, John?" she said cryptically.

Logan slid closer to the edge of the bed as the nurse pulled a chair around in front of him.

"Listen close," she said in a calm and quiet tone. "I've seen on your chart. You have an appointment next Friday with Dr. Elkins."

"That's right, at ten," Logan said.

"After you finish your session, ask him for a day pass for the next day," Nurse Warner coached. "Tell him you have a friend who is going to pick you up that morning and that you feel like getting out of here for a bit will help you."

Logan took it all in, thinking about a possible change in scenery.

"Now all that is the truth," the nurse said. "You won't be telling him anything that isn't so. I'm sure he will give you a day pass. The only problem is you cannot say who your friend is. I think they would frown upon the thought of a nurse taking her patient out for the day. You know, they might take it the wrong way."

"Well, I can understand that," Logan said. "The last thing I want to do is get you in any type of trouble."

"Even if they do find out, I haven't seen a policy that says a nurse can't take a patient out for his best interest and wellbeing," she stated confidently.

"It all sounds good to me," Logan said excitedly. "I'll get that day pass."

"Hey buddy, we're just getting started here," Nurse Warner said impishly, as though she had been plotting a prison escape. "First of all, you've got to have some clothes. You can't go out in those green shorts and T-shirt."

"But this is all I have," Logan said.

"I know, but I'm going to get your size and pick you up a pair of pants and a shirt."

"I don't have any money to pay for that," Logan responded.

"I'm going to pick them up for you, and you can pay me back when you do have your money," the nurse explained. "I know you have some back pay coming your way, and we'll settle up then. Right now I need your measurements."

Logan stared blankly at the nurse. "I have no idea."

"With those broad shoulders, I'm sure your shirt would be a large," Nurse Warner said. "How big are you in the waist?"

Logan said nothing since he had no idea how to answer the question.

"Well," the nurse said. "What size do you have on?"

Logan craned his neck to look at the waistband. Nurse Warner instructed him to turn around, allowing her to turn the band out enough to make out the measurement. "Size 32 it is," she said.

"What size shoe do you wear?" she queried.

"I know that," Logan said with an oversized grin. "It's 11."

"How do you know that?"

"Because it says so on the inside of the shoes I see every morning when I put them on."

"Good point, wise guy," Nurse Warner retorted. "What's the length of your pants?"

"I don't know," Logan said.

"When I come back to pick up your tray, I'll bring a tape and measure you. I've got a few things to figure out first, including how to spring you without anyone seeing us together. It will take a little bit of time, but I'll figure it out."

"I'll bet you will," Logan said with a snicker.

"See, you're feeling better already," Nurse Warner said with a sense of accomplishment as she made her way back to the closed door. "I got a laugh out of you, sure enough. I'll be back later to pick up that tray. Eat it all, you're going to need your strength."

"This certainly gives me something to think about," Logan thought as he opened the Bible to start reading. "What did she mean when she said I'm going to need my strength? It all sounds pretty exciting to me."

Logan was still reading the Bible when Nurse Warner returned nearly two hours later. "You getting caught up on your religion, John?"

"Well I've been told that this book will help me find out the answers to my condition," Logan replied. "So that's what I'm doing."

"Reading the Bible is a good thing, whether you find the answers or not," she said. "Time to put that away, though. Stand up, soldier."

Nurse Warner whipped out a tape measure from the side pocket of her uniform. She handed one end to Logan. She lost concentration as she looked at him, hesitated for a few seconds before refocusing on the task at hand. "Here, put this end where your belt line would be, John," she instructed.

Logan held the tape measure to the top of his shirt, and the nurse extended the line to the top of his left foot.

"Okay I have it," she said. "About 34 ½ inches. That's a long leg. How tall do you suppose you are?"

"I think around six foot three," Logan said.

"That's seems about right," Nurse Warner replied. "You're a good-sized man, John."

The nurse took a second as she stood up to face the patient.

"By the way, I'm going to be out of here on Wednesday and Thursday, but I'll be back Friday afternoon at three," she said. "I'll bring you the clothes. By then I'll have everything figured out for our day off."

"Where are you going during your days off?" Logan inquired.

"I'm planning to visit my mom and dad in Richmond, that's in Virginia," Nurse Warner said. "My mom's not feeling well, so I thought I'd go down and check on her."

"What seems to be the problem?" Logan asked as he sat down on the edge of his bed.

"Not sure. Dad said it might be good if I come home and spend a little time with her."

"Is anybody with her now?" Logan asked.

"Well, dad is with her. He's a physician, so he takes real good care of her."

"Your dad is a doctor?"

"Yep, he's a surgeon," Nurse Warner explained. "He actually worked here at Walter Reed for 17 years. He left when he couldn't take the politics anymore. My folks moved to

Richmond, where he started his own practice. He has just enough patients to keep him busy and happy."

"Is that why you got into nursing?"

"I guess you could say that," she answered, appreciative of Logan's inquisitive mind. "I wanted to be a doctor like my dad, but I only had enough credits from school to come here as a nurse. I may go back later and study to become a physician, but for right now I'm going to stay where I'm at."

"That's good," Logan said. "You should do that. But I'm sure glad you're here right now."

"Only time will tell," Nurse Warner said, slightly blushing. "Right now, we've got to figure out how to get you out of here. I don't think we'll have a problem with that. We just need to be a little cautious, given the circumstances."

Nurse Warner smiled at Logan. "I have all the information I need to get you some civilian clothes, so just take care," she said. "I'll see you again around three on Friday. And don't forget to ask Dr. Elkins for a pass."

"I will," Logan promised. "You just have a nice couple of days off and relax. I hope your mother gets to feeling better."

"I think she will," Nurse Warner said as she left the room.

"It looks like it's going to be a couple of slow days for me," Logan said as he picked up his Bible for more reading. "I can't wait to have a day off."

Thursday morning arrived, and Logan decided to go out onto the patio, curious if Sarge would be out there. As he opened the double glass doors, he could see the wounded warrior sitting in his wheelchair in what appeared to be his usual spot at the far end of the patio. Sarge's back faced the glass double doors. His head was leaning back as he gazed up at the cloud-filled sky, his ponytail hanging straight down. Logan stood there for a moment before approaching him.

"Well, good morning, Sarge," Logan said. "How are you this fine morning?"

"Doing good, John?" Sarge said. "How are you?"

"Physically I'm doing fine," Logan said. "Mentally, I don't know. I've got a lot of questions going through in my head, with no answers to any of them."

"Yeah I know," Sarge said, returning his sights to the sky. "Earth is a big planet, John, but there's millions and billions of planets this size just out there spinning around. Most of them you can't see, but just knowing they're out there sure does make you feel awful small."

"Yes it sure does, Sarge," Logan said, taking it all in.

"Do you think the human body was an accident, John?"

"No I don't," Logan said.

"Sometimes you can't help but think about it," Sarge said. "I've thought about it a lot since I've been here. Was the human body an accident? Well, I'll tell you how I reassure myself each and every day that it wasn't."

"How is that, Sarge?"

"I just look in the mirror," Sarge said.

The comment, like many others from the wheelchair-bound soldier, puzzled Logan.

"Yep, when I look in the mirror, I look at my eyes, knowing they feed vision back to my brain," Sarge continued. "I look at my mouth and nose, realizing that they bring air to my lungs. Even the hair in my nose filters what I breathe. I am amazed at how my ears are designed to trap and send sound. Everything from a small bird chirping, or a whistle at the train station, to raindrops on a tin roof or a storm approaching from the distance. And most of all, John, the heart is your center. It gives life and the ability to feel love, hatred, sorrow and passion, in a way. It will give you feelings throughout your life that you did not know existed."

Sarge looked up at his visitor.

"That being said, and a whole lot more could be said, I don't think the human body was an accident," Sarge said. "So what do you think John? We sometimes wonder why certain things happen to us. Why am I in this chair? Maybe there's a reason why this happened. I just need to make sure I handle it right."

"I have wondered why I lost my memories and what I can do to make it right," Logan said. "Yes, I have thought all about all those things, but I'm at a point where I just don't know what to do."

"Can I give you another suggestion?" Sarge said.

"I get the feeling you're going to anyway," Logan replied. "I'm listening."

"Take a look around on your way back into the hospital. Notice the guy who has a leg missing, or an arm. Some of these soldier are missed multiple limbs. I guarantee that each one is wondering why they are in that condition. It might make you think of that old saying."

"Which one is that, Sarge?"

"There was a man walking down the street, feeling awful sorry for himself because he had no shoes," Sarge said, pausing for effect. "At least that's how he felt until he saw a man in a wheelchair that had no feet. So stop feeling so sorry for yourself. You only lost about 20 years. Hopefully, you have another 50 years ahead of you to make something of yourself. If I were you, I'd start thinking about the rest of my life. So what are you going to do now? That's the question."

"Thanks Sarge, you've given me a lot to think about," Logan said, reaching his hand out to the other soldier.

Sarge stared at Logan's extended hand then looked down at the wheels on the chair, though he did give Logan a slight smile out of the corner of his mouth.

Logan slowly lowered his hand. "See you later, Sarge," he said. As Logan walked away, he noticed that Sarge's gaze returned to the clouds overhead.

As Logan walked down the hall, he noticed hobbled soldiers with only one leg. Others were heavily bandaged, some with patches of blood marking the wounds underneath. Logan looked down at his feet as he slowly realized that he was a lot better off than many of the other patients.

"It doesn't make me happy," Logan reflected. "But it does make me grateful for what I do have."

Chapter 6

Ellen awoke early and anxiously dressed. Her overnight clothes were already packed and loaded in the family's Bonneville. She could hear a light rain tapping on the roof, but it did little to dampen her spirits or deter her from the task at hand.

After having a cup of coffee with her parents, Ellen slipped into Little Logan's room, taking a minute to gaze upon the sleeping child. She bent down to give him a kiss on the cheek, realizing that this would be her first overnight trip without him. As she turned to leave the room she was met by her mother and father, who were waiting by the front door.

"I know y'all think I'm crazy for doing this, but it's just something I have to do," Ellen said, finding her courage. "I've got to know in my own mind. I can feel it in my heart. He's in a hospital somewhere out there, and I'm not with him. I can't imagine leaving him there, wondering where I am. I have to do something. If he's not in the hospital, at least I'll know that I tried. This sitting around doing nothing, thinking of him all the time, isn't helping me or Little Logan. So please just try to understand this, the best you can."

"We understand honey," Mr. Garrison said. "We just want you to be careful. That's all. When you see Debra tell her that we said hello. Y'all just stay safe."

Ellen conveyed her parents' greeting when she picked Debra up later that morning. The rain had lifted and the sun had slowly started to make an appearance. Each minute that passed delivered more anticipation, as Ellen became increasingly anxious of the moment when she and her friend would reach their destination and a possible reunion with her soulmate.

As they neared the hospital, Ellen began to lay out her plan for finding Logan. "We'll walk in together after I find a place to park," she told Debra.

"I called the front desk this morning before I left, and I asked for a Raymond Jones," Ellen said, explaining that she had used the first name she could come up with in hopes of securing a visitor's pass. "The lady told me they had no Raymond Jones, but they had a Raymond Johnson on the third floor. When we go in, I'm going to ask for him in order to get a pass. That should get us in."

Ellen continued to explain her plan. The women would take the elevator to the hospital's top floor, splitting up to spend 30 minutes checking out rooms for any signs of Logan Mackay. They would repeat the process until every floor and every wing of the hospital had been thoroughly inspected.

"If you see an open break room, stop and get yourself a cup of coffee so you'll have a reason for walking slowly through the halls," Ellen suggested.

"Boy, you have really figured this out, right down to the letter," Debra said. "I didn't know you had such a scheming side."

"Sometimes you have to do what it takes to get to where you want to be," Ellen replied as they neared the entrance. Ellen put a few steps between her and Debra as she confidently approached the front desk. "Good morning, ma'am, how are you," Ellen greeted the receptionist, a women in her late 30s. She had good posture, wore dark red lipstick and a trendy beehive.

"I'm just fine, young lady," the receptionist said. "What can I do for you?"

"I need a visitor's pass to see Raymond Johnson," Ellen said, unwavering. "I understand he is staying on the third floor."

"Hold on just a minute," the reception said, stepping away momentarily to rifle through a nearby file cabinet.

"Okay, here it is," she said, returning to hand Ellen and Debra their passes. "Raymond Johnson, he's in Room 334."

"Thank you, ma'am," Ellen said, clutching the pass tightly. "You have a good day."

The lady smiled and pointed down the hallway to direct the duo. "The elevator is that way, over to the left."

Ellen and Debra quietly rode the elevator to the top floor. The door opened with a loud ding, and the women split up, with Ellen making her way down the left wing of the floor.

"See you back here in about 30 to 45 minutes," she whispered. Debra started walking, never saying a word. The plan, though well-intended, made her slightly nervous. But she was a loyal and devoted friend who was determined to see Ellen's scheme through to completion.

As she made her way down the hall, Ellen noticed nurses pushing amputees in wheelchairs, while others were looking down at their clipboards. A nurse darted by Ellen before ducking into a room just a few steps away.

Such a busy place and quite depressing, she thought.

Each floor revealed a different group of soldiers and caretakers, showing the women a side of war that they had never witnessed before. As they met at the elevator one last time, Ellen had decided she had seen all she could see in three hours. The time had come to drive to Virginia, where they would rent a motel room before visiting Walter Reed. Rest was necessary, though Ellen wished she could skip the motel and head straight for the other hospital.

The drive was silent at the pair headed toward Richmond. Each woman pulled deeply into her own form of retrospection, processing all the trauma and pain they had seen just a few minutes earlier. Walter Reed was a much larger facility. What would look like? What would they find when they arrived? Could they handle it?

"I don't know about you, but I wasn't expecting so many horrible injuries," Debra told her friend. "It broke my heart. I feel so sorry for those boys and their families. It must be hell over there. I wanted to just sit down and start crying."

"That's one hell of a mess we're in over there," Ellen said, managing a response, all the while thinking of Logan. "I sure hope it's over soon."

Conversation was scarce as the woman continued north on the interstate. Soon after crossing into Virginia, the women decided the time had come to find a restaurant and a chance to stretch their legs. Any diversion from the day's experience was long overdue.

*****

Ellen and Debra stopped at a small breakfast place off the interstate, grabbing a quick bite and a couple of Cokes for the last leg of their drive. They settled back in the Buick as Ellen angled it back onto the highway.

"How long do you think it will to take us to get to Walter Reed," Debra asked.

"The hospital is just north of Washington," Ellen said, estimating another two and a half hours before they would reach the facility. "I have reservations at the Holiday Inn for us."

"Did you do the same thing you did in the other hospital?" Debra inquired.

"Yep, except I asked for Roger Smith," Ellen said, as a sly smile crept upon her. "No Roger there, but Rodney Smith is set up on the second floor. I figured Smith was as common a name as you can have."

"True, there seem to be Smith's in every neighborhood."

Conversation picked up from there, and soon Ellen was asking her friend about her time at Carolina. Debra had adjusted well to collegiate life, flirting with a 4.0 average. Classes were hard, particularly calculus, but Debra had always been the type of person who sought out a good challenge.

"You have always been good at math, Deb," Ellen said.

"How are you doing in Boston?" Debra asked as she reached into the glove compartment to glance at the map.

"I'm doing fine, though people can spot my southern accent from a mile away," Ellen said. "I catch hell about that sometimes, but it's all in good fun, of course. Grades aren't bad, and mom has been a godsend."

The car got quiet as Ellen again shifted the conversation. "Do me a favor before you graduate, Deb."

"What's that?"

"Let's sit down and talk. I have a business plan for us. No obligation, of course, but hoping you'll hear me out."

"What is the plan?" Debra pressed, overcome by curiosity.

"I can't go into it right now, but I think we would make a great team."

"That sounds interesting, Ellen."

"I know it could be another two years, but promise me we'll have that talk," Ellen said.

"You've got it."

The mood suddenly became light, as Ellen started pressing Debra about social life on campus. "Let's talk about boys," Ellen said, taking a sip of her Coke. "Who have you been seeing?"

"How did I know that's what you were going to ask about?" Debra shrewdly retorted.

They shared a raucous laugh.

"Let's see, I've dated a few guys on campus, but I've settled down to seeing just one," Debra said, taking a gulp from her bottle.

"Tell me about him."

"His name is Don Chilton," Debra said as she tucked a lock of hair behind her ear. "He lives in Greensboro. I met him in an accounting class. His dad is an accountant for one of the textile mills."

"What does he look like?"

"He's tall and fit with light brown hair and hazel eyes with little flecks of green if you look close enough," Debra said. Ellen nursed her Coke, taking in the description.

"I guess you know what the next question is going to be, Deb."

"You're not that hard to read, Ellen," her friend nervously quipped. "All I will say is that he is much more experienced in that area than I am. And that's all I'm going to say about that."

"Well, let me tell you about my first and only time with a man," Ellen said, reflecting on her experience with Logan. "As you know, we never talked about sex at home. The first time I heard about it was in the school bathroom when I was about 13 or 14. All the other girls were talking about it, and I'm sure Logan heard plenty when he was with the boys."

Ellen sighed. "From the time we started walking to school together it never crossed my mind, though I knew I felt something when he first put his arms around me and kissed me. Hormones are a funny thing, jumping off the map in my body."

Another round of laughter overtook the car.

"I know what you mean, Ellen."

"For about five years, it about drove me crazy, and I know it did him, too," Ellen continued. "But he was always a gentleman. We both wanted to, but neither one of us were brave enough to make the first move. By the time he came home on leave and asked me to elope with him to Myrtle Beach, I knew I was ready. I wanted that boy in more ways than one, if you know what I mean."

By now, the women had passed through Richmond and were well on their way to Washington.

"It took me four days of begging to convince my mom to let me go to the beach," Ellen said. "It took more effort to get her to let me drive her car down there."

"I remember that old '60 Plymouth," Debra recalled. "Candy apple red."

"Yep, you could spot that car a mile off. Mom gave in and Logan and I made plans over the phone to meet at the old schoolhouse."

"Come on, Ellen, get to the interesting part."

"Hang on, I'm getting there," Ellen said. "I picked him up at the old schoolhouse. Logan stretched out in the front seat. I drove right through town with my right hand resting on the steering wheel, trying to be as casual as possible, though my heart was racing. I thought it was going to jump out of my chest."

Ellen smiled, caught up in the nostalgia.

"Logan stayed laid down in that front seat until we got all the way to Reidsville," Ellen said. "That's when I asked him to take the wheel. As we switched seats, we looked at each other and that slight smile appeared out of the corner of his mouth. My heart melted, and I slid right up next to him. He put his arms around my shoulders and said, 'I love you, cotton head.' That was the pet name we had for each other, though we never used it around anyone else."

Debra giggled.

"We got our marriage license soon just before we reached the coast," Ellen said. "It only took 45 minutes or so. Then we headed to Myrtle Beach We both wanted to get married in a church, and we found one called the Little Church by the Sea. I love that name. We called and a gentleman named Thomas McDonald answered. After talking with him a few minutes, he gave us directions. We were there within an hour."

Ellen blushed. "At that point, I was getting nervous because my childhood dream was about to become true. Logan was going to be my husband, until death do us part, which you know I take very seriously."

"You can say that again," Debra said.

Ellen described the church, beautiful in its simplicity. The chapel had been built in the 1750s with an A-frame. White and weathered, it had a steeple in the front, double doors and small windows on each side with thick panes. The inlet crested just a few yards away.

"Rev. McDonnell and his wife were standing in the aisle," Ellen said. "Logan and I still had our suitcases in hand. The pastor was tall and portly, with bright red hair. His wife was a small woman, with auburn hair. They could have passed for brother and sister. I ask if there was any place where we could change clothes. Ms. McDonnell directed us to a small dressing room tucked away to the side."

Debra found herself mesmerized by the tale.

"When I came back to the chapel, Logan was there wearing a black suit and yellow tie. I had never seen him in a suit before, much less a tie. He was one handsome man with those blue eyes and short-cut blond hear glistening from the sunlight creeping through those small windows. He looked great. I had grabbed the same dress that I wore to graduation, the light tan one with the flower design, along with matching heels. We looked at each other and took a deep breath as he took my hand and we approached the pastor together."

"How perfect!" Debra bellowed.

"As we stood there, tears streamed down my face as Rev. McDonnell walked us through our vows. My throat got so tight I couldn't swallow. The pastor reached into his navy suit, and pulled out our rings. I wondered where the rings had come from, finding out some time later that Logan had slipped them to Rev. McDonnell while I was getting changed. I was shaking so much, and I could hardly put the ring on his finger. When he placed that ring on my finger, Logan looked at me with that little grin again. I honestly thought my heart would burst."

The miles seemed to melt away as Ellen continued to tell the happiest story of her life. By this time, all the horror of the morning's hospital visit had vanished from the women's minds, erased by the amazing story being told in the Buick that was well on its way to Washington.

"Ms. McDonnell snapped two pictures with a Polaroid camera, one with us standing in front of her husband as we said our vows and another of Logan placing the ring on my finger. She gave them to us before we left. They are the only pictures I have, and boy did they come in handy later. As we left the church lot, headed towards downtown, Logan looked over at me said, 'Well, Mrs. Mackay, where would you like to spend your wedding night? Anywhere you like will be fine with me. I'm happy to just drive until we see one we like.'"

Ellen explained that the newlyweds were only on the road about ten minutes before they found a quaint spot on the beach side of the highway called the Sandpiper Motel.

"Logan asked, 'How does this look to you cotton head?'" Ellen said. "I told him it looked amazing. As we checked in and walked down to the room. I will never forget the room number."

"What was it?" Deb asked.

Chapter 7

"It was 1, 2, 3 … as in 123 go!" Ellen exclaimed.

"My nerves had calmed down a lot, but they quickly returned when we opened the door and Logan picked me up carried me in," Ellen said. "He placed me down on the bed and the nerves only got worse. Logan took off his jacket and tie. It was late afternoon, and we decided to go out on the balcony to watch the sun set. We sat there for about an hour and made small talk. I could tell he was nervous, too. We knew what was coming next, but we both were too shy to say it. Finally, Logan told me he was going to take a shower and then 'go to bed.'"

Ellen described how she slipped into her gown as Logan showered. She could hear the steady stream of water cascading down on her new husband. Her hands shook as she began to unbutton her wedding dress. After just two buttons, she decided to just pull the entire garment off, tossing it onto a high-backed chair before changing into a gown that went from her neck down to her knees. She got under the covers, pulling them up to her chin.

"Finally, I heard the shower turn off, which made me very anxious," she said. "I didn't know what to expect. After a few minutes, Logan stepped out with a towel wrapped around his waist. He pulled the sheets down on his side, choosing instead to sit down on the edge of the bed. He reached over with his left hand and grabbed the bed sheet, while taking the towel off with his right. He slid under the sheets as the towel hit the floor.

"I looked over at him. He didn't say a word, and I could tell he was as anxious as I was. After a few minutes, he rolled over onto his side and put his arm around me. I moved my legs into a position to invite him, and he took the hint. He was very slow and easy with me, as gentle as a man can be. I was frozen stiff and couldn't move a muscle. My heart was pounding as perspiration started running off the side of my face."

Ellen took pause. She could remember that moment so vividly.

"I had both arms locked around his neck so tight. I thought I was going to choke him to death, right then and there. I think it lasted about a minute or two. He rolled over on his back, and I just lay there like a dead fish because I didn't know what to do or say. I just kept wondering if that was all there was to it. You know, after all the expectations and about five years waiting on this to happen.

"I was a bit disappointed, and I think Logan was, too. I just knew there had to be more to it than those two minutes. It hurt, but it wasn't that bad. I rolled over on my side to look at Logan. He was looking at me, and we just laid there for few moments."

Ellen took a moment. "He gave me a light kiss on the lips, as to say all was okay, but it wasn't okay with me. I reached up and kissed him back and, all of a sudden, that feeling, those hormones, started jumping all around. I knew what was happening. I was finally relaxed. Every time before, Logan was the one kissing me, but this time I laid him over on his back and started really kissing him.

"I was determined not to let the moment slip away. After a few minutes, we rolled around, and I was on my back. I was a lot more aggressive, knowing I was ready … ready and relaxed. I kept thinking, '1,2,3, let's go.' And boy did we! I don't know how much time went by, but I do know that when you love someone like I love Logan, and I know the way he loves me, you become one in marriage. I know what that means now, two bodies melding into one."

Deb looked over at Ellen, who was taking a sip of Coke as tears streamed down her cheeks. She struggled to swallow, overtaken by her emotions.

"Are you okay, Ellen?"

Ellen just nodded a response as she trained her eyes on the highway.

"For the next four days, we only left the room to get something to eat, and then it was back to our room. The last night we didn't sleep at all. Checkout was at one o'clock the next day. And we stayed in bed until noon."

"Like they say, it's like riding a bicycle," Debra said. "Once you learn how you never forget."

"I'll tell you one thing, I think Logan and I tried to ride the wheels off of that bicycle," Ellen crowed.

Debra nearly choked on her Coke, and the women shared another lengthy laugh.

"Well, we only have an hour to go," Ellen said. "Do you think we should take a bathroom break before we get there?"

"I think we should," Debra said. "You just about made me pee in my pants laughing."

They stopped at a Texaco station, filling up on gas and using the bathroom. Soon they were back on the road.

"When did you know you were pregnant, Ellen?"

"A few months later, after I got to school, I started waking up throwing up," Ellen said. "I couldn't keep anything down. I called mom and she told me to go to the doctor. He had a big grin on his face and told me I was three months along. I didn't know what to do or say because I hadn't even told my folks that Logan and I had gotten married."

"Why not?"

"Because I was still two months shy of 18, and I knew all hell would break loose with mom and dad if I told them we had eloped," Ellen said. "So I decided to wait."

Ellen turned the car off the highway as they neared the Holiday Inn.

"Now I had to tell mom, and I knew she and dad were going to be disappointed in me. And I didn't know how they were going to take it," Ellen continued. "By this time, I was 18 and I knew there wasn't a whole lot they could do about it. But I also knew that I wanted this baby and I wanted to stay in school. I knew I was going to need mom and dad's help. I thought about it for about a week. It was a Monday, so I decided to fly home that weekend.

"I called mom on Thursday and told her I wanted to come home and needed someone to pick me up from the airport. She wanted to know what was wrong. I told her it was good news and not to worry."

The Buick pulled into the hotel parking lot. The women stayed in the car.

"I had four days to think about how to tell mom and dad," Ellen said. "One morning, it dawned on me that I was a grown woman, married to the man I love. I knew I had done absolutely nothing wrong. I decided I was just going to tell the truth, and let it go at that. When mom and dad picked me up at the airport, dad was driving mom was in the front seat. 'What's going on with you?' mom pressed.

"'I have three things I want to talk to you about,' I told them. 'And since it's going to take some time, I suggest we wait until we get home.' Mom looked at me, and she could tell I was nervous. I think dad could also tell, but he didn't say a word. When we got home, mom went straight to the kitchen and put on a pot of coffee. That's what she does when she gets nervous.

"After putting my suitcase down, I walked into the kitchen and sat down at the table. Dad was beside me. Mom turned the burner on to start the coffee and then pulled out a chair across from me. She put both elbows on the table and clasped her hands together as if she was going to start praying. She looked me straight in the eyes and gave me a stern look. 'Okay, let's have this good news you were talking about,' mom said somewhat sarcastically. I turned and looked at my dad. He was looking at me with a blank expression. Dad could see I was upset, so he assured me that everything would be alright."

Ellen took a deep breath and continued her story. It seemed neither woman was ready to check into the Holiday Inn.

"I reached down in my purse, and I pulled out the pictures that the preacher's wife had taken of the wedding. I placed them face down on the table. I looked at mom and dad and told them the truth about the trip I had taken several months before. I told them about the wedding as I slowly turned the pictures over.

"Mom stood up instantly and grabbed the pictures before dad could see them. Her eyes darted back and forth between the two Polaroids. At first, her face got real red. Then tears started rolling down her face. Dad got up and paced around before putting his arm around mom's shoulder. He took one of the pictures from her, looked at it and then glanced at me. 'I thought this would happen one day, but I always thought it would be after you finished college,' he said.

Debra, hanging on Ellen's every word, slowly took a gulp of her Coke,

"Mom didn't say a word, she turned around, opened the kitchen drawer and took out a towel to wipe the tears that were coming from her eyes. 'I always knew you were going to marry Logan,' she said. 'You know your dad and I think the world of him. I know how much you love him, but it would have been really nice to have a church wedding here.'

"'I know mom,' I told her. 'But Logan only had about a week before he had to go back, and we wanted to spend that time together. We decided then that we were going to get married.'

"I remember mom taking a coffee cup out of the cabinet. After pouring herself a cup, she turned around to sit it down on the table. 'Well, your dad and I will help you and Logan any way we can,' she told me as she caressed her cup with both hands. 'He's a good boy, and he has a great reputation. I think you two make a good couple. I just wished you two would have let us give y'all a great wedding.'

"Mom blew on her coffee to cool it slightly before taking a long sip. 'There's another thing I need to talk to you about,' I said. Dad turned to look at me, while mom put her coffee back down on the saucer.

"'What's that, honey?' she asked.

"'You know when you told me to go to the doctor last week?' I started slowly. 'Well I went, and he told me that I am about three months pregnant.' Dad's chin dropped. Mom looked like a deer caught in the headlights. Neither one of them could manage a word for what seemed like two minutes. 'Yes, you are going to be grandparents,' I said, anxious to break the silence.

"By that point, dad had silently moved his chair closer to mine. He reached over and put his arm round me, pulling me even closer to him as tears start trickling down his face. I had never seen my daddy show any type of emotion, much less cry. I glanced over at mom. She was still just sitting there in a daze. I got up and walked over to her. She turned in her chair to face me, putting her arms around my waist. She laid her head against my stomach. After a few minutes of shared crying, she let go and took a quiet sip of her coffee.

"'You know your dad and I will do all we can for you and that baby,' mom said.

"'I know you will, mom,' I responded. 'I'm looking so forward to having this baby. And I will need help from both of y'all.' I reached into my purse and pulled out the last letter Logan had sent me. I asked dad to read it out loud so mom could hear. After he read it, I looked at my folks. 'I haven't heard from Logan since I got this a month ago, and I'm worried to death.' As I started crying, dad put his hand on my shoulder and mom walked around the table to embrace me, putting her head on top of mine.

"'It's going to be okay, honey,' mom assured me. 'He'll write when he can, but for now you've got to take care of yourself and that baby you're going to have. Yes, you're going to need some help, and we will be here for you. You can count on that.'

"Needless to say, we were up most of the night talking about the situation and how I was going to balance going school to with a baby. There's no way that I could have made it without mom and dad. Even today, as you know, they are the rock that I lean on. Mom has been absolutely wonderful with Logan, and dad just lights up when he sees that boy."

Ellen finished her Coke, handing it to Deb so she could place a few strands of hair behind her right ear.

"The very next day, mom took those two pictures of me and Logan getting married to the drugstore to show everybody. I think she even walked up and down the streets of Draper to show them off. I know she wanted to make sure everyone knew we were married before word got out that I was pregnant. You know how gossip can get started; first you tell a cousin in confidence, but by the end of the day everyone in town knows about it."

Debra burst out laughing.

"You can say that again," Debra said after calming down. "One of the joys of living in a small town. I have to say, you have handled this much better than I would have. And I want you to know that I'm here whenever you need me."

"That's why I asked you to go with me on this trip," Ellen said. "You should also know that you can call me anytime you need me for anything."

The women shared a long embrace, and one last emotional cry, before they headed into the Holiday Inn to check in for the night. Both knew that the next day held considerable potential and promise.

Chapter 8

Logan was up early, had showered and shaved, and was applying his eye drops when Nurse Noble and Dr. Stillman walked into his room.

"Good morning, John," the doctor said.

"Good morning, Dr. Stillman," Logan readily replied. "How are y'all?"

"I thought I'd come by and check on you before you head to Dr. Elkins' office," Dr. Stillman said. "I believe your appointment is at ten, right?"

"Yes sir."

"We've have been discussing your situation, and we think we may have something that will be good for you to try in a few weeks," the doctor announced. "For now, hold your head back and let me look into that eye before you put the patch back down."

Dr. Stillman took his index finger and stretched Logan's eye open as he shined a small hand held light into the cornea. "I see you've been using your drops and wearing your eyepatch," he said. "It looks good."

The focus shifted to Logan's recovering hand. Logan held it up and rotated it based on the doctor's instructions.

"Your hand is responding well to treatment," Dr. Stillman said. "Can you pick up a glass of water?"

Logan nodded. "Yes, sir, and I can hold it tight."

"That's great, John."

"But there are two things I can't do with it."

"What's that?"

"Button my shirts or pull the fly up on my pants."

"You might want to practice those, John," Dr. Stillman said with an understanding laugh. "Well, I have to make my rounds. I'll be checking back in with you in a few days. The only things you need to do now are eat well and exercise. Put on more weight and just keep getting stronger. I'll see you in a few days.

The doctor and Nurse Noble left to continue their rounds.

Logan looked at the clock hanging on a wall across the room from his bed. He had an hour remaining until his appointment with Dr. Elkins. He got up, resolute to take a short walk before his meeting.

Once he left his room, Logan stopped and looked up and down the hall. Everyone was busy. Nurses were darting in and out of the rooms. Doctors with stethoscopes around their necks clutched clipboards as they made their way through the wing. Some patients were being pushed in wheelchairs, while others adjusted to using crutches. A few injured soldiers simply stood in the door ways of their room.

"I think I'll just walk out on the patio and get a breath of fresh air," Logan decided.

As he opened the glass double doors leading out to the patio, he found the courtyard all but empty. The only person out that morning was Sarge, staring straight ahead in his wheelchair in his usual spot in the far right corner of the patio. As Logan approached Sarge, he made sure not to bother reaching out for a handshake, remembering his experience from their first meeting.

"Good morning, Sarge," Logan said. "How are you this fine Friday morning?"

"I feel fine, John, and it seems like you're feel good this morning, too."

"I got a good night's sleep last night, Sarge, with no bad dreams," Logan beamed. "Just slept straight through, but I've been thinking about what you said. It may be time for me to move on, Sarge. I stopped thinking about what I've done, and started thinking more about what I'm going to do with my life. I'm going to talk to Dr. Elkins about it this morning."

"Well that's good, John, I'm glad to hear that," Sarge said, looking up at Logan. "Seems like you're on the right track."

"I can't just stay here and make this my home," Logan said. "It's like you said, I've got to start looking ahead and try to build some kind of life for myself."

"Now you're talking, John," Sarge replied with an affirming nod.

"The sooner I get out of this hospital and start making a life for myself, the better off I'm going to be."

"Hallelujah, John!" Sarge exclaimed. "That's what I've been waiting to hear you say."

"I've got to walk on down to Dr. Elkins' office, and I don't want to be late. We have a lot to talk about today. Maybe I'll see you later today."

"Perhaps so, John."

As Logan started to leave, Sarge called out to him. "It may be time to change that name of yours," Sarge declared.

"I hadn't thought much about that, Sarge," Logan said, looking somewhat puzzled. "Got any suggestions?"

"What would I do if I could change my name," Sarge mumbled to himself. "Let me see, let me see. I got a good one for you."

"What's that, Sarge?"

"Billy Martin," the old soldier said with an oversized grin.

Logan just stared at him, momentarily trapped in silence.

"Billy Martin, Billy Martin," Logan said, repeating the name. "It seems like I've heard that name before. I just can't remember where."

Sarge just kept grinning. "It will come to you someday," he said. "I think that name just suits you."

"You may be right, Sarge," Logan said as he returned to the hospital through the glass doors. "Billy Martin," Logan mused as he traversed the halls to Dr. Elkins' office. "Sure sounds like a good name to me."

Logan walked confidently into Dr. Elkins' lobby.

"You're a little early, John," the receptionist said, looking up from a magazine.

"I didn't want to be late."

"I understand," she said with a smile. "The doctor will be with you shortly. Let me tell him you're here."

The receptionist got up and went into an adjoining room. "John Doe is here," he could hear her telling Dr. Elkins.

Dr. Elkins rushed out to greet his patient, excitedly motioning Logan into his office and imploring him to take a seat in a brown leatherback chair. "Come on in, John, we've got a lot to talk about today. How are you?"

"I've got a lot on my mind, doctor," Logan responded. "First of all, I don't like being called John Doe."

"Let me interrupt you just for a minute," Dr. Elkins interjected. "You're right. John Doe is not a proper name. Dr. Stillman and I have been talking. We unearthed some cases that are something similar to yours, and many of those patients went on to have successful lives, even in instances where they never regained their memories. At your age, you have a lot of living left to do, young man, and staying in this hospital full-time is not going to do you any favors.

"There are some things we can do to help you. One of them is to have your name changed to something more suitable. There are other things we can help you with. We can't predict how long it will take to restore your memory, or if it will come back, but we know you can't make this hospital your home. We think it's time you got out and started trying to make a life for yourself. You need to move on and try to have as normal a life as possible."

Logan sat alert in the otherwise comfortable chair, fixated on every word.

"Starting over starts with a new name," Dr. Elkins continued. "We can get a Social Security number for you. With that, you can line up back pay for at least two years, which should help you get started on the outside. You'll have a lot of decisions to make. Finding a place to live, going to school, buying a car. We can even help you secure a government driver's license until you settle down. What do you think about that?"

"It's a lot to take in, Doc, but it sounds great," Logan said. "I still want to find out where I came from, but I also don't want to give up on the future. I feel like I have a lot of years left in me and that I should find a way to move on. I just can't stay here sitting around thinking about it. It's about to drive me nuts, Doc."

"And it will if you let it keep gnawing at you," the doctor confirmed. "That's why Dr. Stillman and I believe we need to get moving on this. So, you said you wanted a new name. Do you have one in mind?"

"Yes, sir, I do."

Dr. Elkins picked up his pen and pulled out a piece of paper. "Okay, son, let's have it."

"Billy Martin," Logan said with the same confidence he felt out on the patio with Sarge. "That's the name I want. I don't know why, Doc, but for some reason I just like it."

Dr. Elkins wrote the name down on his paper. "Okay, from now on your name is going to be Billy Martin. That's what we'll use for your Social Security number, driver's license, and so on. We're working on a lot of other things, too, which I'll share with you at our next meeting. I have you down for ten next Friday. Just let Ms. Lawson, my secretary, know if you have any other questions before then."

"I do have one more question, Doc," Logan said as he eased out of the chair.

"What's that, John, I mean Billy," Dr. Elkins said with a chuckle. "It will take me a little time, but I'll get it."

"I'd like to get a pass for Saturday."

"Tomorrow?"

"Yes, sir, for tomorrow."

Dr. Elkins opened the top drawer of his desk and pulled out a small pad. He looked over at Logan as he started writing. "I'm going to use your old name, John Doe, on this pass until we get it officially changed by the personnel department," he said, handing the pass to Logan. "I'm not going to ask where you're going or what you're going to do. All I'm going to ask is that you be back here by nine that night. And behave your damn self."

"I'll do that, Doc," Logan said, feeling suddenly free. He glanced back as he left the office to see Dr. Elkins straightening his papers.

"Did you forget something, son?" the doctor asked.

"I just want to say thank you for what you're doing for me."

"No, son, let me say thank you for what you have done for America."

Logan left the office, wondering as he walked back to his room about what he had done for his country. "Maybe I'll have another quick chat with Sarge," he thought, taking a detour to the glass double doors. Only this time, the courtyard was completely empty, though Sarge's wheelchair was parked in the far right corner of the patio.

"Where could he be?" Logan pondered. "I've never seen Sarge without his wheelchair. I guess I'll just check back later."

Logan gave the double glass door a firm push as he clutched the pass in his injured hand. He felt relieved at being cleared to leave the hospital. He was eager to share the news with his gruff, yet direct, friend, but he didn't know Sarge's name or room number.

As Logan returned to his room, his eyes quickly trained on a two-foot square cardboard box resting on the edge of his bed. The lid was taped up with a simple white label that read: John Doe, Room 122. It had no return address.

"What in the world is this?" he thought as he picked the box up and placed it on the table beside his bed. He began to carefully peel off the tape. It made a slow and labored tearing sound as he pulled it across the box.

Removing the lid, Logan found a neatly folded pair of black pants, a white shirt, and a black long sleeve V-neck sweater. A pair of freshly shined black loafers had been placed in a separate brown paper bag. Black wool socks were tucked inside the shoes.

A note, on hospital stationary, fell onto the floor as Logan inspected the contents. He picked it up and started reading.

John,

I hope all of this fits. It's your fault if it doesn't. I did the best I could with the information I had, and I hope you don't mind the colors. I think these clothes will look great on you, see you around 4:30 today.

Terry

Logan looked up at the clock. Terry would be arriving in less than three hours. He went to the closet and pulled out some extra clothes hangers and hung everything up. "I've got to try these on," he mused, admiring the shoes. He could see his reflection in the polish. He turned them over to inspect the soles, smelling the fresh leather. He slipped the shoes on and paced the room a few times. They fit perfectly. Logan smiled as he placed them in the closet.

"Well, I'm set," he said to himself. "I have the pass and the clothes. I'm ready to escape this place."

After a short nap, Logan arose to put in his drops. He was about to raise his patch when Terry entered the room.

"Let me do that," she said with a big smile as she snatched the drops from Logan. "Now hold your head back just a little bit."

The nurse placed her left hand on the back of his neck and eased the black patch up to his forehead. She moved in closer, standing between his legs. Logan slid his hands onto her hips. Terry hesitated for a second before proceeding to apply the drops. She backed away after completing her task.

"Did you try your clothes on yet?" she inquired, looking at him with bright, smiling eyes and a slight grin.

"I put the shoes on, and they fit perfectly," Logan said. "I figured that, if the shoes fit, all the other stuff would, too."

"I hope so," Terry said, giving Logan a wink as she walked back toward the door. "I've got to make my rounds right now. I'll check back with you a little after nine. Visiting hours will be over by then. That will give us a chance to talk. My plan is simple but we should still go over it."

Logan gave Terry a moment to leave before resolving to return to the courtyard to check on Sarge. He was curious to hear what his friend might think of his new identity and the next day's escape plan. As Logan walked outside to the patio, he could see Sarge, this time with a grand smile on his face.

"Good afternoon, Sarge."

"Same to you, Billy," Sarge said. "Heard you're making that name official."

"It makes me feel like I'm somebody now," Logan declared.

"I understand," Sarge said. "It makes me feel better, too."

"I had a good discussion with Dr. Elkins, and he told me that he and Dr. Stillman are working on some things that may help me get out of here and try to start some type of new life for myself," Logan said. "I can't keep my mind on the past all the time. I've got to start looking forward, and that's what I'm going to do. I can't live here for the rest of my life, that's for sure."

"That's great, Billy," Sarge said. "I think you're making the right moves. You can't live here forever. You've got to move on. And I'm happy for you. It's about time."

"Dr. Elkins also gave me a pass for tomorrow, starting in the morning until nine at night."

"Is that right?" Sarge said with a smirk on his face. "What kind of mischief do you have planned?"

"I don't know what I'm going to do yet," Logan said, hesitant to divulge his plans with Terry but unwilling to lie to his friend. "All I know is I'm getting out of here for a day. So I'll probably be talking to you later, maybe Sunday if you're out here."

"Hey, Billy," Sarge said as Logan started to walk away. "You have a good time tomorrow, but be careful."

That last part stuck with Logan as he walked back to his room. Logan wondered if Sarge suspected anything. "He just seems to know so much," Logan said to himself. "Well he couldn't know anything, but he damn well sounded like he did."

Time moved like molasses as daylight eased into evening. Logan was ready to hear about the plan. Terry was supposed to stop by his room in fifteen minutes. The suspense was eating at him when she arrived, holding a clipboard and wearing an oversized grin. She turned to close the door to the room.

"Okay, sit back down," the nurse said as she leaned against the bed.

"This is how it's going to be done," she said. "It's all quite simple. Tomorrow morning, at 8:45, go to the pay phone just up the hall and call a cab. It will take about 15 minutes for it to get here. Then go to the front desk and show the receptionist your pass. She'll check you out for the day. When the taxi arrives to pick you up, tell the driver that you want to go to the bus station. There's only one in town, and that's where I will be waiting for you. I'll drop you off at the hospital's front steps that night so you can check back in. It will be dark by then and no one will recognize my car. What do you think?"

"It sounds easy enough to me," Logan said, pausing momentarily before frowning. "But I have one problem."

"What's that?"

"I don't even have a dime for a pay phone, much less a taxi."

"I forgot you don't have any money," Terry said. "When I make my next set of rounds, I'll bring you a dime for the call and five dollars for the cab. You can pay me back when you can."

"Dr. Elkins told me this morning that he is going to help me collect two years of back pay," Logan said as a smile returned to his face. "I'll pay you back when that comes through."

"I'm not worried about the money," Terry said as they shared a laugh.

Chapter 9

Ellen was up shortly after daybreak on Saturday morning. Debra awoke about an hour later. The women took a pass on breakfast in favor of coffee and an early start on the task at hand. The plan was to arrive at Walter Reed at nine when the hospital opened its doors.

"They'll have a lot of visitors," Ellen informed her friend. "So we'll want to be one of the first to get there. I'd hate to have to wait in line too long."

"Remind me, Ellen, what's the name you're going to ask for."

"Rodney Smith," Ellen said. "He's on the second floor."

"For some reason, I'm nervous this morning."

"I am too, Deb," Ellen said before quickly changing the subject. "Which pair of pants will look good on me?"

Deb and Ellen went back forth over the wardrobe, mindful that Ellen could reunite with Logan wearing those clothes. Ellen settled on a pair of off-white pants, paired with a black wool sweater and matching shoes.

"We'll just work this hospital like we did the other one," Ellen said. "Only this time I'll meet you at the front door when we finish our rounds."

"What time is it?" Deb asked.

"Quarter after eight."

"Let's start packing the car and check out," Deb said. "By the time we're done it should be close enough to nine."

It only took the duo 20 minutes to pack and check out. Ellen drove straight to Walter Reed. They had a few minutes to spare.

*****

Logan spent several minutes admiring his image in the mirror. He couldn't remember ever seeing himself in such nice clothes. He was decked out in black, except for the crisp white shirts that peeked out from behind his black V-neck sweater.

"If there's one good thing about having a black eyepatch," he said aloud as a grin crept upon his face. "At least it matches everything else."

Logan ran his hands through his sandy blonde hair, watching it fall naturally into place over his ears. It might be time for a trim, he thought.

Logan glanced up at the clock; five minutes before he needed to call the cab. With the number and dime in hand, he stepped into the hallway and marched over to the payphone. To his chagrin, someone was using the phone. Anxiety set in as he worried what might happen to the plan if he was unable to summon the taxi.

Three people were already milling around the front desk, waiting for visitors' passes. As Logan mulled over to the desk to pass the time, the patient who had been using the phone, tossed him the handset. "All yours, solider," he told Logan with a smile.

Just in time, Logan thought, quickly popping the dime into the phone and punching up the number. An operator for Central Cab answered after three rings.

"Hi, I'm Billy Martin, and I need a ride from Walter Reed. How soon can you be here?"

"In about 15 minutes," the operator said in a gravelly voice.

"Good," Logan said. "I'll be waiting out front."

As Logan walked past the receptionist's desk, he could see five people waiting for visitation clearance. Surely, it wouldn't take too long to get approved to leave, he thought. The clock struck nine and a heavyset woman opened a door a few feet behind the desk. She had a no-nonsense look on her face as she made her way toward the small, but growing, crowd. Logan had seen her before, but not very often, since she only worked on Saturdays. Besides, she always seemed quite busy. "May I help you?" she asked the first person in line.

*****

As Ellen and Debra entered through Walter Reed's main entrance, they both were amazed at the hospital's beauty and sense of tranquility. The Buick made its way to a circle that surrounded a water fountain. The hospital had an air of architectural majesty that included huge white columns and the white cupola.

"What an impressive looking place," Debra said.

The sun had started to assert itself, yet struggled to warm the pair as a strong breeze whipped through the parking lot. "I'm glad we decided to wear sweaters," Ellen said.

"Me, too," Debra replied, crossing the street as a taxi stopped to let them pass. "But it is a beautiful day."

*****

One person remained between Logan and the receptionist. It was a quarter after nine, and he was sure that the taxi was out in the parking lot waiting for him.

Ellen and Debra took their spot at the back of the line, counting at least a dozen people ahead of them.

"Not too bad, Deb," Ellen said, assessing their place in line. "We ought to be in front of the receptionist in about five minutes."

As they stood in line, the women eagerly looked up and down the hall. They noticed in the distance a pair of glass doors leading out to a patio that seemed to serve as a social area for patients and their guests.

At the same time, people were meeting in the halls, shaking hands and sharing embraces.

Finally, it was Logan's turn. He stepped up and handed his day pass to the receptionist. She mumbled the name on the pass to herself, and then turned around to scour her files. She pulled out a tan folder, brought it back, and opened it in front of him.

"What room are you in?"

"Room 122, ma'am," Logan said.

"My file says there's a Billy Martin in Room 122."

"Yes, ma'am, that's the name that I'm using now," Logan explained. "Dr. Elkins told me when he wrote my pass that it would take until Monday before all my records would be changed. That's why my pass says John Doe."

The receptionist continued to rifle through the pages in his file.

"I wonder what the hold-up is," Ellen said. "It seems as though there's always someone who manages to hold up the line."

"Yep, it sure seems that way," Debra added.

"Ah, yes, I see it here now," the receptionist said. "They marked through John Doe on some of the pages here and put Billy Martin on top."

She pulled out a stamp and slammed it onto the pass. "Have a good day," she said.

Logan grabbed the paper and hustled to the front door. At that moment, Ellen turned, just in time to catch of glance of a patient bolting for the door. She stepped out of line just in time to see the man make his way down the stairs and into the back door of a waiting cab. She was white-faced when she returned to Debra.

"Did you see that?" Ellen stammered, trembling as she placed her hand against her chest.

"Yes, I saw him," Debra responded. "But that man was a good 50 pounds lighter then Logan, and he had a black eyepatch. I didn't get a good look at his face, but he was dressed in civilian clothes. I don't think Logan would be here visiting, so just calm down."

"The way he walked and carried himself reminded me so much of Logan," Ellen said.

The line was starting to move, and soon the women were facing the receptionist.

"Can I help you ladies?"

Ellen fell mute, forcing Debra to step up.

"Yes, we would like to see Rodney Smith," Debra said. "I believe he's on the second floor."

The receptionist calmly turned around and pulled another file from her cabinet. "Yes, you're correct, he's on the second floor," she said. "Will you need two passes, or one?"

"Two please," Debra said, accepting the passes from the receptionist. She put her arm under Ellen's and helped her get to the nearest elevator. "Ellen, get a hold of yourself."

"Just give me a minute, Deb."

"Okay," Debra said, taking charge. "Let's go to the break room and get some coffee."

Ellen settled into the first chair she saw in the breakroom as Debra placed a cup of coffee in front of her.

"Here, drink this," Debra said as she slid the Dixie cup closer to Ellen, who remained silent. "This will wake us both up."

"I guess you're right, Deb," Ellen finally said, taking a drawn out sip of coffee. "That couldn't have been Logan, but you have to admit there was a resemblance."

"I think the odds of it being Logan are slim," Debra said, stroking her friend's hair in an attempt to calm her down. "He did have Logan's walk, for sure, but that was about it as far as I'm concerned."

"Okay, let's get started," Ellen said, as her confidence slowly returned. She finished her coffee, handing the cup to Debra. "We've got to get back to Draper tonight. We have a six-hour drive ahead of us, and we can't get it done sitting here."

Ellen and Debra spent nearly two hours checking rooms and scouring the hallways. Debra made one last pass at the patio outside the two glass doors before heading back to the front lobby. Ellen returned a few minutes later.

"If he was here, he wasn't here today," Ellen said with an air of dejection.

"You can say that again," Debra said as the women made their way to the Buick. The women rode in silence until they pulled onto the interstate.

"It makes me feel better to know something," Ellen declared. "He's not in either one of the hospitals. I knew it was a long shot to find him. Now I can go home and try and focus on other things."

"What's next?" Debra asked.

"I'm going home, getting Little Logan, and heading back to Boston," Ellen said with a sigh. "I have to get my head back into the books and start thinking about our future. I feel like, in a lot of ways, I have neglected Little Logan, so I'm going to put a greater emphasis on raising him and trying to make a life for us. The plan that I envision for us is going to take a lot of my time, so that's where I'm going to need to concentrate."

"I think you're getting on the right path, Ellen," Debra assured. "With the plans I'm making, it's going to take three more years," Ellen estimated. "I'm going to take an additional year for pharmaceutical business courses. Like I said, I've got plans for the future, Deb."

*****

The yellow cab pulled up to the bus station. Logan got out and handed the driver the five dollar bill, imploring him to keep whatever change remained from the fare. Logan stood on the platform, soaking in the sunshine when a bright green Buick Rivera pulled up. Terry rolled down the window, flashing a smile.

"Hey good-looking, want a ride?" she cooed. She was wearing light tan slacks, paired with a dark brown blouse, collared and buttoned down the front.

"Wow, what a fine car," Logan gushed as he got inside. "And I should add that you're looking mighty fine, too. It's the first time I've seen you with clothes on."

"Hmmm," Terry said, clearly amused at Logan's misspoken words.

"You know what I mean," Logan said with a clever wink.

"I know what you mean," Terry giggled. "It's good to get out of that hospital uniform."

"I really like this car," Logan said.

"It's a '64 Riviera," Terry said. "It was my dad's car. He gave it to me when he and mother moved to Richmond."

"Your dad must think a lot of you."

"I'm his only child," Terry explained. "He's got to love me."

Terry turned the ignition and the Buick's engine roared. She put her hand over Logan's as she walked him through her plan for the day.

"Well I had big ideas for us today, but I had to change the plan," she said apologetically. "Mother called me last night. When I was down there earlier this week I was supposed to bring a little gift back with me, but in my haste I ran off and left it behind. Would you mind going with me down there? It should only take about an hour and a half, and we'll take the scenic route so you can see the countryside."

"That's fine with me," Logan said. "I'm fine as long as I am out of the hospital."

"We won't be long, and when we get back I'll take you to my place," Terry said. "And I'm going to fix you a country dinner."

"That sounds great to me," Logan said. "I'd love a home-cooked meal."

"Then we can relax and have a glass of wine, listen to a little music or watch TV."

"I'm looking forward to it!"

Logan and Terry made small talk as the Riviera pulled out of the station. For fifteen minutes, he told her about his meeting with Dr. Elkins and the long wait to check out that morning. She pointed out a few landmarks along the route.

"Okay, we're going to get on Highway 15," she explained. "That will take us around Washington down to Leesburg. There's amazing horse country out there. Then we'll drive past Culpeper to Gordonsville, where you'll get to see some beautiful rolling heels and some beautiful old plantation homes in the distance. This is the way dad goes when he travels to Johns Hopkins."

"I thought he worked at the hospital in Richmond," Logan said.

"He does, but only two or three days a week," Terry said. "He spends a couple of days a week at Johns Hopkins working in the medical research and development department."

"It sounds like he's really dedicated to medicine."

"Oh, he is," Terry replied. "He spends half his time at home reading and studying. It drives my mom crazy."

Logan could not help but notice how attractive Terry was, with her long dark brown hair flowing in the breeze of the open car window. She typically pinned her hair up while at the hospital, tucked neatly under her nurse's cap. Her choice of civilian clothes gave Terry a totally new appearance that appealed to Logan.

As they entered Gordonsville, Logan noticed a small school in the distance on the right. As they got closer, he realized that some boys were playing softball.

"Stop, stop, stop the car!" Logan said excitedly.

Terry immediately complied, pulling the Buick off the road.

"What's wrong, Billy?"

Logan bolted out of the car without saying a word, and with a burst he ran to the chain link fence that separated the highway from the field. He stood and stared at the game that was in progress. Terry, wearing heels, followed behind.

"What's going on, Billy?"

"I don't know, but seeing these kids playing ball hit me like a flashback," Logan said. "I could see myself playing ball. On the back of my jersey was the name of a lumber company."

"Do you remember the name?"

"No, I could just remember seeing the words 'Lumber Company' on the back," Logan said. "I remember running the bases."

Terry let Logan take a moment to watching the boys scurry around the field, hoping more activity would trigger another memory. Nothing else came to mind, so Logan determined that the time had come to get back on the road. When they got back in the car, Logan had nothing to say. After a few miles, however, he looked over at Terry.

"That was strange," he said with a stunned look on his face. "It was like I could see myself hitting the ball and running to first base. While I couldn't see my face, I knew it was me. It was the damnedest thing."

"I think you'll probably see a lot more of those things as you get your memory back," Terry assured. "Just try to see something in them that you can recall that could give us a lead on where you're from.

That would be a big help as we try to figure out your past. Each one of your flashbacks is such a positive thing."

"Yep, that could be a sign that I'm getting my memory back sooner than I thought ."

The Buick meandered its way across the Virginia countryside, drawing increasingly close to Richmond.

"It won't be long now," Terry said, noting that her parents lived just west of the city. "We should be there in about another 15 to 20 minutes."

Soon they were on a single lane road flanked by dense woods. As they turned a corner, Logan saw a paved drive that led to a set of wrought iron gates with brick columns. The forest, along with long winding driveways, obscured any view of homes. Terry turned into one of the entrances, stopped the car at one of the gates and walked over to a brick column. She flipped the lid on a small box metal and pressed a button. The gates creaked as they started to open. As if on cue, she skipped back to the idling car and proceeded to drive through the gate.

"Aren't you going to close the gate, Terry?"

"Mom can close it when we get to the house," Terry said. "She has a button she can push to do that."

Logan looked out his window at the gate with a look of amazement. The woods, heavily populated with a mix of red maples, oaks and tulip poplars, provided a thick canvass that only allowed sunlight in select gaps between the trees.

"Your folks must own a lot of land to have a driveway this long," Logan said.

"We have about ten acres," Terry said. "We have neighbors from Baltimore who raise horses and cattle. They have 20 acres. I think they just wanted a change of pace, so they moved out here to the country."

Chapter 10

After about a quarter mile, the Buick went over a slight hill, revealing the Warners' home, which was carefully built in the midst of the surrounding forest. A small grassy knoll served as the front lawn. As first glance, you noticed the slate roofing, with domes that reached across the front of the house. The residence had diamond-shaped windows and copper gutters that were striking against an exterior of stone and dark wooden boards. Logan marveled at the magnificence.

Terry parked in front of a gray slate walkway that led the pair to a set of mahogany double doors. Terry gave the brass knob a firm twist and they walked in.

"I'm home," Terry said, and immediately a tall middle-aged woman entered the foyer. Attractive with the same dark hair as her daughter, except for a few white strands, Ms. Warner introduced herself with a welcoming smile. She embraced Terry.

"I'm so glad you came back, honey," Ms. Warner said.

"Mom," Terry said, motioning to Logan. "This is Billy Martin."

"I've heard so much about you, Billy," the woman said, reaching over to take his hand. "I'm glad to finally meet you."

Logan gave her hand a firm shake, smiled and nodded his head. "It's my pleasure meeting you, Ms. Warner."

"Y'all come on back to the kitchen and I will fix us a pitcher of tea," Ms. Warner said, beckoning Terry and Logan to follow her down a hallway with a jute rug and more dark wooden panels. "Then we can go out to the pool and catch up."

"Where's dad?"

"He's at Johns Hopkins," Ms. Warner replied as she pulled out a crystal picture of tea. "He told me to tell you that he would try to stop by Washington late Sunday afternoon to spend a few minutes with you before he comes home."

Ms. Warner walked across the spacious kitchen to pick up a sugar bowl and glasses before pouring tea for Terry and her guest.

"Come on, let's go outside," Ms. Warner said. "It looks like it's going be a beautiful day."

Logan was awestruck by the pool, which rivaled the beauty of the Warner's home. A rock structure rose from the pool's farthest point, accented by a water fall that cascaded down past the craggy stones.

Another set of stones formed a wall that wove its way around the pool. Large boulders and strategically placed flowers gave the setting added character. Logan had never seen such involved landscaping.

"Mom, we can't stay long," Terry declared after they had gathered around a circular glass-topped table just feet from the pool's surface. "We've got to get back soon. I have a lot to do, and I'm going to fix a country style dinner tonight for Billy before I have to take him back to Walter Reed."

"From what Terry is telling me Billy, you may want to sit down with my husband," Ms. Warner said. "Did you know that he's a brain surgeon?"

"No, I did not know that, Ms. Warner," Logan said. He could see Terry's face turning a deep shade of red.

"He may be able to give you a little perspective on amnesia," Ms. Warner said.

"I'd love that opportunity."

"Finish your tea Billy," Ms. Warner said sweetly as she gently patted his hand before rising from the table. "I've got to give Terry something to take back with her."

Logan could see the women talking inside as they walked through the house. After a few minutes, they reemerged to join Logan by the pool.

"I'm sorry we had to leave you, Billy," Ms. Warner said

"That's okay," Logan said, gazing out across the pool's crystalline surface. "I was just enjoying the view."

Terry and Logan stayed long enough to enjoy a second glass of tea. As the ice began to melt in the empty glasses, Terry told her mother that she and Logan needed to head back to Baltimore.

"I understand, honey," Ms. Warner said with a knowing smile. "Come on, I'll walk you to the car."

As they made their way back to the foyer, Ms. Warner stopped to pick up a small brown box resting on a marble-topped table.

"Don't forget this again, Terry," she chided. "Take care of it. You see to that."

Terry promised to attend to the box and its contents and, with a wave goodbye, the pair were coasting down the drive back to main highway

"Okay, back to my house we go, Mr. Billy Martin, for some R&R and a home-cooked meal," she quipped.

"That sounds awful good to me, Terry."

Time flew by as the travelers shared tales about the hospital. Logan admitted that he was still adjusting to his new clothing, while Terry shared the story of how her father had the pool's rock structures built with stones that had been dug up as the house's foundation was being laid.

Soon, they were near the outskirts of Baltimore. Terry made a sudden left turn and pulled into an underground parking deck at a high-rise building.

"What's this?" Logan asked.

"This is where I live, Billy," Terry said.

Terry parked the car, and then walked around to the trunk to pick up the small box that her mother had given her.

"Don't want to forget this," Terry said. "Mother would have a fit!"

She walked around to open the passenger side door for Logan. "Are you ready to go in Billy?" she asked.

"I'm ready," Logan responded with anxious excitement.

They entered the elevator, and Terry asked Logan to press the button for the fifth floor. A few dings later, and the door opened up to Terry's apartment. Logan was amazed at the sheer size of the apartment, particularly the huge glass windows surrounding the pad, providing an awe-inspiring view of downtown Baltimore.

"What a view you have," Logan said, stunned at the sight. "I bet it's beautiful at night."

"You'll have that opportunity later, Billy."

The apartment was adorned in ornate furniture with Victorian design. Oriental carpets covered large swaths of hardwood flooring.

"This doesn't look like you, Terry."

"I know," she agreed. "But it sure looks like my mama. Didn't I tell you this was my parent's place before they moved to Richmond?"

"Yep, I remember that now."

"They bought this place years ago when dad started working at Walter Reed," Terry explained. "And when they moved out, they left everything for me."

"How big is it?" Logan asked.

"Not entirely sure, but it has three bedrooms," Terry said. "Dad turned one of the bedrooms into his study. Each bedroom has a full bathroom and there's a half bathroom just down the hall."

"This place is really nice," Logan said.

"Would you like a glass of wine?" Terry said as she made her way to a cabinet at the back of the kitchen. "I'm going to pour myself a glass while I prepare dinner."

"Sure," Logan said with some hesitation.

"Do you like wine?"

"Can't say," Logan said, reflecting on his smoking experience. "But it sounds better than cigarettes."

Terry pulled out a bottle of Merlot and poured Logan a sample, which he slowly sipped.

"It's very tasty," he said, smacking his lips and smiling. "I think I could learn to like this!"

"You can have a seat on that barstool," Terry said with a motion. "We can talk while I make your meal."

After about an hour and a half, and a bottle of wine, Terry placed an oval-shaped bowl of snap beans and a circular bowl of cream potatoes on the bar.

"Do you mind taking this food through the swinging door over there," she said, pointing toward the dining room. "That's where we are going to eat. Be careful because everything is hot."

Terry instructed Logan to hold the bowls by the handles. "I'll be right behind you with the chicken," she said.

Logan's draw dropped as he leaned in with his shoulder to gently push open the swinging door. The room was completely enclosed in glass, providing another amazing view of the city. He could see clippers and barges making their way through the harbor.

"This is one hell of a view, Terry."

"Yes, it is, I love it," she said, joining Logan. She placed a plate of fried chicken in the center of the table. "I have a bowl of speckled butter beans coming up. Just have a seat and enjoy the view."

Terry stopped short of the swinging door to turn on the stereo, and Barbra Streisand started to sing.

People, people who need people

Are the luckiest people in the world

Terry took a moment to soak in the music and assay the ambience before returning to the kitchen. She returned shortly with the beans in hand.

"Okay, everything's on the table," she said, lighting two small candles placed a few feet apart on the table. She took hold of Logan's hand, and bowed her head for a silent prayer. "That one was for you," she told Logan, giving him a wink.

Lovers are very special people

They're the luckiest people in the world

"Thank you, Terry," Logan said. "I need all of those I can get."

"I think we all do, Billy," Terry said. "Now let's eat."

As they ate, the sun was started to set, giving the city an incandescent charm. They could hear the music softly flowing from the kitchen.

With one person

One very special person

A feeling deep in your soul

Says you were half now you're whole

"Everything is delicious," Logan said. "Where did you learn to cook like this?"

"Not from my mother," Terry responded with a giggle before taking another sip of wine. "My dad never liked her cooking. One day when I was a kid, she fixed something – I forget what it was – but made some type of remark that it wasn't good. That's when mom said, 'If you don't like my cooking, you'd better go out and hire you a cook.' That's exactly what dad did!"

Logan was mesmerized by Terry's smile, her face haloed by the sun setting over the Baltimore skyline.

People who need people

Are the luckiest people in the world

"Dad went out and hired a middle-aged black lady, and boy did she know how to cook!" Terry continued. "Dad loved her cooking, and so did I. She didn't try and whip up fancy food. Dad always said she fixed down home cooking, and that's what he liked. Her name was Rosie Lee Benson, but we all called her Ms. Rosie. She was short and stocky, smiled all the time and, to tell you the truth, she practically raised me. Dad worked all the time, and mom was always at some type of gathering.

"Ms. Rosie would always let me go to the grocery store with her and pick out vegetables. We'd fix dinner, and she taught me all I know about cooking. When I was 13, I decided to surprise my dad by fixing him dinner. Dad was so impressed. He even started calling me Little Miss Rosie. Then again, he loved me so much that he would probably eat my cooking even it if wasn't good. I was always dad's little girl."

"You're a wonderful cook," Logan said. "Everything is delicious. Thank you."

"You're so welcome," Terry said. "I'm glad you liked it. You're the first man I have ever cooked for other than my dad. In fact, you're the only man that has ever been here."

With one person

One very special person

A feeling deep in your soul

Says you were half now you're whole

"Well, I feel honored," Logan said bashfully.

"Let's just say I enjoy your company."

"You have made this a very memorable evening, Terry. One that I will not forget anytime soon. Thank you so much."

They stayed at the table a while longer, listening to more music and enjoying their time together. Barbra had stopped singing, and Terry took the opportunity to invite Logan to join her in the den. "I have a TV in there, or we could listen to more music," she said.

Logan took the napkin from his lap and placed it neatly on the table. He got up and walked over to the windows, soaking in the scenery. Nightfall had arrived and the city was alive with cars whizzing down the streets. From a distance they looked like passenger trains racing with their windows lit up, moving around the city like a kid's train set.

Terry walked over to his side. She stood there for a moment, gazing at him. She took another step and placed her arm around his waist as they assessed the beauty of the city at night. After a few minutes, they looked at each other. Terry was beautiful, with her long hair draped over her shoulders and her hazel eyes staring up at him. Logan slowly pulled her even closer. He could feel her small body pressed against his. Her arms clung tighter around his waist. Logan slowly bent down but stopped just as their lips touched, choosing instead to press his cheek against hers. His heart was pounding, his breath accelerating.

Logan slowly whispered in her ear. "I'm sorry, Terry I just can't right now, I'm sorry."

Terry placed her hand on the back of his head and looked into his eyes.

"I understand, Billy," she softly said. "Don't worry about it. Now is not the right time for you. When it's right, you'll know it."

"I've got a lot going on in my head right now," Logan confided. "I know you understand. Just give me a little more time. I'm getting there, but I just want to be sure that it's right for both of us."

"I totally get it, and I want what you want," Terry said.

Logan looked back at the window, staring at their reflections transposed against the skyline. Terry was gorgeous, and he struggled to understand his reluctance. Something was stopping him but he had no clue what that it could be.

"Well Billy, this is very nice, but we've got to have you back by nine and it's a 30 minute drive to the hospital," Terry interjected. "I think we might want to start getting ready for the trip back."

"I'll help you put everything away."

"Oh no," Terry insisted. "I can do all of that after I drop you off."

An awkward silence permeated the car as they made their way back to Walter Reed. Logan had so much to process. The baseball game. Meeting Ms. Warner. His reluctance to kiss Terry. Each thought blurred into the next as he gazed silently out the passenger window.

"Is everything okay, Billy?"

"Yes," Logan managed to reply. "I hope you know just how much I've enjoyed myself today. Meeting your mother was great, and it was nice getting to know you outside the hospital. This is a day I will not forget. It's been wonderful."

"Well, we'll do it again," Terry assured. "And we'll be able to talk every day. You've came a long ways, Billy Martin. Remember that you still have a ways to go. Just know that I will be there for you, if and when you need me."

As they pulled up to the hospital, Logan took another look at Terry. Before he could manage a word, she placed her hand on the side of his face and kissed him on the cheek.

"There, I got my goodnight kiss," Terry said.

Logan got out of the car, and then leaned into the open window. "And I must say I liked it," he responded with a flirty smile and a wink.

*****

Logan was studiously reading his Bible on the next Monday afternoon when Dr. Stillman and Dr. Elkins entered his room.

"What a surprise, both of you here at the same time," Logan said, placing the Bible on his end table. "What's going on?"

"I have some papers for you to sign, Billy," Dr. Elkins said. "This is the first step to getting you out of here."

"What is it?"

"Well, this first document will set you up with a new Social Security number," he said, handing the paperwork to Logan.

"The other one will secure your temporary driver's license. That should suffice until you can get settled in somewhere."

Dr. Elkins set the remaining documents on the end table beside the Bible.

"After you sign those, Dr. Stillman and I are going to sign it and fast track it through the system." Dr. Elkins explained. "So you'll be able to get two years of back pay, which should help with your new start. If all goes well, you'll be able to draw a check until you can take care of yourself."

"The checks will stop after that," Dr. Stillman added. "Have you thought about a college education?"

"Oh yes, I would like very much to go to college," Logan said.

"What would you think about going to Johns Hopkins?" Dr. Elkins asked. "It's just 20 minutes from here. We can see that you get set up with a one-bedroom apartment. That way, we'll be able to check in with you once a month. We certainly want to keep up with your progress."

"Wow, you guys have been working hard," Logan said, pausing briefly. "I don't know how I can ever repay you for your hard work."

"Billy, we know you're a good young man," Dr. Stillman said. "And you have served your country. It is *our* duty and responsibility to help you guys, especially with the situation you're in. We're just glad we can do this for you. We may not be able to cure you, but we can help you start over again."

"I just don't know what to say," Logan said. "This is totally unexpected. I don't know how I'm going to get into college. I honestly can't say how much I remember about schooling, or how much I learned."

"We both graduated from Johns Hopkins," Dr. Elkins said, motioning to himself and his colleague.
We know the right people over there and we'll see to it that you get in."

Dr. Stillman handed Dr. Elkins a third set of paperwork. "There's one more form we need you to fill out, son," the psychiatrist said.

"What's that?"

"Along with your name, you also need a birthdate for your driver's license and Social Security number."

"That's something I haven't thought about," Logan said.

"We'll need something in order to complete all these papers," Dr. Elkins said.

"Let's just go with today's date, since it is the beginning of my new life," Logan said.

"Works for us," Dr. Elkins said, writing October 3 on the form.

"What year should we put down? How old do you think I am?" Logan said.

"Let's think about it," Dr. Stillman said, tapping his finger to his temple. "Basic training typically lasts six months, and you've been here for nearly seven months. You had to be overseas for at least a year. Guessing you enlisted at 18, so I'd be confident saying you're no older than 22."

"If you're 21, that would mean you were born in 1945," Dr. Elkins added.

"Okay, that settles it," Logan declared. "I was born on October 3, 1945."

"It will take up to three weeks to get the paperwork back," Dr. Elkins cautioned. "So you just sit tight and do the best you can to pass the time. Let me know if you need another weekend pass."

"Thank you, Dr. Elkins."

Logan hurriedly signed the papers and handed them back to Dr. Elkins.

The doctors stood up. Before leaving, Dr. Elkins put his hand on Logan's shoulder. "We'll let you know when we hear something," he said. "So hang tight until then."

Logan sat down on the side of the bed, overwhelmed by the realization that he was another step closer to starting a new life.

"Can I drive a car?" he said to himself, his head spinning, filled with unanswered questions. "Can I pass a college exam, or live alone outside this hospital?"

Logan resolved to venture out to the patio. Sarge would help me regain perspective, he thought. Logan made his way to the glass double doors, where he found Sarge in an all-too-familiar corner of the patio. The wheelchair-bound soldier continued to stand his vigil, staring out into nowhere as his ponytail gently swayed in the fall breeze.

"How are you, Sarge?"

"Doing just fine, Billy," the gruff soldier said. "How are you?"

"I just got some good news from my doctors."

"Tell me about it," Sarge said.

Logan began to tell Sarge about his meeting with the doctors, the papers he had signed and the new life awaiting him whenever he left the hospital. Sarge stared straight ahead, listening to Logan. Then he suddenly looked up, flashing a grin. "Well, Billy, it looks like you're on your way out of here."

"It's just a matter of time, Sarge."

"That's great news," Sarge said. "And I know you'll do well in college, or for that matter anything else you set your mind to."

"You think so?"

"I know so, Billy."

"You certainly have more confidence than I do," Logan said with a shrug.

"You're going to be just fine, Billy."

"After I get set up, Sarge, I'll come and get you," Logan said. "I'll get you out of here for a day and we'll just ride around the countryside and, you know, get you a change of scenery."

"That sounds good to me," Sarge said.

"I've got to go now," Logan said. "I've got a lot to think about."

Chapter 11

Ellen turned the knob slowly, opening the door just wide enough to peek around. Her mother, who was sitting on the couch reading a book, looked up.

"Is he asleep?" Ellen asked.

"I just put him down," Ms. Garrison said, watching her daughter take off her coat and scarf. "He's been all over this house nonstop."

"It's getting colder out there, with higher winds," Ellen said, yanking off her stocking cap.

"You are in Boston, dear, so it only makes sense to expect cold weather and harsh wind," Ms. Garrison retorted. "Didn't you put any make up on this morning?"

"Mom, I'm not here to try and impress anyone," Ellen said. "I'm trying to get an education."

"I know, but it wouldn't hurt to have a little makeup on," Ms. Garrison said. "Who knows…"

"Mother," Ellen snapped sternly. "Let's not go there again. The last thing on my mind is a man. I've got more to think about right now than that."

Ellen walked over and joined her mother on the couch. "Mom, can we talk for a few minutes while Little Logan is a sleep?"

Ms. Garrison turned to look at Ellen, carefully placing a bookmark between the pages of her book. "Sure, dear, what's on your mind?" she asked.

"In two months I'll be done with my third year of college," Ellen said. "In just one more year I can get a degree as a pharmacist and go to work in dad's store, just like he always imagined I would."

Ellen paused, collecting her thoughts.

"But that's changed now," she said. "I have more than that on my mind, as far as pharmaceuticals go."

"Oh my," Ms. Garrison said, exaggerating her syllables as an air of disgust set upon her face. "What could that be?"

"I want my own pharmaceutical business," Ellen said. "I don't want just one store. I want several stores."

"What are you talking about, Ellen?"

"Mom, have you heard of Walgreens?" Ellen asked. "It started with one drugstore in Chicago. Now they have about 20 stores in Illinois. They even have one here in Boston. It's a chain now, mom, owned by one man, Mr. Walgreen."

Ellen stood up. "Think about it, mom," she stated, arms stretched out as though she was talking to a choir. "We don't have anything like that down south, but there will be when I start one!"

"Oh, Ellen, that is an awful big idea," Ms. Garrison said, trying in vain to bring her daughter back to her own view of reality. "What makes you think you can do that? It takes money and education to manage a business such as what you're talking about."

"I know, mom," Ellen said, returning to her seat on the couch. "That's why I need to go to college for one more year, in order to learn how to manage a pharmaceutical business. That's what it will take for me to be able to follow through on this."

"Your father only had to have four years of pharmaceutical college to run his business."

"Back then, that was all you needed, mom," Ellen said. "Now they require that extra year to teach you how to manage your own business. Four years just sets me up to fill prescriptions."

Ellen had a determined look on her face that Ms. Garrison knew all too well.

"Mom, I have got to have something new to focus on," Ellen stated. "I know it's going to take a lot of hard work, and a lot of hours, but I've put a lot of thought into this. I have to be able to try and move on with my life, and this seems to be the best way that I can do that."

"I don't know what your father is going to say about this," Ms. Garrison cautioned. "He's been planning on you taking over his business when he retires."

"I know, mom, but I can't see myself standing behind that same counter filling prescriptions all day long for the rest of my life. I just can't see myself doing that. This is something I've got to do, and I'm willing to work hard to accomplish it."

Ellen walked over to the window, where a heavy rain was starting to bear down on the glass panes.

"The next two years are going to be very critical," she asserted. "I'll also be spending a lot of time at school and doing research at home. I know this isn't going to be easy, but I have been thinking about it a lot and I'm confident I can do this with your help and dad's support."

"You know, honey, that I'll do all I can to help you."

"I know, mom," Ellen said as she walked across the room and gave her mother a warm hug. "I don't know what I would have done without you being here to help with Little Logan."

"I'll talk to your father about it when we go home for Christmas," Ms. Garrison promised. "He may just understand."

"It would be a big help if he would work with me on this," Ellen said.

The next day, after school, Ellen drove to the nearest Walgreens, with a notebook and pen in hand. She took a casual walk around the store before heading back to the pharmaceutical counter. For a moment she stood there, observing how quickly the customers were waited on, and the speed by which the prescriptions were filled. There was an order to the traffic flow in the 4,000 square foot store, as customers would walk down the left side of the aisle to get to the pharmacy and exit through an outside aisle.

Walgreens made sure that customers had to pass by tantalizing displays on the way in and out. Many people were picking up items as they made their way back around the store's ten aisles, organized by the types of items sold, before returning to the front counter to pay. Even the checkout counter had pastries and candy on the lower shelves, designed to catch the eye of younger children. Each observation left Ellen tremendously impressed.

She knew that it would take more visits to glean all the ideas necessary to helping her open her own store. I will visit another one later on, she thought, and then another until I have the design laid out just right for what I want to do with my stores.

Ellen arrived home late in the afternoon, meeting Ms. Garrison in the hallway.

"Is he asleep already, mom?"

"Yes, he had a busy day, honey," Ms. Garrison said with an exhausted look on her face that gave way to a slight smile and a chuckle. "He finally gave up and went to sleep."

Ellen took off her winter attire as she made her way to the bedroom. "I've got to take a peek in on him," she said.

Ellen walked slowly over to Little Logan's baby bed. She was amazed how pretty and perfect he looked, and how much he still resembled his missing father. Even down to the birth mark on his calve. She slowly bent down and kissed the young child on the lips, then stood up again to look down at him. The best kisses in the world when they're asleep, she mused.

Ellen returned to the den to find her mother watching TV.

"How was your day, mom?"

"I had a good day, though it seems longer watching an active child," Ms. Garrison said. "How was your visit to Walgreens?"

"I'm amazed at the store's layout and how they direct customers through the store," Ellen said. "One way in, one way out, and no milling around. The people don't even realize they're being herded and sold items as they walk by them! I can see now how they're doing so well."

"Well I hope you know what you're doing, honey."

"I don't know now mother," Ellen confided. "But you can be sure that I'll know by the time I finish school."

After more small talk about the day, and some planning for the week ahead, Ellen decided to go to bed. "I have a lot to do tomorrow, so I think I'm just going to go and get some rest."

"Okay, honey," Ms. Garrison replied. "You sleep well."

Ellen nestled underneath the sheets. Before cutting off the night lamp beside her bed, she noticed the folded letter sitting on the nightstand, recalling the countless times she had taken it out of the envelope to read. It was the last letter Logan had sent her before leaving on his special assignment. By now, she knew every word by heart, and how he must have felt when he wrote it. She read the last sentence out loud.

And remember wherever you go, and wherever you may be, I will only be a whisper away.

And I'll be thinking of you with every breath I take.

After she read it, Ellen laid the letter across her heart. Tears rolled down the sides of her face, followed by a sick feeling in her stomach. She wanted to cry out loud, but instead settled for a quiet whimper. She could see Logan's face, his blue eyes, his dimpled chin, and that crooked little smile he flashed whenever she said something that made him happy.

"Where are you?" she said in a subdued whisper. "Where are you Logan Mackay?"

She folded the letter up, and returned it to the envelope, repeating a process that had become a nightly bedtime ritual. Ellen pulled the covers up to her chin and, after some effort, drifted off to sleep.

Chapter 12

Logan was getting antsy. It had been four days since his doctors had visited his room. He had received no word on the progress of his paperwork, leaving him hopeful that he might learn something during his next appointment with Dr. Elkins. I just want to start moving on, he continuously thought.

Ms. Lawson, the psychiatrist's secretary, greeted Logan as he entered the Dr. Elkins' office.

"Good morning, Ms. Lawson," Logan replied. "How are you this morning?"

"I'm fine, Billy," the secretary said as she quietly arose from her desk. She made a light knock on the doctor's door before letting herself into the study. After a few minutes, she reemerged to tell Logan he was welcome to go in and see Dr. Elkins.

Dr. Elkins stood up from behind his desk, beckoning Logan to enter. He invited the soldier to take a seat in the big brown leather chair.

"Have a seat, young man," Dr. Elkins said. "We have a lot to talk about this morning."

"Well, I hope the news is good, Doc."

"It certainly is, Billy."

As Logan took a seat, Dr. Elkins handed him a sheet of paper. Clipped to the document was a freshly minted driver's license with Logan's name and ID number.

"This license gives you the right to drive anywhere you want to," the doctor said. "It's government issued. I hope you remember how to drive, Billy."

"I honestly don't, but I'm sure I can pick it up again."

"You might want to figure it out before you hit the highway," Dr. Elkins said with a slight smile.

"Oh I will, doc," Logan said. "You can be sure of that!"

"This sheet has your Social Security number on it," Dr. Elkins said, pointing to the paper in Logan's hands. "And this one has your new birth certificate. The final one, which should make you real happy, is a check from the government. There should be enough money there to help you buy a car, get an apartment lined up and start making plans for college."

Dr. Elkins slid a thin booklet over to Logan.

"And here are all the documents you need to get into Johns Hopkins," the doctor said. "It's about 30 pages. You need to fill it all out the best you can, and take your time doing it. It's going to help the faculty figure out where you need to be placed in their system. Dr. Stillman and I have talked to them about your case and they're willing to work with you."

Dr. Elkins opened a drawer and pulled out a card with a typed address on it. He handed the card to Logan.

"You may want to get a taxi to get to this address," Dr. Elkins explained. "It's a one bedroom apartment with a kitchen and den combination. Nothing fancy but you should like it. We can see to it that you get to stay there for the whole duration of your schooling. And it's close enough that you can walk to your classes."

Logan just sat there, his mouth half open, stunned at all that was happening.

"I don't know what to say, Dr. Elkins," Logan managed in a sheepish tone. "I'm blown away at what you and Dr. Stillman have done for me, and I'm going to do my very best not to let you guys down. I know y'all have worked hard and went through a lot of time and trouble on my account. I don't know anything I can say, or do, to show you my appreciation for what you've done for me."

"I'll tell you what you can do, Billy," Dr. Elkins said, leaving his chair to walk around to Logan's side of the desk. "You can get your butt out of here, go to school, get a degree, and make something of your life!"

"I will assure you, doc, that I'll do my very best," Logan said, snatching up the booklet. "And I will start reading this booklet today so I can give it back to you within a week."

"That will be good Billy, but take your time and do the very best you can to double check it," Dr. Elkins said. "And check it again before you bring it back."

"I'll do just that," Logan said, thrusting his hand out to shake Dr. Elkins' hand. "Thank you so much."

Dr. Elkins shook Logan's hand and placed his left hand on the soldier's shoulder.

"Son, Dr. Stillman and I have confidence in you, and we know you're going to do well," Dr. Elkins assured. "It will take dedication and commitment on your part after everything is solidified, but you are welcome to keep checking back in with me. Once a month, let's say, just as a follow-up. I want to know how you're adjusting. And Dr. Stillman wants to see you every two months so he can keep checking on your eye and hand."

"I will do that, sir. Thank you so much."

"Ms. Lawson will show you out," Dr. Elkins said. "Enjoy your weekend, Billy."

Logan returned to his room, sat down in his chair and began flipping through the papers he had just received. When he got to the birth certificate, he stopped and read it out loud: Billy Martin, birth date, October 3, 1945. His doctors had signed the document as witnesses.

Logan couldn't help but let out a chuckle.

"Well, I guess Sarge was right, I've been reborn," Logan quietly mumbled to himself. "It's time to get on with a life, now that I have one."

Logan began thumbing through the Johns Hopkins booklet, reading the questions aloud. He was surprised that many of the answers came fairly easy to him. He ran over to the end table to grab a pencil, eager to start filling out the first page. Time flew by as Logan perused the pages. At four o'clock, there was a light rap on the door

It took a louder knock to get Logan's attention.

"Come in," he said, still captivated by how much he knew.

Terry stuck her head in the door. "Is it okay if I come in?" she asked.

"Sure, I've got something I want to show you," Logan said excitedly while bolting up out of his chair. He handed Terry his new birth certificate. "I am somebody, Terry! I have it in black and white."

"You sure do," Terry said while looking over the documents. "Oh my, look at this check! What are you going to do with this money, Billy?"

"I'm going to buy a car, and I'll need some money to live off of while I'm in college."

"Are you going to go to college?" Terry asked.

"Yep, Dr. Elkins and Dr. Stillman have made arrangements as long as I pass this test," Logan said, holding up the booklet. "They assured me that they could get me into Johns Hopkins."

"That would be great, Billy," Terry said, giving Logan a hug. "You'd be able to see dad sometime. By the way, he told me last night that he is getting ready to trade his old Ford in for a new car. Maybe I could convince him to sell it to you for a good price."

Terry paused.

"I'll warn you that dad has owned it for about ten years," she said. "It has more than a few miles on it."

"Well that's probably all I can afford," Logan said. "I need to save all the money I can. What kind of Ford is it?"

"I don't know a lot about cars, but this one is a 1955 Thunderbird," Terry said. "It's white and got a lot of zip even at its age. Dad bought it new and has kept it in good shape."

"Did you say a '55 Thunderbird?"

"Yes, it only has a front seat," Terry added. "So you can only have one passenger at a time."

"Isn't that an expensive car?" Logan said. "I could never afford a car like that."

"This one is ten years old with a lot of miles," Terry said. "Don't worry about it. I'll talk to dad and see what he has to say."

Logan just looked at her dumfounded, realizing he was overmatched in this conversation. Terry took the booklet from Logan and began thumbing through its contents.

"How are you doing with this?" she asked.

"Surprisingly, it's not hard," Logan said, running his hand through his hair. "And I think the answers I'm putting down are right."

"That's good, Billy," Terry said. "Let me take it home and look over it before you turn it in. I've always been pretty good at this stuff. Or, you could come over to my place and I can help you study."

"How about Sunday?"

"Sunday would be perfect," Terry said. "I'll even fix you lunch."

Terry returned the booklet to Logan and headed back to the hallway to start her rounds. "I'll talk to you later this afternoon," she said before leaving.

Logan sat back down in his chair and resumed his studies.

*****

As promised, Terry came back to visit Logan later than afternoon.

"Listen up," she said with an air of authority. "You need to call Dr. Elkin's office tomorrow morning. Talk to Ms. Lawson and tell her you need a pass to go open up a checking account at Virginia First National Bank. Tell her that you plan to leave the hospital at 10 o'clock. After you're released, go to the far end of the parking lot. Look for my car and I will take you to the bank. Hopefully no one will recognize my car."

Logan walked over to his window to make sure he understood the layout of the parking lot and where to meet Terry.

"We'll go to the bank and get you all set up so you can do the things you need to do," Terry continued. "For starters, you'll need some more clothes. I'm happy to help you with that."

"That sounds like a plan," Logan said. "I'll call Dr. Elkins' office first thing."

"Now let me look at your eye," Terry said, taking a few steps toward Logan. "I'll put some drops in it."

Logan scooted down in the chair and raised the eyepatch. He moved his head backward to look up as Terry squeezed two drops of medicine in his eye. "You are a handsome man, Billy Martin," she said.

"Thank you," Logan said. "And you're an attractive woman, even with all your hair tucked up under your hat."

"That's good to hear," Terry said, blushing as she smiled down at him. She pulled a tissue out of the box on the end table, handing it to Logan. "Now just sit there a few minutes and let that medicine do its job," she instructed.

"I may be able to check in on you before I leave tonight," she added. "But right now I have to complete my rounds. We'll talk later."

Shortly after 11, Terry returned with a light knock on Logan's door. Logan was lying in bed without his patch on.

"In bed already?"

"I've got a big day ahead of me," Logan said enthusiastically.

Terry walked over to the right side of the bed, looking down at the patient.

"You look different without your patch on," she observed.

"Is that good or bad?"

"I think you look good with or without it," Terry said.

"It's a little hard for me to sleep with it on," Logan said.

Terry took her hand and slightly brushed away the hair from his forehead.

"I spoke with my dad today," Terry said. "He's willing to make you a deal on his car. He said he'll stop by on Sunday to visit for a while. That way you two can talk about the car."

"I'd like that," Logan said.

"My dad said he's been looking at the new Thunderbirds, and it's time he got one with a backseat," Terry said. "He's ready to make a change. I told him all about you, and he said he'd work with you on purchasing the car."

"I hope so," Logan said. "I'm going to need a car. Think you so much, Terry. I don't know what I would do without you."

"Oh, I think you'd be okay," Terry said, looking back to make sure she had closed the door. She reached down and kissed him on the forehead. "Get some sleep. I will hopefully see you in a morning."

She squeezed his hand and quietly slipped out of the room.

*****

Logan was energized the next morning, rising early to put on the same attire he had worn during his last "escape" from the hospital. There was a lighter air about him as he made his way down to the front desk. Ten minutes ahead of schedule, he thought to himself. He dashed out to the parking lot. Logan was about halfway across the lot when he noticed the dark green Buick Riviera waiting for him just a few yards away. This time, however, Terry was sitting in the passenger seat.

"What are you doing?"

"I figure that people with driver's licenses ought to know how to drive," she sassed. "So I'm going to handle your driving exam! It's time to find out whether or not you can drive."

Logan slid into the driver's side bucket seat. He stared down at the automatic shift that separated him from Terry. Without hesitation, Logan instinctively fired up the engine, snapped it into drive and pulled out of the parking lot. It all seemed to click, as though he had never forgotten how to handle a car.

"One thing's for sure, you know how to drive!" Terry exclaimed. "I feel more at ease seeing you behind the wheel driving than I did watching you choke on your first cigarette."

"It feels natural to me," Logan said. "Which way do you want to go?"

"Just go straight for now to leave the hospital. I'll give you directions as we go along."

Logan easily maneuvered the highways to get to the bank, comfortably guiding the Buick into a parking space. After about an hour, and a series of paperwork, Billy Martin had a checking account with Virginia First National Bank.

"Man, I'm glad that's over," Logan sighed as he eased back into the driver's side seat of the Riviera. "I feel like somebody now that I have money in my pocket."

Terry laughed out loud.

"You sure do!" she said. "Now let's go buy you some clothes. We can get everything you need at Sears. You can keep all the clothing at my house until you get your apartment. I don't think it would be good to keep it at the hospital. Besides, you don't have any room for it there."

"You're right, as usual," Logan said, nodding in agreement.

In just a few minutes, they pulled up in front of the Sears and Roebuck store. As they made their way back to the men's department, Terry told Logan to find a seat. She was determined to find just the right wardrobe for Billy Martin. She returned shortly with a multi-colored silk shirt and light tan slacks.

"Try these on to see how they fit," Terry said.

Logan went in the dressing room, returning shortly with a puzzled look on his face. "Why are these pants so wide at the bottom?"

"Because that's what's in style," Terry said with a smile. "They're called bellbottoms. The shirt is also in style now. One thing is for sure, people will see you coming from a mile away!"

They shared a riotous laugh that drew the attention of an older couple making their way through the department.

"Now try these boots on," Terry said.

"They've got zippers up the sides," Logan said quizzically, causing Terry to giggle.

"Yes, it's the style."

"I can't say if I like it or not, Terry."

"If you want to fit in at college, this is what you'll want to wear," Terry said.

"Okay, if you say so."

Logan pulled the boots on and yanked the zipper. As he stared at himself in the three-way mirror, Logan realized that he had no belt. "I feel a little funny without a belt," he told Terry.

"You'll get adjusted to it," she said with a wink. "This is the latest fashion."

"It's hard to see myself without having green on," Logan said, referring to his hospital garb.

"You sure do look good, Billy," Terry said. "I'm impressed at how tall you are without boots on."

"Six foot two," he said.

"Those boots add another inch," Terry said, looking him up and down. "You look like you just stepped out of a magazine, Billy. You look real good."

Terry glanced down at her watch.

"Look at the time!" she said alarmingly. "We have to get you back to the hospital by two o'clock. Why don't you change back into your regular clothes and I'll meet you at the register to pay for these."

They shared another laugh as Logan returned to the dressing room.

It wasn't long before Logan pulled back into the back corner of hospital parking lot.

"I'm going to take this stuff home and hang it up for you," Terry said, looking around to make sure no one was near the Buick. "You can come and get it when you're set up."

"I really appreciate your help," Logan said. "It's been great. Thank you so much, Terry."

"I was glad to do it, Billy," Terry said. "I've got to go. I'll see you around four. Bye!"

Terry quickly walked around the Riviera to resume her place behind the wheel. After letting Logan clear, she pulled out and left the lot in haste.

Logan decided to visit Sarge before heading back to his room. It was an exciting day, and he was eager to share his successes with his friend. There was so much to discuss. He had a new life, new opportunities and a new wardrobe. Logan immediately noticed Sarge's absence as he walked through the glass double doors.

I wonder where he's at, Logan thought. The autumn air had begun to turn crisp, whipping a few stray leaves across the courtyard, and Logan figured that Sarge had decided to stay inside. As he made his way down the hall, Logan noticed all the other veterans, confined to wheelchairs or missing limbs, and he started to feel embarrassed about all of his own good fortune in the midst of so much pain and suffering. That moment brought Logan quickly back down to reality. He was fortunate to have a shot at a new life. He was equally determined not to squander that opportunity.

Chapter 13

Logan was sitting in his chair engrossed in the collegiate booklet when Terry walked into the room.

"What are you doing?" she asked.

Logan held up the booklet as though it were a torch. "Just reading," he said, beaming.

"I've got a little bit of news for you," Terry said.

"What's that?"

"There's been a slight change in plans for Sunday."

"What kind of change?" Logan said.

"Dad is still coming over for lunch on Sunday, but he is going to swing by the hospital around noon to pick you up in the Thunderbird," Terry said. "After I told him about the other day, he wants you to drive his car over to my house to see how you like it. He said that, if it suits you, he's going to make you an offer you can't refuse."

"That sounds fantastic," Logan said.

"It will also give you an opportunity to get to know my dad," Terry said. "I know you will like him. He's a down-to-earth kind of guy, and I know he's going to like you, too."

"I hope so," Logan said with some trepidation.

"And it will give you a chance to talk to him about your amnesia," Terry said. "He knows right much about it."

"How is that?" Logan asked.

"He was a brain surgeon at Johns Hopkins," Terry said.

"Yes, that's right. Your mom mentioned that when I met her.," Logan said.

"He was a good one, too," Terry continued. "Now he's into medical research. I don't know if he can come up with a cure, but I'm sure he'll have some theories on how it could have happened."

"Well that's something I would like to know," Logan said, sitting up in his chair.

"Just make sure you get another pass lined up," Terry said. "Ask to check out around noon. Go outside and watch for his white Thunderbird. You won't be able to miss it."

Two days later, Logan was sitting on the top step in from of the hospital, anxiously waiting on Mr. Warner. He was clutching his test booklet, which he had rolled up like a baseball program. The sun helped to offset a seasonal chill, and a number of patients and visitors filed past him along the stairs.

Logan was also filled with excitement. He kept looking out across the water fountain and the car circle. In the distance, he saw the Thunderbird, glistening white with a hard top, slowly coming into view. Logan stood up.

An oversize smile found its way onto Logan's face as the sports car made its way around the circle before coming to a full stop at the bottom of the stairs. A tall man, wearing khaki slacks and a tan suede sports jacket, negotiated his way out of the car. His dark hair was starting to gray around the temples, but there were no wrinkles when he smiled at Logan and motioned for him to come over to the car. He reached out to shake the soldier's hand.

"You're Billy Martin, I presume," Mr. Warner declared.

"Yes sir," Logan responded. "You must be Mr. Warner."

'Indeed," Mr. Warner said, putting his free hand on Logan's left shoulder. "Come on around, Billy, and let's take the car for a spin. I want to see how you like this modern classic."

"Are you sure, Mr. Warner?"

"A man has to know what they're getting into, Billy," Mr. Warner said, waving his hand toward the driver's side. "That not only applies to cars, son. It is an essential life lesson."

Just like Mr. Warner, Logan had to duck slightly to get into the car.

"Oh man, it's beautiful!" Logan said as he settled into the seat. He could hear the engine roar as he tapped the accelerator. With ease, he put the car in drive and started around the circle. In no time, they were out on the open road.

"What do you think, Billy?" Mr. Warner asked, ending a short moment of silence.

"It's a great car and I love it." Logan said.

 After pulling into the underground parking lot of Terry's apartment, Logan stepped out of the car. He took a long walk around the Thunderbird, admiring its curves.

"I'd love to buy the car, but I'm sure I couldn't afford it."

"We'll work it out, Billy," Mr. Warner said as he opened the trunk and pulled out a small box that resembled the one Terry had picked during the recent trip to Richmond. "Let's talk about it after we get settled in."

Mr. Warner rang the doorbell to be greeted by Terry's voice.

"Well if it isn't my two favorite men," she said. "Come on up!"

Mr. Warner handed Terry the box, though she never said a word during the exchange. She gave Logan a hug and told the visitors that lunch would soon be ready.

"Why don't you just go into the den and make yourselves comfortable," Terry said as she made her way back to the kitchen. "You can talk business in there. I'll call you when everything's ready."

Logan handed Terry his rolled-up test papers. "Would you mind holding onto this, too?"

"I'll take a glance and we can discuss it more after dinner," she said.

As the men entered the den, Mr. Warner walked over to a bar built into the wall. Surrounded by glass, the bar had a small stainless steel sink. Logan was impressed by the room's beauty and elegance of the room. He heard the ice rattling in a tumbler as Mr. Warner fixed a drink.

"Would you like a drink, Billy?"

"No, thank you," Logan said. "But I appreciate the offer."

"So I understand you have a problem with memory loss, and that Dr. Elkins at Walter Reed is working with you," Mr. Warner said.

"Yes sir."

"Ken's a fine doctor," Mr. Warner said. "If anyone can help you, he can. Do you mind if I ask you a few questions about it?"

"No sir, go right ahead," Logan said.

"I'm confident that the injury to your right eye is closely tied to your memory loss," Mr. Warner said. "Your memory bank is centered in the middle of your brain. I'm sure you've heard of people losing their memory after falling down and hitting their head."

"Yes I have."

"Well, I know of some people who have never been able to regain their memory," Mr. Warner said soberly. "Then there are some who have recovered their memories, yet certain types of feelings, preferences if you will, never came back. For instance, you may have liked certain foods before the accident. Now you don't.

"The same could apply to sports, though you may not really remember playing them in the first place. Basically desires that used to exist just aren't there anymore. Of course, I've some instances where everything, even the preferences and emotions, come back."

Mr. Warner took a sip of his scotch and took a seat.

"It's strange and fascinating how the brain works," he said, tapping his ring on the side of the glass. "And we still have a lot of research ahead of us as we try the figure it all out. There is still so much to learn. The brain is a complex thing, but hopefully we will figure it out some day. For now, all we can do is put out our best guesses and test them out."

Mr. Warner set his tumbler down on a granite coaster.

"If you ever have any questions for me, please feel free to ask," Mr. Warner said. "I will do all I can to help you, Billy."

"I really appreciate that Mr. Warner," Logan said. "For now I'm just taking life one day at a time. I just hope that I wake up some morning and I'll have my memory back. I know I can't depend on that happening, so I'm just going to keep aiming to build a future for myself using what I have."

"Billy, that's a great attitude," Mr. Warner said. "Okay, let's discuss the Thunderbird. We know you want to buy my car."

"Yes sir, but I'm not sure I can afford it."

"This is what I'm going to propose to you," Mr. Warner said, leaning over and lowering his voice as though he were having a clandestine conversation. "The car is almost 11 years old. I bought it new in 1955 for a little over $2,900. Today, it has 48,000 miles, but it's in perfect shape as far as I know."

Mr. Warner took another sip from the tumbler.

"This is what I'm willing to do," he told Logan. "I'm asking $300, though I'm sure I could get more if I wanted to. You can pay me any way you want, even if it means monthly installments. I want you to have this car and any way you want to handle it is fine with me."

Logan grinned. "The Army has already given me two years of back pay, so I think I can pay it all now and still be okay financially."

"If that's what you want to do, Billy," Mr. Warner said, reaching into the inside pocked of his suede jacket to pull out the car's title. "I've already signed it over to you. Congratulations, the car's all yours. Just take good care of it."

"I really appreciate this, Mr. Warner," Logan said.

"You're welcome, Billy," Mr. Warner said, taking one last gulp of his scotch as the remnants of ice settled at the bottom of the tumbler. "I'm glad I could help you. Now let's go see if Terry has dinner ready."

Terry had already taken off her apron when they met in the dining room. She had a knowing smile on her face.

"Do you have a car, Billy?" she asked slyly.

"Yes I do," Logan gushed as the Warners laughed. "A 1955 Thunderbird!"

"The boy drives a hard bargain," Mr. Warner said with a chuckle.

"Dinner is ready, so let's sit down," Terry said.

"That sounds good to me," Logan said as he claimed a seat at the table.

"It looks like Little Miss Rosie has done it again," Mr. Warner said as he rolled up his sleeves and surveyed the array of fried pork chops, corn on the cob, snap beans and creamed potatoes. "All of my favorites."

"It looks real good, Terry," Logan added.

"I hope it tastes as good as it looks," Terry remarked.

Dinner facilitated small talk about current events, hospital life and, of course, the 1955 Thunderbird. All of the bowls were nearly empty when Mr. Warner proposed how everyone would get back home. Mr. Warner agreed to take

Terry's Buick back to Johns Hopkins, while Terry would drop Logan back off at Walter Reed in the sports car. After getting tags and insurance, Logan would take Terry over to Johns Hopkins to pick up the Riviera.

"My wife can pick me up later that day," Mr. Warner said as he slid his chair away from the table. "It looks like I'm in the market for a new car. Billy, I'd like to stay longer to talk with you, but it's getting late and Terry's mom would raise hell if I don't get a move on."

Terry walked around the table and put her arms around her dad.

"Thank you, dad."

"Thank you for the fine meal, sweetie," Mr. Warner replied. "It was great."

"Be careful driving home," Terry told her father.

"I hope you enjoy your car young man," Mr. Warner said as he grasped Logan's hand. "And just keep moving forward."

"I will sir," Logan said as he vigorously shook Mr. Warner's hand. "Thank you very much for working with me on buying your car. I will take good care of it."

Mr. Warner gave his daughter another hug and let himself out. As soon as the door closed, Terry ducked into the kitchen and returned with the test booklet.

"I'm totally impressed," she said, emphatically pointing the book at Logan as she spoke. "You did great! I couldn't find anything wrong. I didn't know the answers to a lot of the questions, but you did.

You must have been a good student in school to do that."

Terry set the book down on the kitchen table.

"I only have a few more pages to look at," she said, looking up at Logan. "Can I pour you a glass of wine?"

"Sure, that sounds good right now," Logan said.

Terry smiled as she reached for a bottle of red wine. "If it's okay with you, I'd like to take your test over to one of dad's friends when I go pick up my car," she said.

"Dr. Elkins also suggested that I go and check out the apartment they he and Dr. Stillman have set up for me," Logan said. "That is, if I get accepted."

"You're going to be accepted all right," Terry assured. "If you get the address, I'll help you find the apartment. Dad should be able to give us directions. I'd really like to see it."

Terry handed Logan a glass of wine. He leaned over to take a sip. He hesitated for a moment, staring blankly at the glass he was holding before looking up at Terry, who was in the kitchen pouring over the test sheets. He sat the glass down and walked over the counter to Terry, who had her back turned to him. Logan whispered her name as he wrapped his arms around her waist.

Terry slowly turned around to face Logan, still holding the papers in her left hand. She was taken slightly aback, surprised to see him standing so close to her with a serious look on his face.

"What's wrong Billy?" she asked.

Logan hesitated for a second as he looked directly into Terry's eyes. He moved his hands up, placing his left hand on the small of her back and the other on her shoulder. "Words can't express my gratitude for what you have done for me," he said.

"There's no way I could have gotten this far, getting my life in order, without your help," he continued. "You have been a godsend, and there's no way I can express my appreciation for you."

Terry dropped the booklet on the counter, put her arms around Logan's waist, and placed her head on his chest,

"Billy, just let me say that you have no idea how much *you* have done for me," Terry whispered. "I have enjoyed every minute spent with you. Seeing you happy brings me joy. It has been a long time since I have been really happy. You have given me that, and I would like to just think you for it."

Terry gazed up at Logan. Seeing the passion in her eyes, he knew that this was the perfect time to kiss her. Instead, he held her tightly and stroked her hair..

"That time is coming," he whispered. "Just give me a little more time."

"I know," Terry managed to respond. "When the time is right. I'll just have to wait on that time."

Terry gave Logan some distance along with a smile of understanding and veiled disappointment.

"For now, let me finish this paperwork," she said to change the subject. "We've got to get you back to the hospital, boy."

Summoning a grin, she turned around and picked the test up. "Now you just go over there and relax until I'm finished."

"Yes ma'am, I will do that," Logan said.

Terry took fifteen minutes to get the papers in order. "I didn't have to change a thing," she told Logan. "You did a great job, Billy. You should have no problem getting into that school."

"Well, I hope so," Logan said with modesty. "I've got a lot riding on that test."

"It's time for us to go," Terry said, glancing up at the clock. "But hold on a minute, I've got something for you."

She left the room briefly, returning with a pair of pants and a shirt, protected by a clear plastic bag.

"Take this with you," she said, handing the clothing to Logan. "Wear them when I pick you up tomorrow morning. Let's say 10 o'clock. I'm getting a little tired of seeing you in all black."

"Hey, I can do that," Logan said.

"Let's get a move on," Terry said. "I've got a lot to do when I get back."

"I understand," Logan said, as he opened the door for Terry.

Terry and Logan said their goodbyes in the back corner of the hospital parking lot. Logan stayed behind as she drove off, taking a deep breath. What a woman and what a great car, he thought as he turned to make his way across the lot back to Walter Reed.

"I've got to talk with someone about this problem with Terry," he mused aloud as he walked up the stairs. "I wonder if Sarge is out on the patio."

Logan went out the familiar glass doors. Sarge was all alone in the courtyard.

"How are you, Billy?" Sarge asked.

"I've got a problem, Sarge, and I thought you might be able to help me," Logan said, taking a seat next to his mentor.

"With everything going so right in your life, how could you have a problem?" Sarge asked

"It's about Terry," Logan started. "Twice she has left the door open for me to kiss her. Believe me, I want to, but I just couldn't. It's like something stops me, and it's really bothering me. She's been so good to me, and she looks great. I like being around her, and I love seeing her smile and laugh out loud! I just can't get comfortable kissing her."

"Billy, the only thing I can tell you is that your subconscious mind must be telling you to save those feelings for another time, with her or with someone else," Sarge said. "Just take your time and enjoy her company and friendship. You'll know when the time is right, if it is ever right. Don't worry about it right now because you have a lot of other things you need to take care of first."

"You're right, Sarge," Logan said as his spirits slowly lifted. "I've got other things on my mind and, like you said, there won't be a problem when the time is right."

"What's in the bag?" Sarge asked.

"Just a pair of pants and shirt," Logan said. "It's what Terry wants me to wear tomorrow."

"So you're going civilian tomorrow, are you?"

"I'm going over to Johns Hopkins and she wants me to dress up," Logan said.

"I can understand that you want to look your best," Sarge said.

"Sarge, would you like me to push you back to your room?" Logan asked. "It's getting pretty late."

"That's okay," Sarge replied. "I'm going to stay here a few more minutes and then I'll go in."

"I will be glad to push you to your room."

"Nope," Sarge said decisively. "I got it Billy. You have a good night."

Chapter 14

Logan sat upright in bed, sweat running down his forehead. His could tell his pillow was drenched as darkness continued to envelop the room. He fumbled in the darkness to turn on the lamp light, rubbed his eyes and took a quick glance at the clock. It was 5:40 in morning.

In a flash, a third-shift nurse that Logan didn't know entered the room.

"Is everything all right?" she said, rushing to his side.

"Yes, I'll be fine," Logan said as his eyes adjusted to the light. The nurse nodded her head and left.

I wonder if I should go down and talk to Dr. Elkins about this dream, Logan thought. He hesitated. If I tell him about this he may think I'm a nut case. He may not let me out of here. I think I'm just going to wait.

By 10 o'clock, Logan was dressed in his new outfit, sporting dark tan slacks and a light green shirt. He left the hospital and walked to the back of the parking lot, where Terry was waiting in the white Thunderbird.

"Were you waiting long?" Logan asked.

"No," Terry said gleefully. "I just got here, and I must say you look great."

"Thanks," Logan said. "You look mighty fine this morning, as usual."

"We have a lot to do today, Billy," Terry said in a professional manner. "We're going to the bank, and then the DMV, before meeting dad at John Hopkins. He picked up the key to the apartment you'll to be living in."

Terry reached out to open the glove compartment, pulling out the test booklet. "Dad also said that he would take this and make sure it got into the hands of folks who can fast track it to the right people, and hopefully you'll be able to get the results quickly."

"That would be great," Logan said.

Logan withdrew funds for the car, and then secured new license plates from the DMV. Terry turned on to Broadway Street in Baltimore before heading to Johns Hopkins. Logan was impressed by the hospital. It looked like a huge castle, with a large glass dome arising from the center. The interior was equally amazing, with a towering statue of Jesus arms outstretched, keeping watch over the administration building.

Terry explained to Logan that the statue was known as "Christus Consolator" or "The Divine Healer." She told him how employees, patients and visitors would rub the statue's toes in passing, often praying. For many, it had become a symbol of compassion and hope.

As Logan stood there admiring the statue, Mr. Warner arrived sporting a big grin.

"Well, I see you made it," Mr. Warner said as he embraced Terry. Logan wasted no time giving Mr. Warner the cash.

"I just want to thank you again for selling me the car," Logan said. "I love it."

"You're more than welcome, Billy," Mr. Warner said. "I'm glad you like it. Well, what do you think about Johns Hopkins?"

"I'm totally impressed," Logan said. "I think it's a beautiful facility."

Terry handed her father the test booklet. "I think he did very well on it," she said. "I didn't have to change anything on it or make suggestions."

"Excellent!" Mr. Warner said. "I will turn this in as soon as I leave here. You should hear something in about a week."

"That soon?" Logan said.

"I have some people in the administration area that owe me a favor or two," Mr. Warner said. "I'm hoping they're going to send it right on through."

Mr. Warner reached into his coat pocket to pull out a key attached to a metallic chain and a tiny wooden cross.

"This is the key to where you'll be staying at if all goes well," he said, explaining how the buildings were built in the early 1920s. "They are made of brick and rock. A lot of the professors lived in them when they first arrived on campus. There are only about eight units, but everything has been updated. You're going to be the only student staying in one of these, thanks to Dr. Elkins and Dr. Stillman. I think you're going to like it, Billy.

"As you pull out of the parking lot, turn right and go about a mile on the right you'll see a set of rock columns. Drive through them and follow the paved road through the woods until you see driveway eight."

Mr. Warner handed the key to Logan. "I'm sure I'll be seeing you later," he said.

"I really don't know what to say, Mr. Warner, except thank you so much," Logan said. "I will assure you that I will do my best while I'm here."

"I'm counting on you to do just that, Billy," Mr. Warner said. "And I know you will. It was good seeing you, but I've got to get back to work. You two have a good day."

Father and daughter shared an embrace before Mr. Warner headed back to his office.

Terry took the wheel, guiding the Thunderbird as Mr. Warner directed. They drove between the rock columns and started up the narrow winding paved road though a heavily wooded area. Oak trees populated the forest, partially clothed in colored autumnal leaves. A sign marking driveway eight came into view on a small rock column. They turned into the driveway, which led to a small hunting lodge with a rock foundation. Aged bricks ran from the foundation up to a frame roof. The building had a small front porch with its own roof. Perched upon a hill, the cottage overlooked a declining hillside with a mix of wooded area and an open field.

"Boy, this is pretty," Terry said.

Logan opened the car door. Without saying a word he stood beside the car, mesmerized by the building's grandeur.

"It's beautiful," he said.

"I've got the key," Terry said. "Let's go inside."

They walked up on the porch, unlocked the door and stepped inside. Logan and Terry stood there, amazed at the interior. The floor consisted of wide cedar boards, ending at a rock fireplace along the back wall. The furnishings included a dark brown leather sofa, a pair of leather camelback chairs, strategically placed in front of the fireplace. To the right was a small bar separating the galley kitchen. The bedroom had a standard-sized bed and dresser.

"My goodness, I could live here with no problem," Terry said. "Just look at all those throw rugs. I bet they're 50 years old, yet they're in perfect condition. You don't see those anymore."

"I'm home," Logan said. "This place is great. I just hope I pass those tests."

"Oh, you will, Billy."

*****

Logan dropped Terry off at her car before heading back to Walter Reed. For the time he could remember, he was happy.

He could see it all so clearly. Getting out of the hospital, going to college, and having a great place to live all seemed to be within reach. And he already had a fine automobile. And Terry, he thought, what could I do without her?

A week passed, and Logan had yet to hear from Johns Hopkins. Doubt had started to creep into his psyche when Dr. Elkins and Dr. Stillman walked in to pay him a visit.

Dr. Elkins was holding a letter, which he enthusiastically handed it to Logan. Logan could see John Hopkins' seal on the envelope.

"We didn't open it Logan," Dr. Elkins said. "We thought maybe it was your responsibility to do that."

Logan just stared at the envelope, before looking up at the doctors. Each had a stern look that revealed a hint of nervousness.

"Well I guess this is it," Logan said.

He opened the envelope and pulled out a single sheet of paper with a small amount of typing on it. Logan began to read the message out loud.

Congratulations!

You have been accepted in our business management course. Your test score was quite acceptable, placing in the top 12% of our applicants. We're looking forward to seeing you at our Jan. 5 enrollment.

Logan couldn't believe it. He read the letter a second time to be sure before looking up at the doctors in disbelief.

"I just want to say I'm so happy," Logan said, holding the sheet so tight that it creased slightly. "Thank you both for all your hard work on my behalf."

"You don't need to thank us, Billy," Dr. Stillman said. "You're the one that worked so hard on it. I'm just glad that we were able to work this out for you, and I know you're going to do well."

"We're not done with you, son," Dr. Elkins interjected. "You need to come in and see us around the first of every month. I just need to talk with you for a few minutes, and Dr. Stillman wants to keep checking on that eye. If everything works out we can spread those visits out longer. We are going to do is discharge you by the end of this week. Before then, you can come and go as you wish. We know you've got to get that apartment ready to move in."

"Yes sir, I will do that," Logan said.

Logan continued to clutch the letter as the doctors left. I've got to go tell Sarge, Logan thought. I know he's going to be happy for me. Logan walked down the hall through the glass double doors. He looked out to the distant corner that Sarge frequented, but he only saw an empty wheelchair.

"I wonder where he's at," Logan said to himself. "It seems as though he's never there when I have good news."

Every afternoon that week, Logan visited the patio, but Sarge never showed up. Even on Friday, Logan's release day, Sarge was nowhere to be found. Logan spoke with the front desk, but was told that no one had checked out of the hospital during the week. As he said his goodbyes to the staff, Logan slipped a note to Nurse Noble, asking her to give it to his mentor.

"Ms. Noble, tell him that I'm sorry I wasn't able to talk to him before I left," Logan said. "But I'll be back in the next few weeks, and I will definitely look him up."

"I will, Billy, don't worry about it," Nurse Noble said, holding up the folded sheet of paper. "I'll see to it that he gets your letter."

Later that day, Terry and Logan surveyed the apartment, proud of the work they had done to get the place ready for his move in.

"Well, it looks like you're set up, Billy," Terry declared. "You've all new bed sheets, towels and toiletries. I also washed your coffeepot, and there's coffee in that cabinet over the pot. So you can have coffee first thing in the morning. All you need now is a few groceries, which I can help you with tomorrow since I don't have to work. I'll fix your first dinner here, and I will provide the first bottle of wine to celebrate!"

"That's great," Logan said. "A home-cooked meal in my own place sounds great. I can't wait."

Logan woke up early on Saturday morning, blinking as the sunlight hit his face. He sat straight up in bed, initially startled before regaining his bearings. Logan realized he had just spent his first night in his own place. Still wearing just his underwear, he got up and went into the kitchen. As he stopped and looked around, he finally felt at home.

Logan peered out his small kitchen window. There was a thick layer of frost on the ground, and a pair of squirrels were quarreling over a huge tree, leaving tracks as they chased each other. He noticed the coffee pot, sitting beside the sink. After putting a pot of coffee on the stove, Logan decided to take a quick shower. Coffee should be ready by the time I'm done, he thought.

After taking a shower and getting dressed, Logan walked back into the kitchen to find that the coffee was ready. He took a cup out of the cabinet and poured himself some coffee. His smiled broadly as he took a sip. Not too shabby for a man who just made his first cup, he mused.

Chapter 15

Logan got dressed and took his coffee to the front porch, setting his cup down on the top rail. He just stood there for a few moments, watching the steam escape the mug. He enjoyed the scenery. In the distance, over the treetops, he could see the dome at Johns Hopkins' hospital, appreciating the short walk he would be taking to the school. Logan took his left hand out of his pocket and, without thinking, reached for the coffee cup.

He looked down at his hand, realizing he had no thumb and half of his index finger was missing. Logan stopped and held it up, staring at it in astonishment. How did this happen, he thought to himself. How did I do this to myself? What was I doing for this to happen? Logan reflected on the dreams he had been having, and seeing his hand in the dream. He snapped back to attention when Terry pulled into the driveway.

"Good morning Billy!" she yelled out as she got out of the car. "How are you this morning?"

"I'm doing great Terry," Logan said. "What are you doing up so early?"

"I get up early every morning, Billy," she said as she walked up to the porch. "Life's short, and I don't want to waste any time sleeping when I can be up and doing something."

Terry noticed the mug in Logan's hand. "I see you have your coffee ready."

"Yes, I do," Logan said, opening the door to let Terry in.

"I thought we would get an early start," Terry said, walking over to pour herself a cup of coffee. "We've got a lot to do. You need groceries, and we should maybe pick up a few other things while we're out."

She took off her winter coat, laying it across the back of the leather chair. She took a look at the fireplace. "Boy, it would be nice to have a fire this afternoon," she said.

"There's some dry wood on the back porch," Logan said. "I'll fix us a nice warm fire when we get back."

"That would be great, Billy. I would enjoy that."

"Your wish will be granted, my lady," Logan said with a smile and an exaggerated bow. "I'll do just that."

"Oh, listen to you, you charming man," Terry said. "They both laughed."

"Are you ready to get started, Billy?"

"I will be as soon as I cut this burner off," Logan said. "I would hate to burn this place down on my first day."

"I'd hate to see that, too," Terry agreed. "You're going to love it here, and I'm going to enjoy coming over and visiting you."

"Your car or mine?" Logan said with pride, holding up his keys.

"It has to be mine, Billy, since you don't have any room in yours for a lot of groceries."

Logan and Terry returned hours later. Terry started putting the groceries away, while Logan hung up some new clothes, including a new winter jacket.

"I really like this jacket," Logan said.

"Well it's about time you got one," Terry said, looking out the window. "It is November, you know."

"Yep, it's about time I have a coat," Logan said. "There was a heavy frost this morning. I can't believe in about five weeks I'll be going to college."

"That will give you time to check out the campus," Terry said. "I think the sports fields are on the other side of the campus. You can check that out one weekend."

"You can count on that!"

"I'm going to start getting things ready for dinner," Terry said, handing Logan a bottle of cabernet sauvignon. "Do you mind opening this bottle? I'll have a glass while I'm getting the food ready."

"I think I'll have one, too," Logan said as he worked the corkscrew into the bottle.

"I don't think I have any wine glasses," Logan said, fumbling through his cabinets. "Will a water glass do?"

"That will be fine, Billy. Just find the smallest ones."

"Is there anything else I can do to help?"

"Why don't you go outside and grab a few pieces of wood to build us a fire?"

"I did promise you a fire," Logan said. It took him several minutes to get the fire roaring, and then he scrubbed up and returned to the kitchen.

"Done," he said triumphantly. "Is there anything else I can do?"

"You can find some music on the radio," Terry suggested. "When I'm finished here, we will drink some more wine and relax."

Terry picked up her glass and walked over to the sofa. She placed a pillow behind her neck, stretched out and got comfortable. She invited Logan to join her on the couch.

"Have a seat, Billy," she said. "We can talk for a while before I start cooking. Right now, I'm going to enjoy this wine."

Logan sat down at the other end of the sofa. He held his glass up.

"A toast," he declared. "Here's to a warm fire, good food, and a great woman."

"I like that, Mr. Casanova," Terry said as the den filled with laughter.

"I meant every word of it," Logan said with a grin.

Terry stared over at Logan and started to say something. She hesitated.

"What were you going to say?"

"I don't want to get into your personal life," Terry said with a sigh. "And I don't want this conversation to get too heavy. But I was wondering if you have any thoughts on what you want your future to look like."

Logan gazed into his glass of wine.

"Gosh, I can't really say what my future will look like," he said. "I do know that opportunities will be limited without an education. So right now, I'm going to concentrate on getting a business degree and see where that takes me."

"What about your past?" Terry inquired.

"I have worried about that every day since I woke up in that hospital bed," Logan said.

"Of course I wonder about my family. Are they worried about me? Do they think I'm dead? I talked to Sarge about it once, and he said I shouldn't obsess about it too much. He said I need to be thinking about the future and what I need to do to have a successful new life. Sarge said the past will take care of itself, and I think he's right. So I'm looking ahead, trying to establish some sort of career. And if my memory does come back, I hope my family will be pleased with the man that I have become. That's my focus right now."

"Who is Sarge?" Terry asked.

"He's the guy in the wheelchair who sits out on the patio most days," Logan explained. "You know, the guy with the Army Field jacket, ponytail, and beard."

"Oh yes, I remember seeing you talking to him," Terry said. "So he's the one that told you that?"

"Yep, he gave me a lot to think about, and I think he's right," Logan said. "He has encouraged me to move on with my life. I owe him a lot."

"Well, he sounds like a wise young man, though I've never met him."

"You won't forget him once you meet him," Logan said with a smile. "He's a bit unusual compared to everybody else at the hospital."

"I'll keep an eye out for him when I'm making my rounds."

"If you see him tell him I said hello and that I will see him on my next visit,' Logan said.

"I'll do that, Billy."

"Hey, I better put another log on the fire," Logan said as he jumped off of the couch.

"And I've got to get started on fixing some dinner," Terry added. "By the way, how do you like your steak? Well done, medium or rare?"

"Hmmm," Logan responded. "How do you like yours?"

"I prefer medium," Terry said. "Cooked, but a little pink on the inside."

"Why don't you fix mine the same way?"

Terry lit a candle resting on a small round table that sat in front of the front window. Logan could barely make out the front porch and the meadow in the subtle spark

After placing prepared dishes on opposite sides of the table, Terry took off her apron off and tossed it on the counter. Logan, who had replenished the fire, joined her at the table, stopping to pull the chair out for her.

"Well, you are a gentleman," Terry said, impressed. "Even when we're not in public."

"Well, I try."

"And I like that," Terry said.

Logan picked up the steak knife with his right hand, but he struggled to control the fork clasped in his left hand. He kept trying to find a way to use the fork with a hand that was missing a thumb and part of a finger.

"Oh, I'm sorry, Billy," Terry said, reaching over the table. "Would you like for me to cut it up for you?"

"No, thank you," Logan said with a look of consternation that gave way to determination. "This is something I've got to figure out on my own. It always seems like it's the small things that hinder me. I've just got to figure it out in my own way."

After attempting to hold the fork in different angles, Logan decided that the only way he could control the utensil was when he clutched it in a fist. Doing so made the fork secure enough to penetrate the steak.

"I have to admit it isn't pretty, but it's effective," Logan said.

"We're not awarding style points," Terry said supportively. "Just as long as it works for you, Billy. That's what counts."

They finished their meal, and Logan went back in his chair. Terry urged him to relax while she cleaned the dishes.

"Can I help?"

"No, Billy, you'll just be in my way," Terry said with a laugh.

It took Terry some time to finish the dishes. By the time she returned to the den, she found Logan was lying down on the sofa, with his head on the arm rest and his eyes closed. She could tell he was fast asleep.

The only light remaining came from the fireplace, which threw wild dancing shadows across every corner of the room. The only sounds were coming from the radio and the crackling embers from the fire.

Terry stood there for moment, gazing at Logan's face. His wispy blond hair fell down across his forehead. She was intensely attracted to him, even with the black eyepatch. What a handsome man she thought. She inched closer and knelt beside him on the cedar planks. Terry could feel his breath. Curious, she crept ever closer, lightly placed her lips to his.

Logan's eyes opened slowly. He felt her warm and inviting lips on his. He put his hand on the back of her head to hold the kiss that they were sharing. She slowly got off the floor and laid on top of him as they engaged in a passionate kiss.

Chapter 16

Ellen stood in the entry to her bedroom, where she had stored three boxes of research material she had collected for her new business. She paused, suddenly overcome with emotion, and she felt like she might cry. Despite her successes, and potential independence, there was an undeniable feeling of a broken heart. She failed to repress the tears as the trickled down her cheeks. Get a grip girl, she thought repeatedly to herself. You don't have time for this.

Ellen sat down on the side of her bed. Little Logan, who was nearly five years old, realized when he walked in the room that his mother had been crying.

"Why are you crying, mom?"

"I'm not really crying, honey," Ellen fudged. "But mama just feels a little sad right now. That's all."

"We need to be happy now," the little boy insisted. "We are home with pawpaw now."

"That's right,' Ellen said as a smile of joy returned to her puffy eyes. "We're all home now with pawpaw and nana."

"Pawpaw will be home in a little while, mom."

"Yes, I know," Ellen said. "When he gets home, pawpaw and I need to talk about business. So I want you to stay with nana until we're done talking."

"What are you going to be talking about, mom?" the curious child asked.

"It's about business, honey, that you wouldn't understand," Ellen said, rubbing her son's sandy hair. "It is between me and pawpaw."

Mr. Garrison walked in around six in the afternoon.

Little Logan ran up and jumped into his grandfather's arms. Mr. Garrison excitedly whirled the child around in circles in the middle of the room. "How is my little man today?"

"He's been a good boy, pawpaw," Ellen said.

"Well that's good," Mr. Garrison said as he sat the boy down.

"There's something I'd like to talk to you about after dinner," Ellen told her father.

"Is it going to be a good talk or a bad talk, Ellen?"

"I'd like to think it's going to be a good talk, dad."

"Okay, we'll talk right after dinner," Mr. Garrison said. He picked up Little Logan and walked back toward the kitchen.

Dinner went quickly. They sent Little Logan out to play with his grandmother, leaving the dishes on the table.

"Are you ready for that talk, honey?" Mr. Garrison asked. He had a sense about the nature of the conversation, since Ellen had already discussed her plan with his wife, who naturally had shared the pertinent details with him.

Ellen and her father went back to her bedroom to talk business. She opened the door, and Mr. Garrison's immediately noticed a set of blueprints spread across her bed. Additional papers were carefully stacked on a table nearby.

"Dad, don't say a word until I'm finished," Ellen said.

"Lord have mercy," he declared, astonished to see so much research. "What have you got here?"

"That it is my business plan!" Ellen exclaimed. "I have spent a long time working on it, and I would like to get your thoughts on it."

"It looks like we'll be here for a while," Mr. Garrison said.

"Do you remember when I told you that I wanted to start my own business?" Ellen said.

"Yes, I remember that."

"Well, this is it," she said motioning to all the paperwork.

"By looking at all of this, it's obvious you left no stone unturned."

"No sir, I think it's all there," Ellen said with pride.

"Well, I believe that." Mr. Garrison said as he flipped through a stack of documents.

"Dad, I want you to start with this stack," Ellen said, swapping out the papers Mr. Garrison was holding. "Go in this direction. Skim through them and let me know when you're ready to discuss it more. I know it will take some time, but I think you'll walk away impressed."

Ellen closed the door behind her as she quietly left the room.

"Well how did he take it?" Ms. Garrison asked.

"I can't say for sure," Ellen said. "Though he was clearly overwhelmed."

Two hours passed. "He must be really interested," Ms. Garrison said, noting that her husband hadn't even emerged to ask for a cup of coffee.

"Well, maybe he likes it," Ellen said.

"I think you did a fine job, honey," Ms. Garrison assured. "I was impressed. You know I'm with you on this. I know how hard you worked on it."

"Thanks mom," Ellen said as she gave her mother a two-armed hug. "I couldn't have done it without you."

Mr. Garrison called back down to his daughter, asking her to come back upstairs to the makeshift office that doubled as her bedroom. "Ellen, we need to talk."

Ellen looked at her mother, eyes raised. "What do you think, mom?"

"It's hard to say, honey," Ms. Garrison said. "But it had to be interesting for him to take that much time reading it over. I'll keep my fingers crossed for you."

Ellen walked up the stairs slowly. The door was open when she walked in, and Mr. Garrison was sitting in the only chair in the room. He was holding a sheet of paper in his hand, with several more spread out across his lap. He looked at Ellen with a stern look on his face.

"How long did you work on all of this?" he said, looking around the room at all the other stacks of paper.

"About two years," she said. "Most of my work took place in the last year when I started taking business pharmaceutical classes."

Mr. Garrison stared down at the paper he was holding before stealing another glance at his surroundings.

"How in the world did you get all this information?" he said, pouring over her research of North Carolina markets. "You have the populations of Greensboro, High Point and Winston, the number of doctors in each city. You also have locations in mind, along with construction cost estimates and inventory forecasts. Amazing!"

Mr. Garrison reached a second sheet of paper. "This one has the number of people it would take to run each store. My goodness, you even have a breakdown showing what items should be placed along the aisles, all the way down to the individual shelves."

"There is a reason for all that," Ellen said. "As you can see dad, it's a drugstore with one-stop shopping. It's for people who only need a few items when they pick up their prescriptions. It saves them from having to go to the grocery store for everyday items."

Mr. Garrison looked at the first set of blueprints.

"It's going to have a drive-through window for prescription drugs?" Mr. Garrison asked while pointing to a sketch on the oversized sheet.

"Yes sir, that's what's taking place in Chicago right now," Terry said. "People love it. It saves them time without having to leave their car."

"Well, I must say Ellen, you have done your homework," Mr. Garrison said. "How did you come up with these figures?"

"I made some phone calls to contractors in Greensboro," Ellen said proudly. "I sent them copies of those blueprints and asked them for estimates. The costs go down if we build more than one store."

Ellen yanked another sheet out of the stack on the table, handing it to her father.

"Each building would cost about $37,000 to build, excluding land costs," she explained. "I have the locations picked out. All told, it would cost about $154,000 to buy the land, build the stores and stock them both. But I should be able to get a discount on inventory by buying in bulk."

"You've certainly crossed your T's and dotted your I's," Mr. Garrison said. "I'm impressed. It is interesting enough for me to give it serious consideration, but I'll need a few more days to think it over."

"Dad, it will work," Ellen assured. "I have seen it work up north, and it will work down here, too. We just need to be one of the first to get into it before it catches on."

"I understand honey," her father said. "Regardless, you did one hell of a job putting all of this together."

Mr. Garrison looked at his watch.

"My goodness," he said. "It is 11:30 and past my bedtime. I'll think about it for the next two days, and then we'll get back together."

Mr. Garrison stood up and put both his hands on Ellen's shoulders.

"Young lady, you have put together a presentation that would make any father proud," he said. "I just want to let you know that all of your accomplishments over the past five years have impressed me, particularly under the circumstances you have endured. I love you."

"Thank you dad," Ellen said. "And I love you, too."

Two days later, Mr. Garrison walked into the house holding an envelope. Ellen was taking a pan of biscuits out of the stove, and Ms. Garrison was sitting at the table. "Where's Little Logan?" Mr. Garrison asked.

"He's asleep, dad," Ellen said. "That will give us time to talk."

Mr. Garrison pulled up a chair and encouraged his daughter to so the same. He placed the envelope on the table.

"I've been thinking a lot about your business plan," Mr. Garrison said. "And I called Mr. Carter over at the bank. He asked me to bring over the business plan you had put together. He wants to see it."

Ellen stared at him dumbfounded.

"I hope you don't mind, honey," Mr. Garrison continued. "When I came home yesterday for lunch, you and your mother were gone, so I gathered up all the plans and took them down to the bank. Mr. Carter called to see if I could come by to meet. He was so impressed with your plan. He is willing to loan you the total amount you need for both locations, as long as I agree to sign the note."

Ellen threw her hands up in the air. "You've got to be kidding!"

"Nope, I'm not kidding," Mr. Garrison said with a chuckle. "Mr. Carter was very impressed. He said only a fool would reject such a thorough plan. He felt that confident that you would succeed at this. So I signed the paperwork. Here's a note for the entire amount of money you need."

Mr. Garrison placed the document on the table for everyone to see. Ellen leaned over and looked at the figure. Her face turned scarlet as she gazed back up at her dad as tears welled up in her eyes.

"Has the cat got your tongue?" Mr. Garrison teased.

"Dad, I don't know what to say," Ellen said between deep breaths. "Now I'm scared to death."

"Well, I'm not scared, honey," her father said. "I've got all the confidence in the world in you."

Mr. Garrison reached over the table and took Ellen's hand.

"Your dad and I have had a long talk," her mother said. "Everything we've got, and everything we're going to have, is going to be yours one day. So why not let you have it now? This is what we decided to do."

"Mom, y'all are taking a big chance of losing everything you've got on this," Ellen said.

"Honey, we're not looking at this as losing," Ms. Garrison said. "We're looking at it as another opportunity. Your dad has wanted for a long time to go into business with you."

"I've got to get started!" Ellen said, standing up abruptly. "I have a lot of work to do and a lot of people to see. I've got to call Deb and give her the news. Excuse me while I make that call."

Ellen bolted out of the room and fumbled through the numbers to call her best friend.

"Marlow Accounting, this is Debra Marlow."

"Hey Deb, this is Ellen."

"Are you back home, Ellen?"

"Yes, finally," Ellen said, barely able to put two words together. She took a deep breath. "Deb, can I come down to your office in the morning to talk? I can't explain it all over the phone."

"Sure you can," Debra said. "I have an office at the Crabtree Mall. You know where that is?"

"Oh yes I know," Ellen said.

"Stop by," Debra said. "You can't miss my name on the window. Marlow Accounting."

"Okay Deb, I've got to go," Ellen said. "I'll see you at nine in the morning."

"It will be good to see you again, Ellen."

Ellen hung of the phone, and then started jubilantly jumping. She ran back into the kitchen and grabbed her dad around the neck and kissed him on the cheek countless times.

"Thank you!" she shouted repeatedly. "I'm so happy, dad. You have no idea how happy you both have made me."

About that time, Ellen heard Little Logan calling for her from the second floor.

"I'll get him," Ellen said, bounding up the steps, leaving her parents to look at each other and smile.

"She's one happy girl," her father said.

"She has never been this happy since she received that last letter from Logan," Ms. Garrison chimed in.

"That's one reason why I signed that note, honey," Mr. Garrison said, twirling the sheet of paper lying on the kitchen table.

"I know," his wife said. "Seeing her so happy is worth every bit of what we have done for her."

The next morning, Ellen pulled into a parking spot at Crabtree Mall in front of Debra's office. Her friend greeted her with an embrace as she entered the accounting office.

"How are you?" Debra asked.

"I'm great," Ellen said. "How are you?"

"Staying afloat so far," Debra said. "It just takes time to build a business."

"That's why I'm here," Ellen said. "To talk business."

"Come on back and have a seat," Debra said.

"This office looks very professional," Ellen mused.

"Well, it's taken a little while to get set up," Debra said. "I've been here about nine months."

The women sat down at an oval table.

"What have you got on your mind?" Debra inquired.

Ellen enthusiastically shares the previous day's events. Debra hung on every word, letting out a gleeful scream when she heard about the loan.

"What can I do for you?" Debra said after composing herself.

"Do you remember when we took that trip to Walter Reed Hospital?" Ellen said.

"Yes, it was a good road trip."

"Do you remember when I told you that I had plans after graduation?"

"Oh yes, I remember that," Debra said. "But you never would tell me what those plans were."

"Well this is it," Ellen said. "And I want you to handle my books. I'm hoping that, as the company grows, you'll become my full-time accountant.

"Wow," Debra said. "You know I will. We've always made a great team."

"The way I have it figured out, the more my company grows, the more your company is going to grow, too," Ellen said. "Now I just need a good business attorney to help me set up my business."

"You're in luck," Debra said. "I have a good one for you."

"Who would that be?"

"Bob Haywood," Debra said without hesitation.

"Bob Haywood," Ellen said. "Where have I heard that name before?"

"He was the football quarterback at our high school," Debra said. "Remember the tall, good-looking guy with dark hair and the rocket arm?"

"Oh yes, I remember him now."

"He was three years ahead of us," Debra said. "He has his own law practice in Greensboro. He helped set up my business. I must say, he is still gorgeous … and single."

Ellen burst out laughing. "I'm still not looking for a man, Deb."

"I didn't say you were," Debra said. "I'm just saying he's a good-looking man."

"By the way, how did it work out with you and Don?" Ellen asked her friend.

"It didn't," Debra said in a matter-of-fact tone. "We went our separate ways after college. How have you been doing? Are you still looking for Logan?"

"I'm going to always look for Logan, until I know one way or the other," Ellen declared. "I will never stop looking. I don't think I could have made it the last few years if I didn't have Little Logan and this business plan to keep my mind occupied. But to be honest, he doesn't fill my thoughts as much as he used to."

"Well, that's good, Ellen," Debra said. "I will give you Bob's phone number and you can give him a call."

"Let's give him a call now," Ellen said. "There's no point in waiting."

Debra looked a little surprised.

"I guess you're right," Debra said, getting up to walk toward her desk. She fumbled through her Rolodex. "Let me find his number."

"Here it is!" she said, snapped out a card with a flourish. Debra dialed the number, introduced herself to the secretary and asked for the attorney.

Chapter 17

Bob Haywood warmly greeted Debra.

"Hey Bob, I have a friend here that needs to talk to you about forming a business," Debra said. "You may know her from high school. Ellen Garrison?"

"I didn't know her personally but I have seen her around," Bob recalled. "Didn't she and Logan McKay go together in high school? He was such a good baseball player at school."

"Yep, he's the one," Debra said.

I remember them," Bob said.

"Well, Ellen would like to speak with you now," Debra said. "Do you have time?"

Bob agreed to talk to Ellen, so Debra put gave her friend the handset.

"Hello, Bob," Ellen said.

"Hey, Ellen, how are you?" Bob said

"I'm fine, thank you, Bob," Ellen replied. "I'd like to set a meeting up with you as soon as possible. I'm starting up my own business, and I would like you to prepare all the legal documents so I can get started on it."

"What kind of structure are you looking for?"

"I want to form a corporation," Ellen said.

"That will take a little more time, but I can do it for you."

"I need it done as soon as possible."

"When can you come and see me, Ellen?" Bob asked.

Ellen looked down at her watch. "I can be in Greensboro around two this afternoon."

"You are in a hurry," Bob said, pausing to glance at his schedule. "I think I can make that work."

Ellen thanked the attorney for squeezing her in before hanging up the phone.

"Thank you for setting that up, Deb," Ellen said. "It will be great to go ahead and get him started on the paperwork. There's not much else I can do until all the legal filings are made."

Debra wrote down his address and handed it to Ellen. "His law office is located at 203 North Elm Street in downtown Greensboro."

"I can find that," Ellen said. "Well I guess I should get on my way. It'll take me about two hours to get there, and I have a lot more to do today."

"Ellen, I appreciate you keeping me in mind," Debra said. "You know I'll work hard for you."

"I know, Deb," Ellen said as she turned to leave the office. "That's why I'm here. And you're also my best friend. We have to look after one another, right? We'll talk soon, Deb."

"By the way, Ellen," Debra said. "What's going to be the name of your business?"

"I'm surprised you had to ask," Ellen said. "There's only one name that makes sense to me: Logan's Pharmaceutical."

"Why didn't I think of that," Debra said as the women shared a laugh.

It took Ellen about an hour and 45 minutes to reach downtown Greensboro. Bob Haywood's office was located in one of the city's few high-rise buildings. Ellen pulled into the parking deck, and then made her way to the elevator. The office was located on the fourth floor.

A secretary welcomed Ellen as she entered the lobby, signed her in and showed her to the attorney's office.

Bob Haywood was a tall statue of a man, well-tanned with arms that barely fit in the sleeves of his navy blue pinstripe suit. A yellow tie popped against the dark suit's background. Bob walked around his desk to offer Ellen his oversized hand. She noticed his black hair and brown eyes as they shared greetings. To her, he seemed to have stepped out of a men's fashion magazine.

"It's been a long time, Ellen," Bob remarked. "How long has it been?"

"Guessing eight or nine years," she replied. "I think you were in your last year of school when I got there."

"Yes, but I sure remember you and Logan," Bob said. "I remember watching Logan playing baseball. He was great. I suppose he got a great scholarship for school."

"No, he joined the service," Ellen explained. "His plan was to pay his way through college so he could eventually become a high school or college coach."

"Is he coaching now?"

"No, I don't think so," Ellen said, her voice trailing off.

"Oh, I'm sorry to hear that," Bob said. "He would make a good high school or college coach, I think."

Bob looked down at Ellen's hands.

"I see you're wearing a wedding band," he observed. "How long have you been married?"

"Almost six years," Ellen responded instinctively. "We have a son now who is going to turn five soon."

"That's great," Bob said with a smile. "So what is Logan up to now?"

Ellen just looked at him. She hesitated. What do I say now? She decided to go ahead and tell Bob the truth about Logan.

"Bob, we got married while Logan was on his first leave from the Army," she confided. "After our honeymoon he went back to the base. Shortly afterward, he sent me a letter saying he was going on a special assignment and that he would write me as soon as he could. I haven't heard from him since. And that was almost five years ago. He hasn't even seen his son."

"Oh, Ellen, I'm so sorry."

"As you can see Bob, I'm wearing my wedding band until I find out," she explained. "One way or another, I will be married to Logan until then."

"That's very honorable of you, Ellen, and I wish you the very best."

"Thank you," Ellen replied. "What about you? Did you marry anyone I knew?"

"I'm afraid not," Bob said. "After high school, I went straight to college and then Harvard Law. I never had much time for girls. I dated occasionally, but the right one never came along."

"I'm sorry Bob," Ellen said. "I hope the right one comes along one day for you."

"So do I, Ellen."

"Let's get down to business," Ellen said as she reached into her purse to pull out a folder. She handed it to Bob.

"I think all the information you'll need will be in that folder," she said. "My phone number is also there if you need to call me for any additional information."

Bob opened it the folder and rifled through a few pages.

"To be honest, it will probably take me a week are two," he cautioned. "You will be getting a booklet and some information about incorporating a business in North Carolina. Take your time and read through it all. Call me if you have any questions. I'll call you in about a week with an update."

Ellen stood up, sticking her hand out to thank Bob. "I do appreciate your help," she said.

"That's what I'm here for, Ellen," Bob said. "I'm glad you came by."

Ellen got back in her car and began driving north to head home. A lot was going through her mind. I wonder why a nice-looking man like that has never found someone to love, she mused. He seemed nice enough. I wonder if he has to explain himself as much as I do to other people.

Ellen knew that talking about Logan sometimes helped move a conversation along, while other times it created awkward moments and people attempted to sympathize. Seeing Bob, and hearing him talk about Logan, brought back a lot of memories, she thought. It hurt her inside thinking about how much she still loved Logan.

"Stop, stop thinking about it," she said out loud. "You've got a lot to do, and you don't have time to feel sorry for yourself."

Ellen looked down at her watch, realizing that she would make it back to her parents' house in time for dinner.

Ms. Garrison had just finished setting the kitchen table when Ellen walked through the front door. Little Logan was already seated at the table. Ellen walked over and gave the child a kiss on the cheek.

"You're just in time, honey," Mr. Garrison said, putting down a newspaper. "We're just getting ready to eat."

"It has been one busy day, dad," Ellen said as she sat down in front of the meal.

"Did you get anything done?" Mr. Garrison asked.

"Deb is set up to do all of our accounting, and Bob Haywood in Greensboro will handle the legal work," Ellen said. "He said he should have the paperwork filed, and the business set up, in about two weeks."

"Bob Haywood, that name sounds familiar to me," Mr. Garrison. "Isn't his dad Ted Haywood?"

"I believe so," Ms. Garrison said.

"Oh yes, I remember Ted," Mr. Garrisons said. "He helped manage the home lumber company behind the YMCA. His son was the football quarterback, wasn't he?"

"Yep, he's the one," Ellen said.

"So he's going to be our attorney?" Mr. Garrison asked.

"Yes, he said he would be, and I think he'll make a good one, dad."

"Well, if you think so, that's fine with me," Mr. Garrison said. "Have you decided what you want to name the company?"

"There's only one name that will sit well with me, dad."

"What's that," Mr. Garrison said, raising his eyebrows slightly.

"Logan Pharmaceuticals," Ellen declared as she looked at Little Logan. "What else can it be?"

"I like that name," Ms. Garrison said. "It has that ring to it."

"I know the area where I want to build a store," Ellen said. "We could spend the next few weeks scouting out the right locations. It would be great to get your feedback."

"One day this week, I hope," her father said. "I think we can work that out."

"By the way, Ms. Dubois called and asked if you could come by her house in the morning," Ms. Garrison said. "She has something she would like to talk to you about."

"I wonder what that could be," Ellen said.

"I have no idea, honey," her mother said.

"Well, I'll go by there first thing in the morning," Ellen said.

Ellen was up early the following morning. Ms. Garrison had just taken out a pan of homemade biscuits. Ellen grabbed one, cracked it open and laid on a piece of fatback that was lying in a nearby bowl.

"Sit down honey," Ms. Garrison said. "I will have everything ready in a minute."

"Got to go mom," Ellen said as she started toward the front door. "I'll go by and see Ms. Dubois, and then I'll go see Mr. Carter at the bank. I'll be back around lunchtime, I hope. Please keep an eye on Logan. He's still asleep."

Ellen looked out across the Dubois' pasture as she turned onto the driveway. She didn't see Trigger in the horse's usual spot near the fence.

Ellen stepped up on the porch when the door opened. Ms. Dubois had a distinguished look, with pearl ear rings and a matching necklace, dressed as though she was headed to church.

"Ms. Dubois, you sure do look pretty this morning," Ellen said.

"Why, thank you, Ellen," Ms. Dubois said. "Come on in. Let's go in the kitchen and I'll pour you a cup of coffee."

"That sounds good," Ellen said as she sat down at the kitchen table. "I didn't see Trigger as I was driving up."

Ms. Dubois turned her head to gaze out the window overlooking the meadow. She slid her chair out and left the table, making her way over to the window. "Come here, honey, let me show you something," she told Ellen.

Ellen walked over and stood beside her. Ms. Dubois slowly tilted her head up and down as she looked in the direction where her husband was buried.

"Nancy is up there, with Jean," she said.

Ellen looked out at the meadow. In the distance, she could see the granite marker for Mr. Dubois. Another stone stood just a few yards away, on a small hill.

"I buried Nancy on that hill where she liked to spend her late afternoons," Ms. Dubois said. "I could sit at the kitchen table and watch her walk down to the fence, where she'd stand there looking up at Jean's tombstone."

Ms. Dubois stepped away from the window.

"Nancy did that every day, after my husband's passing," Ms. Dubois said. "When Mr. Ross found her lying in that same spot. I think she died looking at his grave. I knew she was heartbroken for him, so I had her buried right where she was found. Someday I'm going to be buried up there on that hill with them. You remember that, honey."

Tears were streaming down the lady's face as the memories flooded in.

"Come on over here and sit back down, Ellen," Ms. Dubois said after composing herself. "We need to talk."

Ellen wondered what Ms. Dubois had on her mind as the women sat at the kitchen table.

"Ms. Simpson is moving," Ms. Dubois said. "Her son was wounded in Vietnam. He and his wife live in Georgia with their two small kids, and Ms. Simpson is going down there to help them out. They need her down there, and I need someone to come over and cook three meals a day, while also driving me to town when necessary. The only good supermarket is Edwards Groceries. I just need a little help here and there.

"Do you know of someone who may be interested in that job? I will pay them well and they can live here if they like. They can drive my old DeSoto. It's an old car, but it is dependable."

"I understand, Ms. Dubois," Ellen responded. "I can't think of anybody off hand, but I'll definitely think about it."

"I already have someone in mind," Ms. Dubois said. "This is where I need your help."

"Of course," Ellen said.

"Do you think Ms. MacKay would be interested in this job?" Ms. Dubois said. "I know she's a great cook, given all the meals we ate at the fire department. Her snap beans and speckled butter beans were just out of this world, and she also made the best pies a person could eat. I know she used to drive, but I see her walking now so I don't think she has a car."

"You're right," Ellen said. "She doesn't have a car. She walks downtown every day to that five-and-dime store."

"Do you think it would insult her to ask her to work for me?" Ms. Dubois asked. "I will pay her as much as she is making at the store. And she won't have to walk to work anymore. She won't need to wear a uniform or anything. It will be like two friends spending time together."

"Well, I don't know," Ellen said. "I'm going by her place this afternoon, and I will mention it to her. We'll see how she feels about it."

"She's the only person in this town that I would like to have in this house," Ms. Dubois said. "I know we would have a good time. And if she is as lonely as I am, it might do us both good."

"I think you're right," Ellen agreed. "I will definitely talk to her this afternoon, and casually mention the opening to see what she has to say."

"Oh Ellen, I would appreciate that."

"I will call you later this afternoon, Ms. Dubois."

"Thank you so much," the lady said.

Ellen kept looking over at the pasture and its rolling hills as she left Ms. Dubois' house. As she drove, memories kept rushing back, forcing her to stop the car before she turned onto the highway. She got out and walked over to the fence, rested her arms on the top rail, and reflected on all the times she and Logan would walk down that path, with Trigger following them to the end of the fence. She could see the little monument resting atop the hill, remembering all the times they would feed the horse apples when they were in season. They would rub his mane, eventually coming to think of the horse as their own. He was our Trigger, she thought.

Ellen stood there for few minutes, thinking of all the good times. She looked back at the monument. "Thanks for the memories, Trigger," she said out loud, wiping away a solitary tear as she turned to walk back to the car. "You will be missed."

The next stop was the bank and a visit with Mr. Carter. Ellen updated the banker on hiring Deb and Bob Haywood and the time required to complete the paperwork for forming a corporation. Mr. Carter was pleased to hear of the progress and that Ellen's business plan was on schedule.

Ellen stopped at the first stoplight after leaving the bank. She saw J.P. Powell standing at the corner, with his trusty flashlight sticking out of his back pocket. He carried that flashlight night and day.

J.P. noticed Ellen, and threw out a big wave and a grin that only he could do. Ellen waved back with a smile, thinking of the time when she and dad were closing up the drugstore. There was no moon and it had gotten dark. They saw J.P. and Jimmy, his regular partner in crime, standing in the distance. J.P. had his flashlight out, throwing beams up in the air toward the stars.

"Let's see you climb to the top of it," J.P. told Jimmy, pointing the ray of light. Jimmy looked at J.P. with a surprised look on his face. "Oooooh, J.P., I know what you're gonna do," Jimmy said. "By the time I get to the top, you're gonna cut it off."

Ellen couldn't help but remember the odd experience. J.P. and Jimmy didn't work because of a form of mental dysfunction, yet they were known and loved by everyone for their simple looks on life.

Chapter 18

Ellen pulled into Ms. MacKay's driveway and walked up to the door. She knocked on the door.

"Hey, honey, come on in," Ms. Mackay said. "Where's Little Logan?"

"He's home," Ellen said. "I left him asleep this morning. I just wanted to stop by and see how you are doing."

"I'm doing okay," Ms. MacKay said, inviting Ellen into the house. "I'm only working three days a week now, Thursday through Saturday. "The five-and-dime is cutting back everyone's hours. They say the business isn't there. I think one of us will have to go."

Ellen saw an opening to present Ms. Dubois' proposal.

"Ms. MacKay, I don't know if you'd be interested are not, but Ms. Dubois might need some help around the home," Ellen said. "She told me that Ms. Simpson has to move down to Georgia to help with her son and his wife. So Ms. Dubois is looking for someone to help with the cooking. The poor lady never learned to cook, and she needs help soon. She is willing to pay more than minimum wage, and would supply a bedroom and cover expenses for the person who helps her out."

"I know Ms. Dubois, and she's a fine lady," Ms. MacKay. "I've always liked her. Anytime I see her around town, she always stops and asks about Logan and how I am doing. She always makes sure to say, with a smile and sincerity, that I should ask her if I ever need help."

"She is a fine lady, and I have her phone number if you'd like to call her," Ellen said.

"That's okay, dear," Ms. MacKay said. "I already have her phone number, and I just might give her a call."

"By the way, do you still have your driver's license?"

"Oh yes," Ms. MacKay said. "I go every four years and get it renewed. It seems like most of the store clerks are always asking for some type of ID these days, so I keep it on hand just in case. It's been a long time since I have driven a car, but I can do it."

"I'm sure you can, Ms. MacKay," Ellen said. "But you need to try to call Ms. Dubois this week, if you can."

Ms. MacKay paused. "I couldn't stay there full time because I have to be here when my Logan comes home."

"I understand that it will be full-time work, and she will treat you as a friend, not an employee," Ellen assured.

"I know you're right," Ms. MacKay acquiesced. "I'll give her a call this afternoon."

"That's great," Ellen said. "I've got to get on back to the house. Logan must be up by now, and I bet he's driving mom crazy."

As they walked down the hall, Ellen stopped at the door that opened up to Logan's bedroom.

"Can I look in his room again?" Ellen asked. "It just makes me feel close to him."

"I understand, honey," Ms. McKay said, opening the door. "I do it every day."

Ellen walked in and sat down on Logan's bed.

"I will leave you alone, honey," Ms. McKay said as she headed back toward the hallway. "You take all the time you need."

Ellen sat there and looked around the room. As the time before, every picture remained where they were when Logan left. The baseball bats were still propped up in the corner, and his baseball glove lay on the dresser. His shined loafers continued to rest beside the bed stand and his jeans were still flung over the back of a chair.

Ellen walked over to the pair of jeans, picking them up before holding them close to her chest. She gazed up at the poster of Billy Martin pinned up to the wall at the foot of Logan's bed.

She slowly laid the pants down across the back of the chair and took one look around the quiet room. For some reason, she didn't feel sad. One day he will be back, she thought, and I will be waiting for him when he returns.

Ellen felt calm and relaxed when she returned to her parents' house. It was an unfamiliar sensation, but there was no doubt in her mind that Logan could come back to Draper. She felt more confident than ever.

It took Ellen and her father very little time to select two locations. They quickly made deposits on both. One site was located on Battleground Avenue in northern Greensboro; the other was on Main Street in High Point. Each location was perfect and the prices were well below their cost estimates.

Ellen was set to leave on Friday morning to go to the bank and sign a few papers, when the phone rang. She picked up the handset to hear Bob on the other side of the line.

"How are you this morning, Bob?"

"I've got some good news for you," the attorney said. "Everything has come back from the state, and you are now incorporated. I have your state tax number. You can check the ledger, but you are ready to operate as Logan Pharmaceuticals Inc.

"That's great," Ellen beamed. "Now we can really get a move on."

"Ellen, I'm coming to Draper this afternoon, around 4:30," Bob said. "I have got to visit my folks for a little while. I can bring to you all the documents that you will need to sign for the state."

"That would be great, Bob."

"Can you meet me at the Mar-Gre Restaurant on Highway 14 around five?" Bob asked. "There are a few more things I need to go over with you. It may take about an hour, if that's okay with you. I can cover dinner."

"That's just fine, Bob," Ellen said with a chuckle. "I'm looking forward to it."

Ellen picked up her keys and headed out. She was about to pull out of the driveway onto the main road when she saw a two-tone green DeSoto pass by. The driver blew the car's horn. It was Ms. McKay, with Ms. Dubois in tow, both waving as they went down the highway.

She could not help but smile. Now there's a pair, she thought. Ellen was pleased that Ms. McKay had accepted the job, knowing that each woman would have support during lonely times.

Ellen spent an hour meeting with Mr. Carter at the bank. She then met her father for lunch, where they discussed more business opportunities and other decisions that needed to be made.

"Well, dad, I've got to go meet Bob Haywood at the Mar-Gre Restaurant at five to pick up all the documents we need to get things moving."

"Okay," Mr. Garrison said. "I'll see you back at the house tonight."

Ellen looked at her watch as she pulled into the restaurant's parking lot. She was 15 minutes early, and, given the early time of day, there were few cars in the lot. She decided to go ahead and find a quiet table near the back to the restaurant so she and Bob could discuss business.

"Table for one?" the hostess asked.

"No, two actually," Ellen said. "I'm meeting a gentleman here by the name of Bob Haywood in about 15 minutes. We've got to go over some business, and I'd like a table where we can talk without too much interruption."

"I understand, ma'am,' the hostess said as she led Ellen to a table at the far end of the restaurant. Ellen started to provide a description of her dinner companion, but the hostess politely cut her off.

"Yes, we know Bob," she said. "He's a regular. Stops by about once every other week. Sometimes alone or with his parents."

The hostess motioned for Ellen to sit down and offered to get her a drink. Ellen asked for a cup of coffee.

"I'll bring Mr. Haywood right over ma'am, as soon as he arrives," the hostess said before heading toward the kitchen.

Bob sure seems familiar with this place, Ellen thought. I wonder how familiar he is with these waitresses.

Ellen looked across the restaurant just as Bob was entering. He was holding a dark brown briefcase. He looked preppy, yet distinguished, wearing tan corduroy slacks, a two-toned tan polo shirt and suede shoes.

As the hostess met Bob at the door, it was obvious they knew each other. She was all smiles and giggles as she waved a menu to point to where Ellen was seated. Bob and the hostess were talking and laughing as they walked over to the table.

"Thank you," Bob told the hostess, flashing a big smile at her as he placed his briefcase on the table. "How are you Ellen?"

"Just fine Bob," Ellen replied. "How are you?"

"Well, it's always good to be back home," Bob said, pausing. "And it's a pleasure to see you again."

Ellen just nodded, unaware of the grin that had spread across her face.

Bob slowly opened the briefcase, and he began to pull out papers, placing each in a small stack in front of Ellen.

"It took a little longer than normal to get these back," Bob explained. "Raleigh is still adjusting to the fact that Leaksville, Spray and Draper are now just called Eden. It took a few phone calls, but we finally got it done. You'll need to sign under the yellow marks before mailing everything back to the state. After that, you're all set to operate Logan Pharmaceuticals."

Ellen excitedly signed the papers. Bob reached over and picked them up, taking time to carefully fold each one before stuffing them into the addressed envelopes. With a quick motion, he placed the documents in the briefcase before sliding the case over the Ellen.

"This is a gift of appreciation from me two you," he said. "If you're going to be the CEO of a pharmacy chain, you'll need a briefcase. Now you're official."

"You didn't have to do that, Bob," Ellen said, given the briefcase a slight nudge back toward her attorney. "I was going to get one. I just haven't had the time."

"I can't take it back, Ellen," Bob said with a laugh. "Not when you're initials are already on it."

Ellen looked down at the briefcase. Her initials, E.M. were already etched in the right hand corner in gold lettering.

"That was really thoughtful of you, Bob," Ellen said. "You shouldn't have."

"It was my pleasure to do it for a high school friend."

The waitress interrupted as she placed a cup of coffee down in front of Ellen.

"May I take your order now?"

"I think I'll just have a garden salad with ranch dressing," Ellen said.

"If you're going to eat healthy, I will too," Bob said without looking at his menu. "Let me have the Cobb salad with ranch dressing on the side."

They handed their menus to the waitress, who darted off to attend to another customer a few tables away.

"Where do you stand now with your business plan?" Bob asked.

"Dad and I have already picked out two lots that we want to build on," Ellen said. "Hopefully dad will talk to the contractors today. As soon as we get the contracts signed, I will mail them to you to look over. And then we should be well on our way to building two facilities."

"You haven't wasted any time," Bob remarked.

"I've been planning this for three years, Bob," Ellen said. "I see no need to drag my heels now."

Ellen noticed that Bob's smile remained, and perhaps grew wider, as she talked. She had to look down and away at times to avoid eye contact. Often, she felt as though he knew what she was going to say before she had even uttered the words. It made her slightly uncomfortable.

Most of the meal was spent making small talk about high school and where old acquaintances had gone. After about an hour, Ellen told Bob she needed to leave to meet her father to discuss the next steps for the business.

"I understand," Bob said. "Thank you for meeting me here. By the way, if you have time when you get those contracts, feel free to run them by my office. No appointment necessary."

"Thank you Bob, I appreciate that," Ellen said. "And thank you again for this beautiful briefcase. I will definitely use it."

Bob stepped forward as if he planned to embrace Ellen, who stepped back and stuck out her hand for a professional handshake.

"Tell your parents I said hello," Ellen said. "And I hope you have a good weekend."

"You, too," Bob said.

Ellen decided to leave the briefcase in her car, reluctant to explain to her parents why her new attorney gave her such an unexpected gift. Mr. Garrison was getting up from the dinner table when she walked in the front door.

"I talked to Eric Hendren today, and he's ready to get started on the properties," Mr. Garrison said. "Eric said he could have both buildings completed within five months, if he can get started right away."

"That's great, dad," Ellen said. "Bob gave me the paperwork to send back to Raleigh, so it looks like we're on our way. I'll call Eric tomorrow and ask him to take the contract by Bob's office for final review. I know it's probably a standard contract, but I'd like to just play it safe."

"I agree," Mr. Garrison said, stopping in the middle of his sentence to grab a magazine off the kitchen counter.

"This is the pharmaceutical journal that I get every month," he said, handing the magazine to Ellen.

"A Whisper Away"

"This month's edition has an article about a pharmaceuticals seminar and tradeshow at the convention center in downtown Baltimore. It may give you the opportunity to meet some new vendors and learn about some of the newest drugs. Who knows, maybe you'll even pick up more marketing inspiration."

"That sounds great, dad," Ellen said, looking at the article. "When can we go?"

"I can't go," Mr. Garrison said. "I have got to work at the store. The show is on Saturday, so maybe you could go and make a weekend of it."

"Why don't you call Deb and ask her to go with you?" Ms. Garrison shouted from the other side of the kitchen. "I bet she doesn't work on the weekends."

"That's a great idea, mom," Ellen said. "I'll give her a call."

Ellen called the contractor first thing on Monday morning to discuss the start date. He sounded professional and eager to begin, and Ellen was pleased with the projected completion date. He also agreed to take the signed contracts to Bob Haywood's office in Greensboro.

Her next call was to Debra.

"You're up mighty early," Debra said.

"Yes, Little Logan always rises early," Ellen said. "When he gets up, I'm the first person he wants!"

They both laughed.

Ellen told Debra about the trade show in Baltimore and, given the fun they had on the last road trip, she wanted her friend to go with her to the conference.

"It would give us an opportunity to talk business and catch up some more," Ellen said. "All the expenses will be covered by my new company. I'm planning on leaving Friday afternoon and staying through Sunday."

"That sounds good to me," Debra said. "I need a weekend off."

"Let's plan to leave for Baltimore around noon," Ellen suggested.

"That sounds like a plan to me," Debra said enthusiastically. "I'll be ready."

Chapter 19

Logan was partially raised up on the bed, resting on his elbows. The morning sun was just beginning to peak through the curtains, throwing out a light orange light tint as its light bounced off the few remaining leaves on the trees outside.

Logan eased out of bed, careful not to wake up Terry. He was thinking about the dream that had just ended his slumber, confused by its meaning and repetition. Logan picked up his pants and a shirt that was lying across the back of a chair and made his way to the kitchen. He grabbed his shoes and walked out onto the deck. The dawn's light embraced him as he pondered the same old dream that continued to pursue him since he first woke up at Walter Reed.

He was lost in thought as Terry quietly joined him, wearing her nightgown.

"Are you okay, Billy?"

"I'm fine," he said, trying to hide his anxiety. "I just couldn't sleep."

"Did I cause you to wake up?"

"Oh no, I just had that weird dream again," Logan said. "That's all."

"Do you want to talk about it?"

"Not right now," Logan replied. "I think I'll go to the hospital this morning and discuss it with Dr. Elkins."

"It would be good to get it off your chest," Terry said as she rubbed his shoulders. "It may help you to sleep better."

"Maybe so," Logan agreed. "I think I'll leave after we eat. I'd like to be there when Dr. Elkins gets in. Hopefully he'll see me if I'm the first one there."

Terry volunteered to fix breakfast. Logan decided that he would call his professor to explain that he would be late coming to class. After making the call and taking a quick shower, Logan ate breakfast and grabbed his car keys.

"I'm going to take my time and get dressed before going back to my apartment," Terry said. "I need to pick up a few things before I go to work. I'll see you here if you're back by 11. Otherwise, I'll call you before I go to work."

Logan started to open the front door. Terry stopped him. She gave him a light kiss on the lips. "You be careful," she said.

Logan was waiting outside Dr. Elkins' office when Ms. Lawson, the secretary, walked up.

"Good morning, Billy," she said, greeting him with a smile. "How are you?"

"I'm doing fine," Logan said. "Is it possible to see Dr. Elkins this morning when he comes in?"

"I think it can be done," Ms. Lawson said as she unlocked the door. "Just have a seat. He should be here shortly."

Ms. Lawson had barely finished her sentence when Dr. Elkins walked in.

"Good morning, Billy," the doctor said, opening the door to his study. "This is a surprise. What brings you in so early?"

Billy sat down as Dr. Elkins hung up his coat and took a seat behind his desk.

"How is your baseball team going to be next year?" he said, inquiring about Johns Hopkins' baseball team, where Logan had recently joined the coaching staff.

"Coach Barrett is working everybody hard," Logan said. "Unless we improve, it is going to be an uphill climb for us this year."

"How long have you been with Coach Barrett and the Blue Jays?"

"I started helping out the second year I was there," Logan said. "I think he just got tired seeing me sitting alone up there in the stands, cheering the team on, even during practices. Finally he walked up to me and asked if I would like to come out on the field and help out.

"I must have done a good enough job to become an assistant coach. They don't pay much, but it's enough to cover my books, which suits me fine. I just love being on that field, Doc."

"How well can you field without your thumb?"

"I use what they call a first baseman's glove," Logan explained. "It looks a lot like a lobster claw. I have no problems with it. Dr. Stillman did a great job with my hand so I could have enough of a grip to close it."

"That's great Billy," Dr. Elkins said. "I hope the Blue Jays have a good year."

"I do, too, Doc," Logan said. "But I'm not promising anything. We have all new players this year."

Dr. Elkins laughed before shifting the subject, curious to know why Logan would show up at his doorstep first thing in the morning.

"So Billy, tell me why you're here," the doctor inquired.

"I had that bad dream last night," Logan said. "You know, the one I had been telling you about."

"To be specific, you mean the one you would *not* tell me about," Dr. Elkins said in a correcting tone.

"Yes sir, that's the one," Logan said. "I think I'm ready to talk about it now. You know why I haven't told you? There's an old saying that says if you tell about your dreams to someone you'll never have them again. I didn't want that to happen. I love the dream, but I just don't know what it means."

"Superstition is a powerful thing," Dr. Elkins said, his voice trailing. "But now, for some reason, you think the time is right to share the dream with me?"

"I just can't get it off my mind."

"Okay, let's hear it," Dr. Elkins said

"I will start from the beginning," Logan said, taking a deep breath before talking in slow, succinct sentences. "I'm in North Vietnam. It is early morning. Not sure if it rained that morning but the ground is wet. I wake up on my side. Guess I had been knocked out. The first thing I see is my hand. My thumb is hanging onto a small piece of skin, with blood slowly draining out.

"My head feels like it is going to burst open. I know that I need to stop the bleeding. I take my belt off and wrap it around my arm above the wrist. I keep tightening it until the blood stops running. There's so much pain in my head, and all I want to do is just lay there and die. I'm hoping the good Lord will just take me out of my misery and pain. As I'm settling in to meet my faith, I happen to look up, and there's a little girl dressed in white. She has long white hair and a glow around her.

"She is smiling at me. Oh what a beautiful smile! Just looking at her makes me relax. The blood stops running out of my hand. She raises both her hands out, seemingly in slow motion. She is beckoning me to come to her, and my head stops hurting. I start crawling in her direction. I crawl for a while, but every time I look up she is still the same distance from me. She keeps waving and I keep crawling. It happens over and over again until I pass out.

"The next thing I knew I'm in a cave somewhere, with the mountain guards and that Angel that led me there. It's as though I would've died if I hadn't followed her. I was ready to give up, but she kept right on waving me on.

"The general premise of the dream stays the same, though there have been some changes each time. For instance, early on the young girl has gone from being seven or eight years old to a grown woman in her early 20s. She still has her arms open, waving for me to come to her. She's so beautiful; her smile is unbelievable. At the beginning, she was in the jungle but lately she has been standing in a beautiful green meadow. There's a house on a hill in the distance. There's a white fence that I have to climb over to get to her, but she isn't there when I get to the other side. When I wake up I feel a love and passion that I have never felt before. I think she's my guardian angel.

"I have feelings for her, and I have been afraid of telling my dream for fear of never seeing her again. And I don't want you and Dr. Stillman to think I'm losing my mind."

"I wouldn't worry about that, Billy," Dr. Elkins said with a slight chuckle. "If you've been having that dream for about five years, it is quite possible that you may continue having it for the rest of your life. I don't think you're losing your mind, and I know Dr. Stillman would agree with me."

"The dream just seems so real, Doc," Logan said. "It takes me two or three days to get my mind off of it and to shake off my feelings for the woman. It seems so strange and I felt like I needed to tell someone, so I chose you. What do you think?"

"You say this is the only dream you have?"

"Yes, sir, I have no other dreams but this one."

"Hmm," Dr. Elkins said, while tapping his pen on his notepad. "Your subconscious could be telling you something. Let's think about it. You said there was a house on a hill. Could it be a place from your past?"

"If so, I don't remember it," Logan said.

"This could be a good sign, Billy," the doctor said. "It could reflect a memory from your past, which I'd view positively. The next time you have the dream, try opening your mind. Take in every detail. Something there could open doors for you to remember your past."

Logan looked at him without saying a word. He just looked down at his hands.

"I hope you're right," he finally said quietly. "So what you're saying is this dream could be a good thing."

"Yes, I think so, Billy," Dr. Elkins said. "You just keep right on doing what you're doing. You still have two more years left in college. Focus on your grades. Keep helping Coach

Barrett with the Blue Jays. And you may wake up one morning remembering everything."

"If that happens, you'll be the first to know," Logan said.

"Any time something comes up like this, feel free to stop by," Dr. Elkins said. "I will always make time for you."

"Thanks, Doc, I appreciate that."

Logan left Dr. Elkins office and headed to the patio in hopes of finding Sarge. As he walked through the swinging glass doors, he looked in the distance where Sarge used to hold court. A wheelchair was there, but no one was in it. Logan went back indoors and walked the halls in search of his mentor and friend, but he didn't turn up. Looking at his watch, Logan realized that it was just past 11. Realizing that Terry had likely left his place, Logan decided to go home and fix a sandwich before heading to class.

*****

Logan was on his way to class when he saw Mr. Warner coming down a nearby spiral staircase.

"Hey, Billy," Mr. Warner said.

"How are you, Mr. Warner?"

"I'm doing fine," Mr. Warner said. "I'm glad I ran into you. The pharmaceutical research and development group is having a showcase of the latest medicines over at the downtown convention center. They could have new information on eye transplants and treatments for amnesia. I can get three passes if you can talk Terry into going. It's really going to be interesting."

"I would like to attend that Mr. Warner."

"Just check with Terry," Mr. Warner said. "If she decides to go, I'll meet you guys there with the passes."

"I'll give Terry a call later," Logan said.

"By the way," Mr. Warner said as he turned to head down the hallway. "How are the Blue Jays doing?"

"We've got our work cut out for us this year," Logan said.

"Hang in there," Mr. Warner said as he walked off at a hastened pace.

Logan was walking home after baseball practice. As he neared his apartment, he noticed Terry's car parked in front. Isn't she supposed to be working, Logan wondered.

Terry met him at the door running. She jumped up, wrapping her arms around his neck and her legs around his waist.

"Guess what!" she said.

"What?" Logan said, shocked by Terry's wild enthusiasm.

"I'm now on first shift," she beamed. "And I have the rest of this week off to prepare for my new duties."

"That's great," Logan said. "How did you swing that?"

"I put in a request for first shift over a year ago," she said. "The hospital has so many veterans, and the first shift is shorthanded, so they asked me if I wanted to switch! I think I can be of some help on the second floor. Moving to first shift means I can spend more time with you."

"That is great!" Logan said, slowly setting Terry down on the floor.

"I'll also be able to go and watch your baseball practices in the afternoon," Terry said.

"I didn't know you liked watching baseball," Logan said.

"I'm not going to watch baseball, silly," Terry said. "I'm going just to watch you."

They burst out laughing.

"You're something else, little lady," Logan said. "By the way, I ran into your dad today. He invited us to go with him to a pharmaceutical conference downtown."

Terry's face inexplicably soured.

"I really don't care about going to that seminar, Billy," she said curtly. She walked back into the house and sat on the sofa. A solemn look remained on her face.

"Why would you pass this up?" Logan asked, following her over to the couch. "I would think you'd like to get caught up on the latest medicines."

"Some medicines are good, and some aren't," Terry explained. "I've seen some medicines do more harm than good. It might help one thing in your system, but tear down others. When that happens, you have to take another medicine to heal the new problem. Next thing you know, you're taking all types of medicines like some type of lab experiment."

Terry took Logan's hand.

"That irritates me, Logan," she said. "Trust me. I have experienced that time and time again."

"I can understand why you feel that way," Logan said. "But there could be something at the convention that could help me with my amnesia. I would like you to go with me. We have to let you know something by tomorrow in order for him to get the passes."

Terry stared at him with a stern look on her face.

"Okay, Billy," she said after some hesitation. "But only if you think there's a possibility that we could find something that would benefit you and your condition. I will go just because you want to go, but it's something I'm not looking forward."

"I understand, and I appreciate you going with me," Logan said, rubbing Terry's hand.

"Okay let's change the subject," Terry said. "What would you like for supper?

Chapter 20

Debra bounced out of her office, a suitcase and garment bag slung over her shoulder, as Ellen pulled up in front of the accounting office. She tossed her luggage into the back seat and hopped into the passenger seat.

"Let's get the hell out of here," Debra urged. "I'm ready for a break, Ellen. I had two people walk in thinking I was open, even though I had the 'closed' sign on the door."

"I agree," Ellen said. "I also need some time off. I think dad recognized that. Maybe that's why he suggested this trip."

"How's your business coming along?" Debra asked.

"The contractor is working the ground over as we speak, and he says he can have both sites completed within five months," Ellen said. "That's really when the work starts for me."

Ellen pulled out onto the highway.

"I'm looking to hire three pharmacists," Ellen said. "Dad is looking at several retired pharmacists that he thinks would be willing to come in and help look after his store in Draper. Both of us will have our hands full for several months after we open the stores. I know I'll be working 18 hour days just trying to get things started up and organized."

"Let's change the subject," Debra said. "How's your love life?"

"I still think of Logan every night before I go to sleep, and first thing in the morning," Ellen said. "I'm so busy during the day working on the business that I can keep my mind clear of him. But it is a different story at night."

"It has been about five years now," Debra said.

"And three months," Ellen added.

"That's a long time," Debra said. "Do you ever think about other men?"

Ellen slowly turned her head to glance over at Deb, flashing her friend a grin. "Only with my Logan, Deb, only with my Logan," she said.

Debra started laughing. "Well I had to check you out girl," she said.

"A new man is the last thing I have on my mind now," Ellen asserted. "The business is the only thing that keeps me going."

"I got a call from Bob Haywood the other day," Debra said. "He told me that y'all had dinner together. What did you think of him?"

"Bob seems like a real nice man, and yes, Deb, he's handsome," Ellen said. "But that's as far as its going to go. He's my attorney, and I plan on keeping things very professional between the two of us."

"Well, you know I had to ask," Debra said.

'There's one thing I know for sure, Deb," Ellen said. "I have enough on my plate right now, and a man is the last thing I have on my mind."

"Let's turn the table," Ellen jeered. "How is your love life, Deb?"

"Same old, same old," Debra said in a casually dismissive tone. "No one special."

The women laughed.

"Have you heard anything from the military, about Logan?" Debra asked.

"I saw on TV that the president is trying to negotiate a peace deal in Vietnam," Ellen said. "If that works out, prisoners could be coming home, and hopefully Logan will be among them."

"I hope it all works out," Debra said. "We need to get our boys back home, and I'm going to pray that Logan is one of them."

"I'm praying, too, Deb."

"Where are we staying in Baltimore?" Debra asked.

"Downtown on Lombard Street, at the Holiday Inn," Ellen said. "It is a short walk to the Civic Center."

"I like that we don't have to drive," Debra said.

"Some of the sessions are reserved for physicians and pharmacists," Ellen explained. "Those will only last about 30 minutes or so. I'm afraid you won't be able to attend those with me."

"That's okay," Debra said. "I just use that time to go get drink and a nice place to sit and people watch until you're done."

"We may not stay all day," Ellen continued. "That all depends on how interesting the conference is and how many contacts I can make."

"That sounds good to me," Debra said.

"I reserved two side-by-side rooms with an inside door connecting them," Ellen said. "That will give us time to talk and catch up on old times, but we'll also have our own space. That way we won't have to fight over the first shower."

"It used to take you forever to take a shower," Debra said with a laugh.

"Yes, I remember," Ellen said. "That's one of the reasons why I got us two rooms."

*****

"Dad left two passes in the front seat of my car yesterday," Terry said as she pulled out a pass and handed it to Logan. "Just clip this pass onto your belt, or you can attach this lanyard to it and wear it around your neck."

"I think I'll clip it on," Logan said.

"Do you want to drive or walk?" Terry asked.

"How far is it?" Logan replied.

"Maybe three blocks or so," Terry said. "We should be able to walk it in about 20 minutes."

"Let's walk," Logan said, looking up at the sun. "It looks like is going to be a pretty day. Besides, it would take up a lot of time just parking."

"That's one reason I wanted to spend the night here at my place," Debra said. "We won't have to worry about parking."

Terry and Logan entered the venue. There were aisles of vendors, looking professional with suits and ties.

"Maybe I should've worn a suit, Terry," Logan said, amazed at just how many people had gathered at the convention.

"Those folks are mostly doctors and pharmaceutical reps," Terry said. "Don't worry about it. You look better than them, even in your casual clothes."

"I don't see how you're going to be able to see much with this many people here," Logan said.

"You're just going to have to worm your way in and out," she explained. "If something interests you, just grab a brochure. We can read about it when we get back to my place."

Terry and Logan started making their way down one of the aisles, passing a display for defibrillators. Another representative was marketing a drug to treat blood pressure.

"Don't forget that I have to meet dad at 11 o'clock at his suite," Terry said. "He wants to attend a talk featuring a colleague of his, and he wants me to come along. It will likely last an hour or so. If you want to, you can go over to the cafeteria and have a cup of coffee. I'll meet you there when I get out and we can leave if you've seen all you want."

"I'm sure I can't see it all in two hours, but we'll see how I feel when you get back," Logan said.

"We still have an hour before I have to meet dad," Terry said, taking Logan's hand as they kept making their way down the aisle. "So let's just start walking. Stay close. I'd hate to lose you out here."

Terry and Logan must have walked by dozens of tables offering cures for a number of conditions, though none seemed ideal for Logan's maladies. At the end of the hour, Terry showed Logan where to find the cafeteria, and then headed off to meet her father.

Logan walked into the cafeteria. There were tables everywhere, and most would accommodate up to eight people. He relished the breathing room, and he managed to find a smaller table for two. It was tucked away in a corner. He sat down, ordered a cup of coffee, and began skimming over some the brochures he had picked up.

*****

Ellen was standing in front of a full-length mirror when Debra walked into her hotel room.

"What do you think of this outfit, Deb?" she asked her friend.

"Very professional looking," Debra responded. "Those cream-colored slacks and matching jacket look great on you, especially with your light blonde hair. And what a great fit! It really shows off your figure."

"I'm not thinking about my figure, Deb," Ellen chided.

"Well, you know the old saying," Deb said with a giggle. "If you have it, flaunt it."

"You look nice too, Deb," Ellen said. "Who knows? Maybe you'll catch some man's eyes while you're out there."

"A girl can only hope," Debra said. "I think a doctor in my family would be a good thing."

The women laughed as Ellen reached over to pick up her briefcase.

"Let's go!" Ellen said. "It's almost 9 o'clock. The conference center is about to open."

Ellen and Deb walked into the room, astonished at the sophisticated displays and all the professionals pitching their products and services.

"Deb, I'm going to take this aisle," Ellen said, pointing to the right. "Why don't you take the one beside me? We'll just pick up the business cards and brochures. We can check them over tonight when we get back to the hotel."

Each woman spent about two hours networking with doctors and pharmaceutical reps. When they reunited, they decided it was time to get a bite to eat, and Ellen suggested walking over to the cafeteria.

"Makes sense to grab lunch before the noon crowd gets hungry," she said.

"That sounds good to me," Debra said as she looked around for the cafeteria entrance. She pointed toward a set of double wood-paneled doors over in the back corner of the complex.

"There it is, Ellen," she said. "Let's go."

The cafeteria was already breaming with people as they arrived. A few tables offered an isolated chair or two, so the women chose to make a pass around the cafeteria before deciding on a table.

"Let's find a table near the best-looking men," Debra half quipped.

It didn't take that long for Debra to spot a table in the middle of the room with three vacant seats.

*****

Logan was reviewing the brochures and sipping his coffee, while periodically keeping a lookout in case Terry walked in. He glanced up and saw two women, and one of them made his eyes open wide. His body felt as though he had been shocked. Logan was virtually paralyzed. The only part of his body that could move was his eyes, which followed the women as they made their way to a table in the middle of the cafeteria. One of the women said something to two men, who promptly made room at the table. The woman with the light hair, the one who had caught his eye, had her back toward him. All he could see was her long hair flowing down her back.

Could this be the angel in his dreams? All that was lacking was a bright aura. He stared at her as his palms began to sweat. Logan tried to take a sip of his coffee but his hands were shaking so badly that he couldn't pick up the cup. He took a deep breath. I guess I'm going crazy, he panicked.

Logan was so distracted that he didn't notice Terry as she walked over to him.

"Hey you good-looking man," she said playfully. "Why are you sitting over here all alone?"

Logan didn't look up until Terry placed her hand on his shoulder.

"Are you okay, Billy?" Terry asked, noticing the perspiration that had collected on his forehead.

Logan tossed her an awkward smile before picking up a napkin to mop off his face.

"Is it hot in here or is it just me?" he said clumsily. He stood up and looked at Terry.

"I think it's probably that hot coffee you've been drinking," she said. "Are you ready to go?"

"Yes, I'm ready to go," Logan said, finally feeling calm. "How was the talk you went to?"

"It was okay," Terry said, letting out a yawn. "Dad got more out of it than I did."

As they made their way out of the cafeteria, Terry locked arms with Logan and put her head on his shoulder. Logan took one last look back in hopes of catching a glimpse of his angel. The eyepatch made it difficult to see from certain angles, forcing him to crane his neck a bit. There she was, smiling as she talked to the other woman. He was so fixated that he almost stumbled over Terry as they were walking.

"Are you okay, Billy?" Terry asked.

"I'm fine," he said several times. "I'll be okay in a minute, just as soon as I get some fresh air."

Logan didn't have much to say as they walked back to Terry's apartment. All he could think about was the angel's face. The resemblance was uncanny and it made him anxious and optimistic.

Terry gave Logan much-needed space as they walked before breaking the silence as they entered the apartment.

"I think dad's coming over when he leaves the show," Terry said. "I told him that he could spend the night here and drive back in the morning."

"I think I'm going to just go on home then," Logan said. "We can talk more tomorrow."

"Are you sure you're okay?"

"Yes, I'm fine," Logan managed to say. "I think I just need to go home and get some rest."

"You're acting weird," Terry said.

"I'll be okay," he assured. "I think I just got overheated in there, and drinking that hot coffee didn't do me any favors."

"Just be careful driving home, and call me when you get back," Terry said as she reached up and gave him a kiss on the cheek.

Logan sat in his parked car for a moment. He took a deep breath. His hands were still damp from sweat.

"What in the hell did I just see?" he muttered to himself.

Logan revved up the Thunderbird's engine. He needed to go see Dr. Elkins, even though it was almost 2 o'clock on a Saturday afternoon. Unsure if the psychiatrist would be at his office, Logan still resolved to drive to Walter Reed to find out.

Logan parked his car and sprinted up the steps, skipping some of them, until he reached the hospital wing where Dr. Elkins welcomed patients. The halls were crowded with weekend visitors as Logan navigated the wing. Along the way, he ran into Ms. Lawson, who looked surprised to see him.

"What's wrong with you, Billy," she said, quickly detecting that Logan was upset. He was winded, though the secretary was unaware that he had dashed from his car to the office.

"I need to see Dr. Elkins," Logan said, panting.

"He left about an hour ago, Billy," Ms. Lawson said. "What's wrong?"

"I really, really need to talk to him, Ms. Lawson."

"Come with me, Billy," she said, taking him by the arm to walk him back up the hall. She took the keys out of her purse and opened the door to Dr. Elkins' office. She walked around to her side of the receptionist's desk, picked up the phone and started dialing a number.

"Dr. Elkins," she said. "Billy Martin is here."

Ms. Lawson turned her head away from Logan in hopes of being discreet.

"Yes, that's right," she told the doctor before pausing. "Okay, we'll see you in about 30 minutes.

Ms. Lawson hung up the phone and looked at Logan. She could tell he was extremely upset.

"Sit down, Billy, and I will get you a glass of water," she said.

"That's okay," Logan said, realizing that his breath had returned. "I'm going down to the patio to take a chance on Sarge being there."

"Dr. Elkins will be here in about 30 minutes, Billy," Ms. Lawson said sternly.

"I won't be long," Logan assured her as he grabbed the doorknob and left. Ms. Lawson followed to watch him meander through the hall, dodging people as he walked toward the courtyard. She just shook her head and walked back inside the office.

Logan opened the patio doors and looked toward the back corner of the patio for Sarge. The corner was completely empty. Logan took a deep breath and slowly returned to Dr. Elkins' office.

Chapter 21

Ms. Lawson was waiting for Logan with a cup of water.

"Have a seat and calm down," she said. "Dr. Elkins will be here in about ten minutes."

Logan sat down on a comfortable leather couch and closed his eyes. His breathing slowed as he began to calm down. "Thank you for the water and for calling the doctor," he told Ms. Lawson.

In a short while, Dr. Elkins walked into the office. He looked almost excited and as breathless as Logan appeared a half hour earlier. He relaxed once he realized that Logan was again in a tranquil state.

"Come on into my office," Dr. Elkins said as he opened the door. With a wave of his hand, he offered Logan a seat in the well-known chair in front of his desk.

"I'm really sorry for having to call you at home, Doc" Logan said. "But something happened today and I felt like I had to talk to someone. You're the first person to come in my mind."

"What happened, Billy?"

"I really don't know how to begin," Logan stammered. "It was the damnedest thing I've ever seen."

"Why don't you start from the beginning," Dr. Elkins suggested.

"You probably won't believe this," Logan said.

Logan paused, struggling to find a way to discuss Terry with Dr. Elkins. The situation was certainly complicated by her job at the hospital and her desire to keep her relationship with Logan confidential."

"I went to the convention center in downtown Baltimore this morning," he said. "It was hosting a conference."

"You mean to the Pharmaceutical Expo?"

Logan looked at him and hesitated.

"How did you get a pass to get in there?" Dr. Elkins pressed.

Logan felt like a deer caught in the headlights, worried that any wrong word could out Terry.

"I see Mr. Warner at the college and he asked me if I would like to go," Logan said as he felt slightly shifty. "He thought there might be some drugs coming out that could help with my amnesia."

"Did you take Terry with you?"

Logan looked at him, wide eyed and determined to confront the truth head on.

"Yes, sir, I did," he said.

Dr. Elkins stern face evolved into an affable grin.

"Billy, it's okay if you and Terry see each other," he said. "You're out of the hospital now and on your own. What you do is your business, and Terry's a grown woman. You two make a nice couple."

"How..." Logan said, trying to compose himself. "How did you know we were seeing each other?"

"She came by last week and asked me about Sarge," Dr. Elkins said. "She said you wanted to find him, and she asked for my help. I told her I would talk to you during your next visit."

Logan breathed a sigh of relief.

"We can talk about Sarge later," Dr. Elkins said. "For now, let's talk about what got you so upset today."

"I was sitting in the cafeteria, waiting on Terry," Logan started. "She and her dad had gone to a lecture that I couldn't attend. We agreed to meet in the cafeteria after the lecture. The cafeteria was basically full when I got there, but I found a seat in the back of the room where I could watch the front entrance for Terry.

"I had been there about 45 minutes, reading brochures and occasionally looking up at the entrance, when I saw my angel walk in. The one from my dreams! She had long wispy blonde hair that flowing down over her shoulders. She didn't have a bright glow around her like she does in my dreams, but I know it was her. I felt a numbing shock across my body. I could literally feel my heart pounding, and my hands were sweating.

"She was joined by another lady and they were looking around in the room before sitting at a table in the middle of the cafeteria. A man got up and pulled chairs out for the ladies. By this time, she had her back to me, so I couldn't see her face. I just stood there staring, hoping for a better look, when Terry walked over and punched me on the shoulder. I couldn't say a word.

"As Terry and I walked to the front of the cafeteria, I looked back to try and get one more look at my angel. Sure enough, she was looking across the table at someone with that smile I have seen so many times before in my dreams. I felt as though my legs were going to give out from under me. It might have happened if Terry hadn't been holding onto me so tightly."

Logan stopped and took a gulp of water.

"It scared me so badly," he said. "I didn't know what to do. I dropped Terry off at her place, but I know I wouldn't be able to get the encounter off of my mind. I had to talk to someone about it, so here I am. Do you think I'm going crazy, Doc?"

Dr. Elkins sat behind his desk, arms folded, while looking down at his desk.

After some hesitation, he looked up at Logan.

"Billy, there's no doubt that you saw a lady walk into that cafeteria," Dr. Elkins said in careful, measured words.

"This lady could have looked like the angel from your dreams, especially since you had just had a dream about her a few nights ago. The subconscious mind sometimes has a way of playing tricks on us," the doctor continued. What you saw, and what you believe you saw, could be totally different things. Some of this could be occurring because of the time you spent in the jungle. It could have something to do with the drugs you were given for your pain. The opium may have cleared your bloodstream, but you still maybe having some mind-altering effects. It could make you see images that aren't actually there."

"What are saying, Doc?" Logan said. "Do you think she was a figment of my imagination?"

"No, not exactly," Dr. Elkins said. "I'm saying you may have seen a lady who resembled the woman in your dream, and your subconscious mind is projecting the image of your angel from your dream."

"That's hard for me to believe," Logan said, clinching his fists. "To me it was as real as you are sitting right in front of me."

"Well," Dr. Elkins said. "I was waiting for the right time to discuss something else with you, so I guess now is as good a time as any."

The doctor took a deep breath.

"Let's talk about Sarge," Dr. Elkins said. "What did you talk about with him when you were out in the courtyard?"

"We had several conversations," Logan said. "Some of the advice he gave me made a lot of sense. I followed through on some of it, and look at where I am now."

"Give me an example, Billy."

Logan sat in the brown leather chair, reflecting on all his chats with the veteran in the wheelchair.

"I guess the one I remember the most came at a time when I had been walking and trying to think of my name and where I was from," Logan said. "I was wondering if I had a family. It was all that I had on my mind, and I was struggling to move on.

"I told Sarge about it. He listened and finally he told me that my condition was like being reborn. He said it was time for me to start thinking of my future and not my past. He suggested that I focus on my future by getting an education and making something out of myself. He told me that sitting around thinking of the past wouldn't help me move forward. He gave me a firm kick in the ass and helped me accept that my memory may never come back.

"It got me thinking, and I realized that, should my memory ever come back, my parents should be proud of my accomplishments. So I went out in search of a new start."

"That was good advice, Billy," Dr. Elkins said. "You were wise to follow Sarge's advice. The only problem is that Sarge did not give you that advice. You gave that advice to yourself."

Logan struggled to contemplate the doctor's words as a puzzled look crept upon his face.

"Look Billy, the person you had been talking to, Sarge, was a figment of your imagination," Dr. Elkins said. "He never existed. You made him up in your mind, and the advice he gave you was actually coming from your own subconscious."

"That just cannot be, Dr. Elkins," Logan said, banging his hand on the desk. "Now you're saying I am crazy."

"No, Billy, I'm not saying you're crazy," Dr. Elkins assured. "You're a smart young man. You asked the questions and you answered them. Though at the time, Sarge was the person you needed to talk to. Did you ever shake his hand? Did you ever make any contact with him at all?"

Logan stared into Dr. Elkins' eyes as he slowly accepted the truth. His eyes began to well up and his bottom lip started to quiver. Tears ran down the side of his face as he began to feel sick to his stomach.

"So you're saying I was out there on the patio talking to an empty wheelchair the whole time?" Logan said as he wiped the tears away with back of his hands.

"To you, Billy, that wheelchair wasn't empty," Dr. Elkins explained in a calming voice.

"Did everyone know I was out there doing that?" Logan asked.

"Billy, think about where you're at," the doctor said. "You're in a hospital with a lot of wounded soldiers with a lot of mental problems. Other men here have bad dreams at night that have them waking up screaming. I see it all the time. I have sessions with men who are going over the same Territory every day, trying to reconcile where they have been and what they have done. A lot of those boys will never get over it. They will probably have those dreams for the rest of their lives.

"What I'm trying to say is that you're not the first soldier to experience this, and believe me you will not be the last. Sarge was there for you when you needed him. You will probably always think of him, but you've also got to know that you gave yourself the tools to move on and find success."

Dr. Elkins smiled at Logan.

"Billy, you have a mild case compared to what I see here," the doctor said. "So, using a baseball phrase that you're familiar with, it's time to step up to the plate and move on. You have a lot of living to do, and I haven't given up on you reclaiming your past. And all will still be well if it never comes back. You will continue to make a new life for yourself. So far you seem to be doing a good job of that."

Logan couldn't help but feel relief.

"Right now, I think I'm going to walk down the hall and get us a Coke," Dr. Elkins said as he stood up and reached for his billfold. "I'd like you to just sit here and think about what we've discussed. We can discuss any questions you have when I get back with those Cokes."

Logan just nodded slowly. Dr. Elkins left the office, closing the door behind him quietly. He looked at Ms. Lawson and asked her in a low voice to make sure Logan stayed in the study. It took him 20 minutes to return with the sodas. He handed one to Logan and say down on the edge of his desk.

"Okay, Billy, how are you feeling?" Dr. Elkins asked. "Did you have enough time to think about what we discussed?"

"I feel like I have lost a good friend, Doc," Logan said. "Knowing I did it on my own makes me feel somewhat better, and knowing that I haven't seen Sarge in nearly two years seems to be another sign that I'm getting better. And I can also see how I could've been wrong about seeing my angel today. You're right, though, it could have been someone who just looked like her. Maybe it was something that my subconscious really wanted to be real."

"Just keep in mind that you have come a long ways and the only thing you're dealing with now is that dream," the doctor said. "And you only have that dream occasionally. When you are finally free of the nightmares, we can continue working on your amnesia. You're doing great, Billy. Keep going to school, and continue helping the coach. Enjoy your time with Terry. Truth is, you have a lot to look forward to."

Dr. Elkins walked over and shook Logan's hand.

"Now you go back home and get some rest," he urged. "And forget about what happened today."

Three hours had passed when Logan pulled into his driveway. Terry's car was there, and she met him on the porch as he approached the steps.

"Where have you been?" she said with a sense of urgency in her voice. "You didn't call me when you said you would. I was worried to death since you didn't act right today."

"I had to go see Dr. Elkins and I got a lot straightened out," Logan said. "I think just maybe I can now move past some things that had been bothering me. It's all going to be fine now."

*****

It had taken Logan four long and arduous years to make it to graduation day. But there he was, in January 1972, a recent college graduate who finished with a respectable 3.50 average and a business degree. His confidence was high. Two years had passed without any disturbing dreams.

His relationship with Terry had grown stronger. After all, she was the encouragement he depended on as he pursued his degree. Now, at 27 years of age, Logan was eager to establish some type of career and a bright future, regardless of the unanswered questions about his past.

Logan knew it was time to make a change, find a job, and another place to live. He just hoped that Johns Hopkins would give him time to do that before he had to move out. The administrators had been very generous, letting him live in the cottage the entire four years.

He wanted to stop by the ballpark to thank Coach Thorne for bringing him on as an assistant coach. Logan had been longing to stay on the coaching staff for a second year. While the past season was challenging for the team, he had seen improvement from the year before that made him optimistic about the year ahead, even though several good players had also graduated. It helped that he seemed to understand Coach Thorne's outlook on life and his approach to coaching.

Before Logan could get to his car, he looked up to see Coach Thorne pulling into his driveway. The coach, a hulking man in his late 40s who weighed nearly 300 pounds, struggled to get out of his car. He did the best he could to hide his stomach with a tight leather belt with a big buckle. His once black hair was graying, but he could move pretty fast for a man of his size and age.

Coach Thorne stepped up on the front porch.

"I was hoping to be able to catch you at home, Billy," he said. "Do you have a few minutes? We need to talk."

"Funny thing, I was just on my way over to see you, coach," Billy said. "Come on in and get out of the cold. I've got a fire going inside."

"That sounds good to me, Billy," the coach said as he shook Logan's hand and entered the house. "It's nice and cozy in here, Billy."

"Yeah, I've enjoyed living here for the last four years," Logan said. "It's been a nice place to live."

"I'm going to get right to the point, Billy," Coach Thorne said as he pulled a chair out from the kitchen table.

Billy joined him at the table, wondering what the coach had on his mind.

"I must admit that we didn't have a good season last year, but then again it wasn't all that bad, either," Coach Thorne said as the fire crackled behind him. "And I must say that you put in a lot of hard work for the team. I've never seen anybody so dedicated and conscientious. You worked so hard to make us a better team, and you did one hell of a job for us. You were definitely an asset."

"Thank you, coach," Logan said. "I was on my way over to thank you for providing me with that opportunity. I thoroughly enjoyed being with you and the team this past year, and I must say you taught me a whole lot."

"I've seen some improvement in you, too, Billy," the coach said. "That's why I'm here. I just left out of a board meeting with the president and the rest of the faculty concerning our team. I had requested a permanent assistant coach. I need someone who can take my place if necessary. I need a leader who can command respect from the players and teach them discipline. I told them that you were the man for the job. The president and the faculty agreed with me, and they authorized me to make you this offer. First of all, you can stay here, or you can live on campus. Either way, your house will be free, and food at the cafeteria will be covered, too."

Coach Thorne reached into his shirt pocket. He pulled out a folded piece of paper and slid it over to Logan, face down. "This is what we're willing to offer you to stay and be my assistant coach," he said.

Logan slowly opened the piece of paper to see the one-year salary offer. He stared at it with a somewhat surprised look on his face. "Are you serious with this figure, Coach?"

"You're worth every penny, Billy," Coach Thorne said. "I would be pleased if you would accept and be my assistant coach."

"I couldn't be any happier than what I am right now," Logan said. "There's nothing that would please me more than to stay on as your assistant coach. I will accept this, with gratitude to you and the school, and I will do my very best for you and the team."

"I can't ask any more of you than that," the coach said, rising from his chair to shake Logan's hand. "I think next season is going be our year, Billy, now that you're staying on,"

Logan walked the coach back to the front door.

"Billy, I'm going to give you a few days to settle in," Coach Thorne said. "Then I want you to come by my office. First, we'll set you up with your own office next to mine. There are a lot of decisions to be made about players. So rest up. The heavy lifting starts next week.

Chapter 22

Debra had just parked her car in the Garrison's driveway when Ellen came out of the house, her briefcase in hand.

"Let's take my car over to the bank," Ellen said.

"Oh, so you want to show off your new station wagon?" Debra said.

"It's not new," Ellen replied. "It's six months old. This wagon has also turned out to be my office. I talk more business in this car than I do anywhere else, which reminds me that I need to look into some office space. It's hard to work here with Little Logan running all over the place and mom chasing after him trying to get him to stop!"

"How do you like this wagon?" Debra asked as she looked in the backseat. Several rolled up tubes of blueprints were strewn across the seat and floorboard, mixed up with clipboards that had writings and drawings on them.

"Yep, I'd say you need an office somewhere, Ellen," Debra agreed.

"I asked you to come with me to the bank because I'd like you to show Mr. Carter our financial statements," Ellen said. "And I wanted some time to talk with you about another business deal."

Debra could tell that Ellen was ready to get serious.

"Deb, you have been with me and Logan Drugstores from the beginning," Ellen continued. "You have always been on top of things concerning the business, helping me out with the tax laws and the dos and the don'ts. You bailed us out several times, and you've always been there to keep me straight day and night. I don't think we could've made it without your help.

"So I was curious, Deb. How much of your business comes from our company?"

"I'd say that about a third of my revenue is tied to your drugstores," Debra estimated.

"What do you think will happen when I open these other two drugstores?"

Debra started to respond, but Ellen decisively cut her off.

"What I mean is that dad and I would like to hire you as our executive vice president, in charge of finance," Ellen blurted out. "You would attend all our board meetings and work one-on-one with our attorney, Bob Haywood."

Debra just smiled.

"If you would take this job, Deb, I'll set you up in an office," Ellen said. "I could possibly set you up in the same building Bob is in."

"Boy, you really do want me to take this job, Ellen."

"I can also give you a company vehicle," Ellen pressed. "We'll reimburse you for all company expenses, and we'll start you out with a salary that is 5% more than what you're making now."

"You drive a hard bargain, Ellen."

"Come on Deb," Ellen said. "We've been together since the second grade, and there's nobody that I trust more than you. And remember that I told you on our way to Walter Reed hospital six years ago to keep an open mind because I was working on a long-term plan. Do you remember that?"

"Believe it or not, Ellen I do, but who would have believed that this would be coming true today," Debra said.

"Me, Deb, me," Ellen said gleefully as she pulled up in front of the bank ten minutes before it was set to open.

"Deb, you don't have to give me your answer now," Ellen said. "Just think it over. Take as much time as you need. Get back to me as soon as you make a decision."

"Are you sure you want to do this so soon Ellen?" Debra asked as the women stood in front of bank.

"Why not?" Ellen said, just as Mr. Carter unlocked the doors.

"Come on in ladies," the banker said, waving them back to his office.

Debra quickly opened her briefcase and pulled out a folder file before they could all get settled in.

"Well, Mr. Carter, we're getting ready to do it again," Ellen began.

"Do what again, Ellen?"

"I'm going to open up two more stores," Ellen said. "I want to open one in Winston Salem on Stratford Road, and another one on Church Street in Burlington."

Mr. Carter started carefully thumbing through the paperwork.

"I don't see a problem," he said. "After all, you paid off the last loan in less than two years. How well are your stores doing now?"

Debra reached into the folder and slid a piece of paper in front of Mr. Carter. "This is the gross profit, and here is net," she said, sliding her fingers across the numbers as she explained them.

The banker looked at it, slowly moving his head back and forth. "I have never seen such a quick return on investment," he declared.

"So now you want to open up to more stores?" he asked.

"Yep, two more," the women said in unison.

"Based on these numbers, you should have enough cash flow to do it on your own, Ellen," Mr. Carter said.

"I know, but I would prefer to use your money rather than mine," Ellen said. "I'll use my money for other projects that come along."

"Well, I will go ahead and draw up all the paperwork and mail it to you," Mr. Carter said.

"You can just mail it to my attorney," Ellen said. "You know Bob Haywood, right?"

"Yes, I know Bob, and I have his address."

"Thank you, Mr. Carter," Ellen said.

"Thank you, Ellen," the banker said as he shook each woman's hand.

As they started out of the office, Debra turned to Ellen.

"I guess you'll need to call the contractor and tell him to get started," Debra said.

"Honey, he got started four weeks ago," Ellen said with a laugh. "We're already ahead of schedule."

"You had him to start before you got the money," Debra said, dumbfounded.

"I knew that the construction timeline was going to be more difficult to wrangle than getting another loan," Ellen explained. "You have to move when the time is right, and the timing was right for Eric to get started."

Debra just shook her head and took a deep breath. As they started to get in the car, Ellen heard someone call her by name. She turned around to see Mr. Carter waving at her.

"You have a phone call, Ellen," he said. "It sounds urgent."

Ellen rushed back inside, with Debra close behind. Mr. Carter's secretary handed her the phone.

"This is Ellen."

Debra couldn't tell who was on the other line, but there was a frantic tone to the individual's voice.

"I'm on my way, Ms. MacKay," Ellen said. "I'm leaving the bank now and will be at the hospital in a few minutes."

"What's wrong, Ellen?"

"I'll tell you when we get in the car to go to Morehead Hospital," Ellen said.

Ellen pulled out of the bank's parking lot and drove the car onto Draper Road.

"What happened?" Debra asked again.

"Ms. MacKay tried to wake Ms. Dubois this morning and she didn't respond," Ellen said. "They're on their way to the hospital with her now."

Ellen hurriedly parked the car and the women sprinted for the hospital entrance. The receptionist at the front desk wouldn't let them go back to the emergency room since they weren't relatives, but she assured Ellen and Debra that someone would come out at some point to give them an update.

It took Dr. Clarke about 20 minutes to come out to the waiting room. He had been Ms. Dubois' doctor for years, along with about 90% of the town.

Ellen jumped up from her seat.

"How is she, Dr. Clarke?"

"We couldn't resuscitate her, Ellen," he said soberly. "Her heart finally gave out. If it's any consolation, she went peacefully and quietly. She must have passed in her sleep."

Tears swelled in Ellen's eyes as she sat back down, when she realized that Ms. MacKay was going to be coming home to an empty house. "Let's make sure we're home when she gets back," she told Debra.

They buried Ms. Dubois four days later on the hill in the pasture, beside of her husband. Most of the town showed up for the ceremony; cars were parked along the winding drive to the house, lining up all the way to the main highway.

Five officers from the Draper Police Department, and every member of the volunteer fire department, were there. Ms. Dubois had been a big contributor and supporter of both organizations.

"She would have been proud, Debra, that all these people come to say their farewells to her," Ellen whispered during the service.

Ellen, and Debra and Ms. MacKay started walking back to the house when they ran into Mr. Ivey, an attorney in the neighboring town of Leaksville. He was looking for Ellen.

"Ms. Dubois' will has you down as the administrator of her estate and financial affairs," Mr. Ivey said. "I was wondering if we could meet on Monday morning to go over the will. She didn't make a lot of requests, but most of her plans involved you."

"Yes, that would be fine," Ellen said. "What time suits you?"

"Would 10 o'clock work for you?" the lawyer asked.

"That would be fine," Ellen said. "I will see you on Monday."

Debra looking at Ellen as the lawyer walked off. "Boy, are you going to have your hands full."

"I don't mind," Ellen said. "She was a fine lady and we had a chance to get close over the last two years. Little Logan loved her so. He's really going to miss her."

Ellen quietly turned to Debra and Ms. MacKay and suggested going to the library for a quick conversation.

Ms. Dubois' library had 12-foot ceilings with thick crown molding and dark mahogany paneling. An oversized oriental rug added a splash of color, with its dark maroon, blue and tan threads. The walls were covered with bookshelves, filled with tomes dedicated to winemaking and raising thoroughbred horses. A huge Victorian-era desk with a pair of wing-backed chairs was positioned in the middle of the room.

"I've got to go home and stay with Little Logan so mom can come by and visit," Ellen said. "Ms. MacKay, would you mind staying here until everybody leaves. I can come back when mom returns home."

Ellen turned to Debra.

"Debra, would you be okay staying at my folks' house tonight?" she said. "I'd really like you to go with me in the morning to Mr. Ivey's law office. I think I may need your support in the morning since you know more about legal terms than I do."

"I'll be glad to," Debra said as the women turned to rejoin the gathering of people paying their respects.

The next morning, Ellen and Debra stopped by Ms. Dubois' house on their way to the law office. Ellen knocked on the door and let herself in.

"I'm in the kitchen, honey," Ms. MacKay said. "Come on back."

Ms. MacKay was having coffee with Mr. Ross, the property's manager and the caretaker, when Ellen entered the kitchen.

"How are you this morning, Ms. MacKay," Ellen said. "And it is nice to see you, Mr. Ross."

"We were just sitting here talking about how much Ms. Dubois did for this town," Ms. MacKay said. "There are a lot of people that are going to miss her."

"Debra and I are on our way to meet with the attorney to go over Ms. Dubois' will," Ellen said. "I wonder what she wanted to do with this place. As soon as we get back we'll discuss her wishes with you."

"For right now just sit tight," Debra added. "We'll be back as soon as we can."

"Would you like a cup of coffee before you leave?" Ms. MacKay asked.

"No, thank you," Ellen told her mother-in-law. "We have to get to Leaksville in 30 minutes to make the appointment."

*****

Debra gave Ellen directions to get to Mr. Ivey's office on Bridge Street.

As they neared Leaksville, they noticed a row of older homes lining both sides of the road. They were large, with 1920s architecture and beautifully landscaped lawns.

"Those are beautiful old homes," Debra said in awe. "They don't make houses like that anymore."

Ellen pulled up to a two-story yellow house with black shutters and white window trim.

"Here it is," Debra pointed out. "Let's pull into the driveway."

They noticed a white post with a sign hanging from two small chains that said "Richard Ivey, Attorney At Law, 313 Bridge Street." A small arrow on the sign pointed to a winding sidewalk leading to the back of the house.

"Well, this is it," Debra said. "Let's go."

Ellen was quiet as they walked up the sidewalk and around to the back door. The stoop had a small A-framed roof hanging over it. Ellen rang the doorbell. Mr. Ivey opened the door, his white hair parted in the middle and combed back over the collar of his pin-striped suit. He wore a blue bowtie and a pocket watch with a chain that looped into his vest pocket. He looked as though he had stepped out of the roaring 20s.

"Come on in ladies and have a seat," the lawyer said as he walked around to sit behind an old four-legged oak desk. "Which one of you is Ellen?"

"I'm Ellen, sir."

"May I see your driver's license," he asked as he reached down to pull out a leather folder. He reviewed the license and handed it back to Ellen. His eyebrows furrowed. It seemed as though he was sizing her up.

"You're a very lucky young lady," he said, pulling out a sheet of paper. "This is Ms. Dubois' last will and testament. I signed it two years ago. I'm going to read it out loud, if there are no objections."

"That will be fine," Ellen said.

Mr. Ivey read the following message from Ms. Dubois.

Ellen,

I hope this does not come too much of a shock for you. I have known you for all your life. You and your parents have always been like family to me, although we have become closer in the last year. As you know I have no relatives or family living, and neither did Mr. Dubois.

I cannot think of anyone else that I had rather have managing my estate and my affairs. You proved to me at such a young age that you had the maturity, honesty, and integrity to do what's right and to follow these requests that I ask of you.

First of all, I want you to continue to maintain my house, the horses and our gravesite. I would also like to see Ms. MacKay and Mr. Ross stay employed as long as you see fit. They have been very loyal employees and personal friends. I love them both. I would also like to see you continue to contribute to the Fire Department and Police Department, as well as my church, every year. I would also like to see set up a college fund for one high achiever at the high school. Perhaps Logan wouldn't have gone into the service if I had done that years ago. I've always regretted that I did not do more to help him.

I would also like to see Little Logan get the best education that money can buy. He is such a great child, and I love him dearly.

All of my assets, including the deed to my house and all of my financial accounts, now belong to you to make all of these things happen. If Logan should ever return, he is to have equal shares of whatever is left when he comes back. Should you die, I want my estate transferred to Little Logan and handed down to his heirs.

Thank you and Logan for being the children I never had. I love you both.

P.S. Be sure that Ms. MacKay gets my old DeSoto. I know she will cherish that old car just like I did.

Mr. Ivey looked up at Ellen and Debra after reading the will.

"Well, you are probably the wealthiest woman in the area," he said as he closed the leather folder and slid it over to Ellen. "This folder has all of Ms. Dubois' account numbers and the financials for the estate. I have handled Ms. Dubois' affairs for over 40 years. If there is anything I can do to assist you in any way, please call me or come by anytime. I will do whatever I can to assist you as well."

Ellen sat there mute. She was in a fog as Mr. Ivey shook her hand. When they got outside, she handed her keys to Debra.

"Oh, so you want me to drive?" Debra quipped.

Ellen just shook her head up and down with a stunned look on her face.

Debra had driven halfway home without Ellen saying a word. She could tell Ellen was engrossed in deep concentration. Suddenly Ellen stared at Debra.

"You have no choice, Deb," Ellen said. "You have to become part of this company. I need you now more than ever.

"Actually, this is bigger than the company. I need you to meet with Bob and start working with him on setting up a scholarship at the high school in the Dubois' name. And we'll need to set up payroll for Mr. Ross and Ms. McKay, along with some type of benefits and maybe a retirement plan. We'll need to line up donations to the fire department and the police. There's so much to be done! Just remember that you're not just doing this for me. You're also doing it for Little Logan."

"That's right, Ellen, throw Little Logan on me as well," Debra said. "It looks like you're going to get your way. When do you want me to start?"

"You started last week, Deb," Ellen said. "All of the finances can be transferred into my name, but I want to make sure the funds are only used for payroll and caring for the farm. I don't want any of this money used for the drugstores. I want my business to succeed because of our effort and not because of Ms. Dubois' kindness."

"I understand, Ellen," Debra said. "That's the way I will set it up."

"Now let's get back and talk to Ms. McKay and Mr. Ross," Ellen said. "There is so much to discuss!"

Chapter 23

It was mid-June, 1973, and Logan had just finished another season coaching the Blue Jays, winning the last game over Lynchburg College by a run. Although it was a mediocre season, with eight wins against six losses, Logan had developed a reputation among the other coaches for the job he had done for Johns Hopkins. Still, he was disappointed as he drove home from Lynchburg, upset that Terry wasn't there to help the team celebrate as she had done so many times before.

Terry had decided to stay home, worried that she was coming down with a bug that had weakened her with a fever. Winning was great, but it wasn't the same in light of her absence. Logan decided he would risk infection by paying her a visit. He stepped off the elevator and rang her doorbell. Terry opened the door, in her pajamas and with eyes swollen from crying.

"What's wrong, Terry?"

"I'm just running a fever and my nose won't stop running," she sniffled.

Terry walked back into the den and threw herself back down on the sofa. Logan followed her and sat on the edge of the sofa. Terry put her head on his lap and looked up at him.

"How did the game go tonight?" she asked. "We won the game by one run, but it wasn't the same without you there," Logan said.

"That's sweet, Billy," Terry said with a sigh. "You always did know how to say the right things to me."

Logan could see just how pale Terry was in the light of a nearby lamp.

"I think I'm going to spend the night here with you," he said.

"You don't need to do that, Billy," she said, looking up at him "I'll be okay in a couple of days."

"No, I'm going to spend the night here with you," Logan insisted.

"You may want to sleep in the other bedroom," Terry warned. "I may keep you up all night."

"That's okay, I'm going to sleep in the bed with you," Logan countered. "If you get worse during the night, I will know it."

"I don't feel like arguing with you, Billy, you do what you think is best."

Logan woke up early the next morning and eased himself out of bed to avoid waking up Terry. He slipped into the kitchen to fix a pot of coffee. He then ducked into the shower, shaved and got dressed before returning to the kitchen. He could see that Terry had her way to the couch. She was already holding a cup of coffee.

"I've poured you a cup," she said. "It's on the bar."

"How are you feeling this morning?"

"I just feel weak and tired."

"I've got a meeting with the coach at nine," Logan said. "Do you think you will be all right until I get back? I can get back here around noon."

"You don't have to come back, Billy," Terry whispered. "Mom and dad are going to be here in a little while, and I'll call you later this afternoon."

Logan got the impression that Terry wanted to be with her family, which puzzled. Why wouldn't she want him to come back? He assumed that she was just trying to keep him from catching her virus.

"Okay, I'll get on my way then," Logan said, setting his coffee cup on the counter. He walked over to where she was sitting, reached down and kissed her on the forehead. "I sure will be glad when you're feeling better."

"Agreed," she said.

Logan turned and started to walk away when he heard Terry call his name. He looked back at her.

"I just wanted to tell you that I love you," she said with a solemn face devoid of a smile.

Logan just stared at her. "That's the first time you have said you loved me," he said.

"I know, and I do," Terry said.

Logan got down on his knees and put his hand on top of hers.

"Well, I just want to tell you..." Logan started, but Terry interrupted him by putting a finger to his lips.

"Don't say it now, Billy, just wait," she said.

Logan tried again, but Terry put her entire hand over his mouth.

"Now, you get on out of here, and go meet the coach before you are late," she insisted.

"Okay, I'm on my way," Logan said. He stood up and hurried to the door.

Logan pushed the button to summon the elevator. Terry's words kept cycling through his mind. Not just what she said, but how she expressed her love. Why now? After all those years and all the late night conversations in bed, she chose this morning to say those words.

Maybe she's delirious and talking out of her head, Logan hypothesized. No, no, she knew what she was saying. The elevators doors opened with a loud ding.

Logan could see as he pulled into the college parking lot that the coach was already there. Logan looked at his watch. He was five minutes early, Still, he hastily walked up the sidewalk to the front entrance. As he walked into the office, he could see Coach Thorne standing near the window with his back facing the door, holding a mug of coffee in his right hand.

"Good morning coach," Logan said.

"Good morning to you too, Billy," the coach said. "Winning the last game of the season always makes for a good morning, doesn't it?"

"Yes it does," Logan said. "Thank you for letting me be part of it, coach."

"By the way, Billy, you may be getting some calls from other colleges."

"What do you mean, coach?"

"Word has gotten out about your coaching ability," the coach said. "And you could be getting a call from one of them."

"I think I'm fine where I am," Logan said.

"We're not talking about an assistant coaching position," Coach Thorne said. "People are talking about you as a candidate for head coaching jobs, Billy."

"Are you serious coach?" Logan said, disbelieving.

"Yes, and don't be surprised if you get a call."

"I'm surprised, but I feel comfortable where I'm at for now," Logan said.

"I'm not one to hold a man back from bettering himself," Coach Thorne said. "If you do get that call, I'll be glad to sit down, discuss it with you, and give you all the advice that I can."

"Thanks, coach I would appreciate that."

Logan spent two hours filling out end of season paperwork and examining the locker room before returning to the coach's office.

"Everything checks out coach," Logan reported. "The locker rooms have been cleaned out and all the paperwork is up to date for next year."

"Are you headed out, Billy?"

"Yes, I'm going home and get some rest," Logan said. "I didn't sleep too well last night, and I've also got some studying to do."

"Did you say studying?" Coach Thorne asked. "I thought you were done with school."

"I'm going to summer school to get a head start on my business courses," Logan explained. "I'm going to try to get my master's degree next year. I don't know what I would do with my spare time if I wasn't in school."

"That's good, Billy," the coach said. "Have a good weekend."

"Thanks coach," Logan said. "You do the same."

"A Whisper Away"

Logan pulled into his driveway, hopeful that Terry's car would be there. No such luck, he quickly realized. So he went inside, dove into his books, and tried to clear his mind of Terry, while still hoping she would call.

Two days passed with no word from Terry. Logan wondered why she wouldn't call. He decided to give her another day before calling the hospital to check on her.

Logan left his office the next morning to use the phone in the coach's office to make the call. A pleasant voice answered the phone at the hospital.

"I would like to speak to Terry Warner," Logan told the receptionist. "She's a nurse on the second floor."

"I'm sorry, sir, but Ms. Warner no longer works here," the lady said.

"Ma'am, Terry Warner is a nurse on the second floor," politely repeated.

"Yes, sir, I understand," the receptionist replied. "She turned in her resignation last Friday."

Logan was shocked, hanging up the phone without saying another word. What is going on, Logan wondered, as he started feeling sick to his stomach. I have to get to her house, he decided. I need to know what's going on.

Logan started sprinting down the hall, bounded down the steps and raced across the parking lot to his Thunderbird. His hands were shaking to the point that he couldn't put the key in the ignition. Slow down, slow down, he repeated to himself. He took a few deep breaths and managed to insert the key, start the engine and drive out of the lot.

He could feel his heart beating faster and faster as he pulled into the underground lot at Terry's condo. Slow down, slow down, he repeated. Everything is going to be okay.

Logan stepped off the elevator and walked over to Terry's door. Positioned perfectly in the center of the door was a "for-sale" sign by Century 21, marketing the upscale condominium with "a beautiful view of the city." The agent's number was printed at the bottom.

Confusion overtook Logan, and he had no idea what to do next. Slow down, slow down. I'll just go back home and wait for her to call. No, no, I'll go see Mr. Warner tomorrow at school, and he'll tell me what's going on.

Logan raced home and dashed directly to his phone. He called the college but there was no answer. There's nothing I can do until the morning, he realized. Slow down. Slow down.

Logan arrived at the campus early the next morning. He was sitting on a step overlooking the parking lot when a white 1972 Thunderbird pulled into a reserved spot. Mr. Warner got out of the car and started making his way to the front entrance. Logan stood up.

Mr. Warner saw Logan and stopped momentarily before continuing to walk across the street. Logan chased after him, forcing him to stop.

"Before you say anything, Billy, let's just go to my office where we can talk," Mr. Warner said. The men walked in silence until they arrived at Mr. Warner's office.

Mr. Warner carefully set his briefcase down as the entered the office.

"Sit down, Billy," Mr. Warner said as he sat down and leaned back in his reclining chair. He had a sincere, but sad, expression on his face.

"Billy, I'm sorry that Terry didn't call you," Mr. Warner said. "It wasn't right, and I told her so. I don't have to tell you this, but when she makes her mind up there's no changing it. She has moved back home with us, and that's where she's going to stay for a while. She knew you come to see me, so she asked me to give you this letter."

Mr. Warner opened the center drawer of his desk and pulled out a white envelope. He handed it to Logan.

"If you would like to read it here I will go outside," he told Logan. "Or you can read it at your home. Whatever you would like to do is fine."

Logan knew bad news was lurking in the envelope, so he decided to take it home and read it by himself. He was unsure of his potential reaction and he didn't want anyone around when he learned what was in the letter.

So he stood up and thanked Mr. Warner, who walked around the desk and placed his hand on Logan's shoulder.

"I'm sorry, son," he whispered.

Logan didn't remember much about his drive home. He was preoccupied with the words he would read and the truths that might be revealed in them. He slowly opened the door to his home and sat down on the sofa, clutching the letter in his hand.

Logan tried to steel himself, taking deep breaths, before ripping the envelope to reveal a one-page note.

Dear Billy,

When you receive this letter, I will be at mom and dad's. I didn't want to call you and tell you this. I guess I'm just a coward taking the coward's way out, but this is the only way I know how to do this. I have thought long and hard about what to say to you, but I think what I'm doing is the best thing for both of us.

I know you have another life out there, and I pray every day that you will find it and be happy. More than anything, that is my wish for you. Please understand, Billy, this gift I am giving to you is going to make us both happy in the long run. Just know that my feelings for you were true.

Always remember the last words I told you. I meant every word. I know it's going to be hard to move on, but you can do it, Billy. It will take you time, but I know you can do it.

Please do not try and contact me. It is my wish that you would continue just as you are doing right now. Go back to school, play ball and enjoy your life! You owe that to yourself. Just know I will be thinking about you every day, and I wish you the very best in whatever you find in life ... and happiness.

I will always be thinking of you,

Terry

Chapter 24

Logan could not believe what he was reading. His mind was racing. She's saying farewell with no explanation. Why would she tell me she loved me, then quit her job, sell her home and move back with her parents? None of this makes any sense. There has to be a reason for it. Logan decided he needed to have another talk with Mr. Warner.

Just like the day before, Logan was sitting on the steps overlooking the campus parking lot, waiting for Mr. Warner to arrive. He sat there holding the letter, reading it over and over again trying to make sense of it all.

Mr. Warner pulled into the parking lot. As he got closer to stairs he saw Logan sitting there, holding the note.

"We need to talk, Mr. Warner," Logan said. "Just give me five minutes and I will leave you alone. I promise you will not hear from me again."

Mr. Warner looked at Logan. He could see the sadness and pain in the young man's eyes.

"Okay, Billy, let's go back to my office," Mr. Warner said.

Logan again took a seat in front of Mr. Warner's desk.

"This letter doesn't make any sense at all," Logan said, holding the note up with trembling hand. "She told me the last time I saw her that she loved me, and the next thing I know she quits her job, leaves her condo, and moves back home. The letter says she doesn't want to see me anymore. All I want to know is why."

Mr. Warner could tell that Logan was unsatisfied with the letter.

"Okay, Billy, I'm going to give it to you straight," he said. "Since Terry was 16, she has always wanted to be a physician, but she quit after four years of medical school. She had enough education to become a nurse, and that's what she did. And that's how she ended up at Walter Reed.

"Something happened after she met you, Billy. She saw how you were moving forward with a new life, getting an education and following your passion for coaching baseball. I think you inspired her to do the same thing. She has decided to go back to school to become a doctor. In order to do that, she had to quit her job. I invited her to move back home so I could help her with her studies, so there was no need to have the condominium any more. Terry is 27, Billy, and she needs to keep her mind on her studies. It will take her another five years to complete her education. At this point in her life, she needs no distracts."

Logan didn't say a word. After a minute, he stood up to face Mr. Warner.

"I can respect that, Mr. Warner," Logan declared. "If that's what she wants, then I will do my part. Thank you for taking the time to explain it to me. I wish her the very best. Please tell her I said that."

"I will, Billy, thank you for understanding."

Logan walked out the door, still holding the letter in his hand. As he neared the steps, he saw a trash can. He walked over and tossed the letter in the can. If she doesn't want to see me again, that's fine, Logan thought. If staying away would help Terry become a doctor, that's fine.

Logan resolved to devote his full attention to studying for his business courses. He filled his free time exercising and running laps around the ball field, intent to do all he could to keep his mind off of Terry. Days turned into months, and by October it was time to prepare for a new baseball season. Logan was eager to begin, knowing that a busy schedule would help keep Terry out of his thoughts.

It was a Thursday morning. Logan was sitting at his desk when Coach Thorne walked in, closing the door behind him. The coach pulled up a chair in front of Logan's desk.

"Okay, Billy, it has happened," Coach Thorne said.

"What's happened?"

"I got the call last night," the coach said. "You've got a big decision to make."

"What kind of decision, coach?"

"Whether you want to go to Blacksburg and become the head coach at Virginia Tech. Or Liberty Baptist College. They're also keen on you."

"Are you serious, coach?"

"Yes, I'm serious," Coach Thorne said. "Congratulations, Billy."

"Wow, I don't know what to say, and I sure don't know what to do."

"I knew this day was going to come, Billy," the coach said. "Even with one eye and a half of a hand, you will do a better job than most coaches out there. I think you should go home today and think about those offers. Just make sure that you decide what is right for you."

Coach Thorne stood up.

"We'll discuss it when you come in the morning," he added. "You can let me know which school you want to talk to first."

Logan was up half the night, walking the floors thinking about the job offers. He was grateful for the opportunities, and for what Johns Hopkins had done for him. So naturally he felt an obligation to the school. He also knew that a new job would further the distance from Terry, and he was still holding out faint hope that she might come back. What if he passed on the opportunity and she didn't want to come back? Logan also realized that, by staying at Johns Hopkins, he would regularly cross paths with Mr. Warner, which would bring back a lot of unbearable memories.

Maybe it's time to move on, he thought. After all, Terry wants to be left alone.

Logan walked into the coach's office the next morning to discuss his options.

"Good morning, Billy, I bet you slept well last night."

"Maybe about two hours, Coach," Logan said.

Coach Thorne let out a hearty laugh. "I can understand that," he said.

"Sit down and we'll talk about it," the coach said, offering Logan a seat. "I've been thinking about it, to, Billy. Liberty Baptist is a good school, but I think Virginia Tech, the Hokies, is the place I'd seriously look at if I were you. They already have a good program that would best suit a first-time head coach. And the three assistants are pretty good coaches. You may have to make a change or two down the road, but the first year I'd tell you to hold on to what you have."

"Well, you have helped me make my decision coach," Logan said, nodding in agreement. "That's where I'll go then."

"I will call Coach Bryan and set it up for you," Coach Thorne said. "I'm sure he will be glad to see you. He's been eager to retire for the last two or three seasons, and his last two years in Blacksburg have not been good ones."

After meeting with Coach Bryan, Logan was pleased with the deal that Virginia Tech had presented him. The money was great, and the house he was set to live in was near the college. Time was of the essence, though, Virginia Tech needed him on campus within two weeks. Logan wasted no time, resigning as the Blue Jays' assistant coach, while having his studies transferred to Virginia Tech, where he would continue his education.

It took Logan a few weeks to fully settle into his new house and office and to get fairly acquainted with his trio of assistant coaches. The most likeable assistant was Jim Walker, a tall slender man in his early 40s who had joined the staff a few years earlier from Wake Forest College. Walker, who coached third base, was extremely knowledgeable about baseball and shared Logan's passion for the game.

The team's pitching coach was Roger Stackhouse, who had been at the school for two years. In his mid-30s, Stackhouse had ties to Richmond College. A respectable student of the game, Stackhouse was better known at Virginia Tech for his hustle, and he was eager to do whatever was necessary to get a job done.

Randall Cook handled first base responsibilities. A local boy who played his college ball in Blacksburg, Cook had stayed at his alma mater after graduation. Mostly used as a glorified gopher by Coach Bryan, Cook was content as long as the players, and the other assistants, addressed him as coach.

*****

It was the first week of December, and Logan was hopeful about getting caught up on paperwork and recruiting during Christmas break. He was in his office talking with Tommy Jackson, the program's baseball recruiter. Jackson had been at Virginia Tech for years. He had just turned 61 and was looking forward to retirement. He was responsible for most of the high school and, from what Logan had seen and heard, Jackson had simply been marking the days until retirement. The complacency bothered Logan, who knew he had to come up with something to address the recruiting issues. The window had closed to address the upcoming season, but there was still a chance to salvage recruiting for the next year.

Logan could tell from the conversation that Jackson was uninspired, but he decided to wait until after the holidays to make any major moves.

"I think I'm going to go home and get ready for Santa Claus," Jackson said, unaware of the changes that were afoot. "You have a Merry Christmas, Logan."

"You do the same, Tommy," Logan said. "Be safe out there."

Logan was set ready to leave his office. It was a few minutes after six, and about time he started his winter break. He started to pull his winter coat on when the phone rang. Who in the world could that be, he thought. He answered the phone to find Mr. Warner on the other line.

"Yes, Mr. Warner," Logan said with some hesitation.

"Billy, I realize it's late and I'm sure you're busy," Mr. Warner said. "But it's imperative that you leave now and come to my house."

Logan's mind was racing. His heart started pounded to the point he could hear and feel it.

"What's going on?" he said. "What's wrong, Mr. Warner?"

"I don't have time to explain over the phone, Billy," Mr. Warner said in a stern, but calm, voice. "Just get in your car and come up here as soon as you can."

"I will leave right now," Logan said.

Logan rushed to his car and, as quickly as possible, got onto the interstate. His mind was wandering. What could have happened? Is Terry hurt? Or maybe something happened to Ms. Warner. Something didn't add up. Mr. Warner made it clear that it was urgent, yet there wasn't a sense of urgency in his voice.

It took about three hours for Logan to cut across Virginia backroads to get to the house nestled in the woods just west of Richmond. He drove down the long driveway. All the lights in the house seemed to be on, including the bulb illuminating the front porch.

Logan guided his Thunderbird around the circular drive and parked awkwardly in front of the house. He took a deep breath and reached out to ring the doorbell. Mr. Warner flung the door open before Logan could press the button. There were no formalities. Instead, he laid his hands on

Logan's shoulder. In a low voice he instructed Logan to follow him into his personal study, closing the door behind them.

"First, let me apologize to you for the story that I told you about Terry leaving you to go back to medical school," Mr. Warner said. "That wasn't the case at all."

Mr. Warner stopped as his eyes welled up with tears. "The truth is that she's dying, Billy."

Logan felt his knees buckling, quickly grabbing hold of nearby chair to get steadied. He slowly found a way to sit down in the chair as the room spun around him.

"My wife and I have been preparing ourselves for this day for over 10 years, Billy," Mr. Warner continued. "She has lung cancer. I quit my job at Walter Reed to go to Johns Hopkins to conduct research in hopes of finding a cure. I found a treatment that slowed down the cancer's advancement. Terry wasn't supposed to make it past 18. The regimen I gave her bought her time, but the cancer has finally has caught up to her.

"My wife and I didn't support your relationship because we knew this day would eventually come and we felt like it wasn't fair to you. But I have got to say, Billy, you found a way to make these last few years the happiest of her life."

"Can I see her now?" Logan asked.

"That's the reason why I called you, Billy," Mr. Warner said. "She has been asking for you."

Logan stood up gingerly. His legs, while weak, were able to stand on their own. He was calm again. He just wanted to see Terry and put his arms around her.

Mr. Warner guided Logan down, past a huge den and through another hallway before stopping at a door on the right.

"Don't appear to be surprised by her appearance, Billy," Mr. Warner cautioned. "She asked her mother to put on some makeup and fix her hair so she could be ready for you. And I would like to thank you, Billy, for coming. My wife and I certainly appreciate it."

Logan just stared at him and nodded his head slowly.

Mr. Warner opened the door, and Logan stepped inside. Ms. Warner was sitting in a straight back chair, holding her daughter's hand in her lap. Terry was in bed, her eyes closed. She was very pale, except for the light makeup on her cheeks. Ms. Warner turned and looked up at Logan. She stood up and motioned for Logan to take her seat.

Instead, Logan moved the chair aside and sat down on the side of the bed. At that moment, Terry opened her eyes and a slight smile come across her face. She attempted to talk, but it came out as a barely discernable whisper.

Logan moved closer so he could hear her.

"I'm so glad you came, Billy," Terry said in a thin raspy voice "I have missed you."

Logan could not speak. He just leaned over and gave her a kiss on the lips and smiled. He nodded his head and he tried to swallow the lump in this throat.

"I have missed you too, baby," he said. "I am so sorry."

"I'm not sorry, Billy," Terry said. "You gave me a life I thought I would never have. You showed me what love felt like. I had never felt so alive in my life. How liberating to go to bed happy. I'm grateful for being able to wake up happy with you by my side, and looking forward to spending the day with you. Just seeing you smile brought me joy."

Terry's voice was getting weaker as she struggled to speak.

"I…" she started. "I just wanted to tell you thank you for loving me and making what time I had left beautiful."

Terry tried to raise her arms as tears streamed down Logan's face. He moved close enough so she could place her arms around his neck. Logan gently moved his arm around her back and raised her frail body up to his. Terry laid her head on his shoulder, while placing her hand against his chest. He heard her whisper, "I love you."

Logan felt her body relax, and her hand limply fell away from his chest. He knew she was gone, but he didn't want to let go. He just sat there, holding her as tears dripped off his chin.

Mr. Warner quietly walked over and put his hand on Logan's shoulder

Logan gently laid her head back down on the pillow, and lightly kissed her on the lips, and stood up beside the bed. She looked so peaceful and beautiful. Logan turned and looked at the Warners but he couldn't speak. Instead, he just slowly nodded his head with tears in his eyes, mouthing the words "thank you."

Logan silently excused himself from the room, went out to his car and drove to the end of the driveway. He put the car into park and broke down sobbing, crying so much that he couldn't get his breath.

His drive back to Blacksburg was a blur, obscured by his pain. When he got home, he stayed inside for two weeks, avoiding contact and conversation over the holidays. Truth be told, all he wanted was time to himself to think. Finally, New Year's Day was nearing, Logan got up, took a bath and shaved. He decided that the time was right to walk to campus. As he headed down the steps and crossed the street toward the college, he looked up at the morning sun. What a beautiful morning, he thought as Terry lingered on his mind.

Chapter 25

It was 11 o'clock on a Sunday night. Ellen poured herself a glass of wine and slowly walked up the spiral staircase that led to her bedroom. She slowly opened a door across the hall and walked across the room to look down at Little Logan as he slept. She marveled at how big he was at 10 years old. With each day, he looked more and more like his father. She slipped out into the hallway and into her bedroom, walking across a thin shaft of light to the small terrace overlooking the backyard.

Ellen took a relaxed sip of her wine as she gazed up into the sky. The bright stars sparkled over a dark tree line that cut across the horizon in the distance. In the stillness of night, she could only hear her own soft breathing. Two years had passed since Ms. Dubois' death, and Ellen had finally started to feel as though the estate was her own home.

Little Logan was happy here. Mr. Ross had seamlessly stepped up to become a role model for the child, teaching him how to ride horses, while making him feel like he was the man of the house by giving him chores around the farm and teaching the importance of accepting responsibility. Ms. McKay was a godsend, continuing her role of overseeing duties around the house, while almost becoming a surrogate mother to Little Logan, preparing his breakfast before school, packing his lunch, and driving him to school in that old De Soto.

Ellen wondered, as she took another sip of her wine, if she was doing the right thing by putting most of her time and energy into the business. While she didn't see Little Logan that much, the child was far from neglected.

Her thoughts turned again to Logan. Ellen had just turned 28 and she was eager to move on, either with Logan or possibly by building a life with someone else. I need to make a decision, she thought. I need to know if he's dead or alive. If he's alive I will find him. If he's dead, and it can be verified, then at least I'll have closure.

It was 1974, and most of the prisoners of war had been exchanged. Still, more than 20,000 soldiers were still missing half a world away, and it was certainly within reason that Logan could be among them.

If I'm going to find out Logan's fate, I need to know about that damn secret mission he went on, Ellen thought. That would require getting to the right people, with the right connections. A politician, maybe? If so, it would take money, which I certainly have now, to get things done. The war is over, right? Now is the time to get answers.

Ellen took a final sip of wine, put her glass down, and resolved to visit her Congressman in hopes of solving the riddle that had vexed her over the last decade.

The next morning, Ellen walked into the library that now served double duty as her office. Ms. MacKay opened the door and peered in as Ellen was settling into a chair behind her desk.

"What would you like for breakfast this morning, sweetie?" Ms. MacKay asked.

"I'm fine," Ellen said. "I may just get a cup of coffee in a little bit."

"I'm getting ready to take Little Logan to school," Ms. MacKay said.

"Will you please have him come in here for minute before he leaves?"

In short order, Little Logan was bouncing into the room.

"Hey, mom," he said.

"Good morning, sweetheart," Ellen said motioning her son over. "Come here and give mommy a hug."

The little guy dashed over and threw his arms around his mother, who planted a kiss on his cheek.

"You do well in school today, you hear," she said.

"I will, mom," Little Logan said.

"And listen to your teachers," she instructed as he made his way to the door.

Ellen picked the phone up and called Debra, who surprised Ellen by answering on the first ring.

"Why are you in so early?" Ellen said. "It's not even eight."

"Because Ms. CEO there's a lot to be done here," Debra said. "I'm getting an early start."

"I'm coming to Greensboro today," Ellen said. "I should be there around 11:30. Will you ask Bob to come by your office? I need to have a brief meeting with you two."

"Is your dad coming with you?" Debra asked.

"No, he's in Raleigh today working on a few things for me."

"Okay, we'll be there," Debra said. "Maybe we can go to lunch afterward?"

"It sounds great," Ellen said. "I will count on that."

*****

Ellen walked into Debra's office a few minutes early. The women walked through a side door into the conference room to meet Bob.

"It was a challenge to get him here, Ellen, but I did it," Bob said.

"Yeah, right across the hall," Ellen said with good-natured sarcasm. "I know it was hard on you making those 20 steps."

Everyone burst out laughing.

"How are you guys this morning?" Ellen asked.

"That depends on why we're here, Ellen," Bob said.

Ellen placed her briefcase on the conference table, walked over, and poured herself a cup of coffee. She ambled back over the briefcase, opened it, and handed folders to Bob and Debra.

"I see we're building again," Bob said.

"Yep," Ellen confirmed. "One store in Durham and another in Raleigh. Dad is down there today signing all the paperwork so we can get started. Deb, you might want to start looking to hire three or four employees to work directly with you. I've got bigger plans for down the road."

"That's not new Ellen," Debra said. "Of course you have."

"I want to train those new employees in the Burlington store," Ellen said. "The contractor says he'll have the Durham and Raleigh stores ready in six months. He would have it done earlier, but he had to demolish a building in Raleigh. But it was worth it since it is a great location near the college with a lot of traffic. The same can be said for the Durham store. I think both locations are going to be very profitable."

The meeting, as promised, was brief. Bob left, leaving Debra and Ellen to make plans for lunch. Breakfast for each woman consisted of coffee, so they wasted no time settling on Elm Street Bar and Grill, a diner around the corner from the office.

"How long will it take me to walk to the federal building, Deb," Ellen asked as the waitress brought out their orders.

"It's about two blocks, so I'd guess it's a 10-minute walk," Deb said. "What have you got going on in the federal building, Ellen?"

"I have an appointment with Congressman Powell," Ellen explained.

"I called his office before I left this morning and his secretary set it up," she continued. "It might cost me a contribution to his upcoming re-election campaign, but I think he can help me find out what happened to Logan. I want to know what type of a secret mission he went on and what his chances of survival were. It's been over 10 years now, Debra, and I've got to find out one way or the other if he's alive or dead, even if it takes going to the president. I feel like the government owes me that. I can't move on with my life until I find out. The war is over, so there's no need for them to hold that information back."

"I certainly can understand that, Ellen," Debra said.

"Okay, Deb, I'm going to give you a call tonight after you leave work," Ellen said. "I will give you an update on what he had to say."

"Yes, I would be interested in that," Debra said.

Ellen left the diner and walked toward the federal building. Two men in navy blue coats and gray pants directed her to the legislator's office. She walked in and was immediately greeted by the receptionist.

"I am Ellen MacKay and I have appointment to meet with Congressman Powell."

"Yes, ma'am, I have you down to see him," the receptionist said. "Please have a seat. I will take you to his office in just a few minutes."

The receptionist called through to the Congressman to let him know that Ellen had arrived. She stood up and directed Ellen back to the office. The Congressman walked over from behind his desk, shook Ellen's hand, and offered her a seat.

Ellen had never met Congressman Powell, though she had seen his pictures in the newspaper. He wore the traditional garb of a politician; politician navy blue pinstripe suit, white shirt and red tie. He was much shorter than Ellen had imagined, with black hair parted on the high side of his head.

"Ms. MacKay, I must say I'm very impressed on what you have done for the last few years," he said. "How many Logan Drugstores do you have now?"

"We're getting ready to build stores in Raleigh and Durham," she replied. "That will give us six."

"That's great," Congressman Powell said. "I understand they're doing very well."

"Yes, I'm very pleased."

"What can I do for you?" the politician asked.

Ellen reached into her pocketbook and pulled out an envelope, handed it to the Congressman, and asked him to read the letter inside. He carefully opened the envelope, noticing it was old and worn, and slowly unfolded the note within. He took his time to read the letter.

"What would you like for me to do, Ms. MacKay?"

"Two things, sir," she replied. "I would like to know what type of secret mission Logan went on. But most of all I would like to know if he is alive or dead."

"Oh my, that is a big request," Congressman Powell said. "I think there are over 20,000 soldiers that are unaccounted for over there."

"Congressman, I know there's got to be some paperwork somewhere describing the mission and the expectation for survival," Ellen said with determination.

"If I knew that much, I might be able to reach my own conclusion as to whether he made it out or not. The war is over. Shouldn't those papers be easier to access? As his wife, I feel like I have the right to know that much, and I'd like your help. If you can do that, I would be totally indebted to you come November."

Those final words caught the Congressman's ear, and he sat up straighter in his chair.

"I'll tell you what, Ellen," he said. "Why don't you give me Logan's full name, social security number and any information on his basic training? I will take it from there. I have a four-star general in the Pentagon that should help me get some answers."

"Congressman I really would appreciate all the help you could give me," Ellen said. "I'm not going to give up on this until I get that information. I'm determined to find out what happened."

"I understand Ms. MacKay," the politician said. "And I assure you that I would feel the same way if I was in your situation. Just send me that information and I promise you that I will start working on this. It may take me two or three weeks to get back to you, but I will find something out."

"I really would appreciate it," Ellen said. "Thank you very much."

"I'm going to start making calls today," Congressman Powell said as he shook Ellen's hand and gave her back the yellowing envelope. "We're going to find out something, Ellen, I assure you."

As Ellen walked back to the car, she seemed pleased with how the conversation went. He seems sincere, she thought. I will give him those three weeks. If I don't hear from him, then he will see me again in Washington.

Two weeks went by. Ellen had been passing the days by focusing on construction in Raleigh and Durham. She filled her evenings playing and reading to Little Logan. Each night, before she went to bed, Ellen would gaze up at the dark blue sky and wonder if Logan was doing the same thing. She couldn't accept that he was dead.

Chapter 26

Ellen was in her office on a cloudy Monday morning, getting ready to drive to Durham, when her phone rang. She quickly answered to find Congressman Powell on the other end of the line.

"I have a bit of information for you," Congressman Powell said.

"I'm not through yet, but I wanted to let you know I'm still working on it," he continued. "What I know right now is that Logan was at Fort Bragg in Fayetteville, where he was transferred to a special Green Beret unit. He went to Fort Benning in Georgia, completed jump training school, and received his wings as a paratrooper. Next, he was transferred to Fort McKinney in Kentucky where he went through Ranger training. He completed a jungle survival course and became an expert marksman. Logan also spent two weeks in a survival school in the Everglades.

"Ms. MacKay, the only thing I can tell you is that the Army spent a lot of time and training on your husband. I still don't know what his mission was, but I know it had to be very important for them to put him through all that training. I'm still digging and will give you an update as soon as I have one."

"Thank you so much, Congressman, for what you have already done," Ellen said. "I'm looking forward to hearing from you. Thank you again."

Three weeks went by without another word from the Congressman. Then, at about 10 o'clock on a Tuesday night, Ellen's downstairs phone rang. She sprinted down the stairs, wondering who would call on her business line that late at night. As she picked up the handset she heard the Congressman Powell's voice on the other end of the line.

"I can't explain much over the phone," he said curtly. "I need for you to come to Washington. How soon can you get here? I also need you to bring your marriage license with you. We will need that."

"I can be on a plane this morning, Congressman, with my marriage license."

Congressman Powell gave Ellen his phone number and instructions to call him with an arrival time. He agreed to dispatch a driver to pick her up at the airport.

Ellen could not sleep that night, unsure of what information the Congressman had for her. She was up at 4 o'clock. She hurriedly got dressed and, after leaving a note for Ms. MacKay, she drove to the Greensboro airport. She was so nervous that she almost missed her exit into the airport. I've got to calm down, she thought. If I don't, God knows where I'll end up.

Ellen managed to book a seat on one of the earliest flights to Washington, with an arrival time before 10 o'clock. She used a payphone to check in with Congressman Powell's office and boarded the plane. She deplaned and walked into the airport lobby to find a young man standing there holding a sign with her name on it.

"This way, ma'am," the young man said as he escorted Ellen to a limousine parked outside. "Congressman Powell is waiting on you at his office. We'll be there in about 15 minutes."

Ellen's heart begin to beat a little faster as she viewed all the traffic on the highway, and a lot of black limousines, headed towards the capital. The driver stopped in front of the Pentagon, and a neatly dressed woman in an Army uniform greeted Ellen as she got out. Without saying anything else, the woman led Ellen into a side entrance back to an office. Congressman Powell was standing in the doorway.

"Come on in, Ellen," he said.

As Congressman Powell quietly closed the door, Ellen looked up to see a four-star general standing next to a large mahogany desk.

"I'm General Gates," the man said. "I hope you had a pleasant flight."

"I did, sir, thank you for asking," Ellen replied.

General Gates offered Ellen a seat. He walked over and put his hands on the back of a nearby chair. Ellen was impressed with his appearance. He was well-decorated, and she wondered about the accomplishments required to collect so many metals. He was tall and appeared very athletic.

Congressman Powell sat down, prompting General Gates to walk back to his desk.

"Do you have your marriage license with you, ma'am?" the general asked.

Ellen reached into her purse and pulled out a folded envelope, which she handed to General Gates.

"This was dated after Logan first enlisted," he observed.

"Yes, we got married when he came home during his first leave," Ellen said

"I only bring this up because, when Logan enlisted, he noted that he was single in all the paperwork," General Gates said, handing the license back to Ellen. "We have no other documentation that says he ever got married."

"I understand, sir," Ellen said.

"We just have to be sure that any information I give you remains confidential," General Gates said sternly. "It must not leave this room."

"I understand, sir, and I give you my word it will not."

General Gates opened the middle drawer on his desk and pulled out a folder. "Top Secret" was written in large red letters across the front of the folder.

"Wait a minute general, I've got to stand up for a minute," Ellen declared through heavy breaths. "I have waited a long time for this, and my heart is pounding 1,000 beats per minute right now."

Congressman Powell stood up and offered to get Ellen a glass of water before ducking out of the room. She was still standing when he returned. He handed her the water, and Ellen slowly started to calm down after taking a few sips.

She quit pacing and returned to her seat.

"Okay, General, I'm ready."

"Ms. MacKay, the first set of information will reveal what his mission was," General Gates said. "The second segment will tell you the results."

General Gates started to hand the folder over to Ellen, but he paused before completing the hand off.

"First of all, I have to explain the scenario our military was in when this mission was planned," he said.

"Every time we would get into a skirmish, all the high command generals of the V.C. would cross over into Cambodia," General Gates explained. "The U.S. government wasn't allowed to cross over the border to pursue them. Needless to say, it was very frustrating. At one point, we received intelligence that a high command general, Tran Quang Binh, had been directing the V.C. war effort from an underground bunker right across the border in Cambodia.

"We knew he had all the war plans, and a map of the tunnels, hidden in his bunker, along with a list of all the generals under his command. We also believed he was in possession of a list of weapons stockpile locations and information on espionage activities across Vietnam. We wanted that intelligence, realizing that possessing that information could give us a major advantage in the war.

"While we had a general knowledge of his location, we weren't 100% sure where the bunker was. And we didn't know how many guards he had securing his location. So we drew up a very simple, but highly dangerous, plan to have one highly trained soldier infiltrate the bunker. We stripped the soldier of all identification and supplied him with a modified M-16 rifle that we scrubbed of all distinguishing markings. We strapped him down with about 20 pounds of C-4 plastic explosives before dropping him down at night along the Vietnam-Cambodia border. He was instructed to make a low-flying parachute jump into the jungle, where the chute opens just a few seconds before the solider hits the ground. To succeed, the aircraft must have a perfect altitude.

"The soldier was ordered to hide his parachute, locate the general's headquarters, and do whatever was necessary to gather the intel before blowing the bunker up. We gave the soldier three days to make his way back into South Vietnam, where we had a location selected for a helicopter to pick him up. He never showed up. We went back several times, but he was never there. After three days, we sent out a search team, which found the burnt-out shell of the bunker and several dead V.C., giving us confidence our guy had accomplished that part of his mission. The bodies showed signs of injuries from hand-to-hand combat but we didn't find our soldier's body.

"The team started checking the outer perimeter of the jungle, where they found and followed blood drippings for about a mile. It led them to a cave, where they found his rifle. It was severely damaged and splattered in blood. The gun's brace had been basically shot off and there was a circle of blood on the end of the scope. Our best guess was that the solider had been holding the gun when it was hit by a bullet or charge of some kind, which would have also driven the scope back into his eye. We don't know the severity of the injury, but we do know he lost a lot of blood.

"A V.C. shoulder bag was a few feet away from the gun. It held all the information we needed, along with bandages and animal bones. We are confident that the Montagnards, local mountain people, found him and took him to the cave. The Montagnards had been helping our Green Berets and Rangers since the beginning of the war. I'm sure they tried to help him, but we don't know whether they were successful or not. We do not know where he is located, or if he is even alive."

General Gates hesitated as he looked into Ellen's eyes. She was motionless; it was if she was daydreaming. The general called her name and she slowly and silently looked up at him.

"So we don't know where he is, dead or alive," the general said. "I don't want to give you false hope. It was a very risky mission. The Montagnards could have been found by the

V.C. and killed. It is also possible that our solider was slowing the mountain people down and they left him behind. I will say this, it has been nearly 11 years, and I feel fairly confident that if he was alive he would have found his way out. We would have found him. To be sure, your husband is a hero. He did the job that was asked of him, even if that meant giving his life for this country. For that, I would like to give you something."

General Gates opened another drawer and placed a small blue box on the desk. He lifted the lid and held it up for Ellen to see its contents.

"This is the Congressional Medal of Honor," General Gates said. "It is the highest honor any military serviceman can get."

Congressman Powell handed General Gates a sheet of paper. "And this is a document, signed by the President of the United States, recognizing your husband for his service."

General Gates took out another box, revealing a Purple Heart. "Though we don't know the severity of his injuries, we know your husband was wounded. He deserves this metal."

"I hope this has helped you and your family to move on," Congressman Powell added. "You have a lot of benefits coming your way from the Army if he is declared dead. I would like for you to just go home and talk it over with your family. If you decide you want us to do that, we will take care of it, and hopefully you and your family can move on."

Ellen just looked at the men as her lips tightened and her eyes welled with tears.

"I understand what you are saying," she said. "And after what you have told me, and what the Army expected him to do, it's hard to believe one man could do all of that and come out alive."

"He was the best of the best, Ms. MacKay," General Gates said with reverence. "He accomplished his mission and I hope you would be proud of that. He was a true American."

Ellen stood up, clutching the Congressional Medal of Honor in her hand. She shook the hands of both men, thanking them for their efforts and the information.

"I appreciate you telling me the full story of my husband," she said. "I will go home and talk it over with my family, and get back with you on what we decide."

"I will honor your wishes, Ms. MacKay," General Gates said. "We will carry out whatever you decide."

General Gates opened the door to the office. The neatly dressed woman was waiting in the hallway to take Ellen back to the airport.

As Ellen sat on the plane, she reflected on all that General Gates had told her. She could visualize everything that Logan had done, and how he went about doing it. He had that type of determination and fearlessness.

Ellen took a deep breath as the clouds wafted past her window. I've got to go home and talk this over with Little Logan, she thought. I don't know how he would feel about declaring his dad dead. It has been more than ten years. Like General Gates said, if he was destined to come home, he would be back by now.

Chapter 27

A sick feeling settled into Ellen's stomach as she headed home from the airport. She wondered about how she could tell Ms. MacKay about Logan's fate. It would be like telling someone that their son had died.

It was late afternoon when Ellen pulled into the estate's driveway. She drove slowly up to the house, delaying the inevitable. She decided to talk to Little Logan first, but not right away. No one at the house knew where she had been, and she was determined to keep it that way until she found the proper way to share her grim news.

That night, as Ellen tossed around in bed, she could hear General Gates' words in her head. *It has been nearly 11 years, and I feel fairly confident that, if he was alive, he would have found his way out. We would have found him.* Ellen knew he was right, but she was having a hard time letting go of her last sliver of hope.

Ellen took the next two days to stay at home and devise a way to talk to her son and mother-in-law. The next morning, she was having breakfast with Little Logan, who was home for summer break, and Ms. MacKay.

"Well Logan, what are you plans now that school is out?" Ellen asked.

"I don't know, mom, all my friends are at the beach this week."

Ellen looked at him and hesitated for a minute.

"How would you like to go to the beach with me for a few days?" she asked.

"Can we, mom?"

"I don't see why not," Ellen said. "Lord knows I need to take a break. I haven't had a real vacation in a long time."

"That's a great idea, Ellen," Ms. McKay said. "Y'all need to spend some time together."

"Yes we do," Ellen said, looking at Little Logan.

"When can we go, mom?"

"Just as soon as you can go upstairs and pack," Ellen said. Don't forget your trunks."

"I'll give him a hand," Ms. McKay said as Little Logan jumped from the table and bolted up the steps.

I better get some things together, Ellen thought as she sat alone at the table. She decided to give Debra a call first.

"Good morning, Deb," Ellen said.

"How are you doing, Ellen?"

"I'm doing okay," Ellen replied. "We have a lot to talk about when I see you next, but this time it is about personal stuff."

"I'm here for you whenever you need me," Debra assured.

"I know Deb," Ellen said. "I'm going to take Little Logan to Myrtle Beach for a few days. I'd like you to run the business while I'm gone. If you have any questions, just give dad a call. I'll let him know you're handling things for me. I will call you when I figure out where we're going to stay."

"I won't call you unless it's an emergency," Debra said. "You and Logan go have a great time. Get some rest, Ellen. Lord knows you deserve it."

Ellen loaded up her car and they made their way to the beach. Ellen called ahead to get a reservation to the Sandpiper Inn at North Myrtle Beach. They pulled into the inn's parking lot, and, before Ellen could open her door, Little Logan had excitedly grabbed his suitcase, jumped out of the car, and headed across the parking lot.

"Hold on, Logan, I'll be there in just a minute," she bellowed out to him.

After checking in, Ellen found herself staring at a familiar room number. She couldn't help but smile, thinking of when Logan picked her up and carried her across the threshold of Room 123. More memories started flooding back as she and Little Logan made their way to another room.

The next few days were filled with one activity after another. Swimming in the ocean, playing putt-putt, and going to the amusement park. All the while, Ellen was struggling with finding the right time to talk to Logan about his father. Soon it was their last day, and Little Logan was putting his bathing suit on for another trip to the beach.

"A Whisper Away"

"You can leave your trunks on, just put your shirt on over it," Ellen said. "There's somewhere I would like to take you before we go to the beach."

After driving for about 15 minutes, Ellen pulled into a grassy parking lot in front of a little white church with a small steeple. The entrance had a little white sign that said, in Old English letters, Chapel By the Sea.

"Mom, this is a church," Little Logan, clearly confused by the destination.

"Yes, it is Logan," Ellen said. "Your dad and I got married at this little church. Isn't it beautiful?"

"If you say it is, mom."

"Let's see if we can go in," Ellen suggested.

Ellen and Little Logan walked in, and she immediately noticed that nothing had changed from her wedding day. They slowly walked down the aisles. There were only about 20 benches on each side, all short in length. The altar awaited them at the end, looking just as it had all those years before.

"Your dad and I stood right here, son," Ellen said with a motion. "He stood exactly where you are standing now."

"Right here, mom?" Little Logan said as he looked down at his feet.

"Yep, right there," Ellen said. "The day we got married was the happiest day of my life at that time. It has only been topped by the day you were born."

They just stood there for few minutes, as Ellen held Logan's hand.

"Your dad looked so nice," she recalled. "He wore a black suit and tie. It was the only suit he ever had. Of course, he had to tell me that he originally bought it for a funeral. Your dad could be so funny, and he always knew how to make me laugh."

Ellen pointed to a bench at the front of the church. She realized that now was as good a time as any to talk to her son. "Let's have a seat," she said.

"There are some things I need to talk to you about," she started. "Last week I was in Washington meeting with a Congressman and a four-star general. They explained to me the type of mission your dad had gone on. It was a very dangerous mission, but it had the potential of saving a lot of soldiers' lives. Your dad is the type person who would honor an oath and not tell anyone about the mission, not even me. He accomplished the mission, but they couldn't find him afterwards. They knew he had been wounded but they didn't know the extent of his injuries."

Ellen took a deep breath and cleared her throat, as she put her hand on Logan's shoulder.

"Son, they seem to think that, had he survived, he would have been home by now," Ellen said. "You know, Logan, that it has been 11 years."

Logan looked up at his mother's face. "Are you saying that you think he's dead?"

Ellen gazed into Logan's blue eyes and gathered her thoughts.

"Well, they can't say for sure that he's dead, son," she explained. "They just think that he should have been home by now. They sent out several search parties to look for him."

"Do you think he's dead, mom?"

Ellen could see the hurt in the child's face as a small tear slowly worked its way out of the corner of his eye.

"Mom, I will never say that my dad is dead," Logan said defiantly. "When some of the other ballplayers ask me where my dad is, I just say he's in the service and hasn't come home yet. The reason I play baseball so hard, and work at it to be good, it's because of him. I want my dad to be proud of me when he comes home. And I'm going to keep right on working hard to be the best I can be."

Logan paused.

"Have you given up on him, mom?"

Ellen started crying, too. A lump in her throat prevented her from replying. She could not swallow as tears streamed down both sides of her face. She put her arms around Logan and pulled him to her.

"No, no, I have not given up on him, honey," she said.

Very little was said as they drove back to the inn. Finally, Little Logan looked over at Ellen and broke the silence.

"Mom, tell me some things about dad that you liked about him," he said.

"There were so many things I liked about your dad," Ellen said.

"The one thing that I loved about him the most was his heart," she said after some reflection. "He was respectful to adults, and he was always kind to people. I can remember one time, when the coach asked him and another boy to choose the players for their team, your dad used his first pick to select the smallest kid in the lineup. All the other kids started laughing as Logan motioned for that little boy to come over and stand beside him. The next time around, your dad chose another small kid. He found out that those little fellas were pretty good and they played their hearts out for your dad. They still lost the game, but it was closer than what any reasonable person would have expected.

"I asked Logan after the game, as we were walking down to the soda shop, why he picked those kids. He looked at me and smiled. He knew that those boys were always the last ones to get picked and he didn't want them to feel bad and embarrassed any more. He said that selecting them made them feel good, and it made me feel good just to be around him. I knew he had a good heart, but he also had passion for those who lacked the talent that he had.

"That's just one example. There were plenty of other things that he did for others. I knew he was a good person, and that's the main reason why I loved him so much."

"I've heard my coach and other people say that I was a chip off of the old block," Logan said with a smile. "I think they meant that I was like my dad. I like that, mom. What do you think?"

"You're like your dad from the top of your head down to your toes," Ellen said. "I am so proud of you."

"Sometimes, mom, when no one is around, I get your school yearbook down and look at his picture," Logan confessed. "I love the one of him in his uniform standing on first base. It makes me proud to be his son. When he comes home, do you think he'll be proud of me, too?"

"There's no doubt about that, son," Ellen said. "He's going to love you until the end of time."

"I hope so, mom," Logan said. "I can't wait until he's back. He will be coming home one day."

"Yes, son, he will," Ellen said as she reached over and rubbed Logan's hair.

For days after that, all Little Logan wanted to talk about was his dad. He had never shown so much interest before. It was as though he had been holding all his questions inside, and now he was eager to get them all out in the open. It allowed Ellen to share all the feelings she had been hiding. She felt free, reliving her life with Logan as she explained just about every detail of their lives to her son.

Little Logan had helped her to cleanse her soul of all the memories by speaking them out loud to someone who wanted to listen. She felt a sense of relief that had been missing for years.

Little Logan seemed happier than she had seen him in a long time. He said he felt like he knew his dad for the very first time. He was proud of his father, and anxious to see him for the first time.

By the end of August, Little Logan was enthusiastic about returning to school. He approached his classes with newfound vigor, turning his typical B's to straight A's. His baseball coach also noticed a change, remarking that Logan's enthusiasm for the game had risen so high that he really acted like he enjoyed playing. He was also doing remarkable things on the field that overshadowed the accomplishments of his teammates.

It seems as though Little Logan is finally in a good place in life, Ellen thought, quickly realizing that she needed to do the same.

*****

It was a Wednesday morning, and Ellen was drowning in a deluge of phone calls. The first was from Eric, the contractor, who had hit a construction snag. She told him to do whatever was necessary to fix the problem.

The next call was from Debra, who was headed to the Durham store. After assuring Ellen that everything was fine, she asked her friend to meet her at the location.

"I have some good news for you," Debra said.

"There's nothing like good news, Deb," Ellen said. "I'll be leaving here in five minutes. See you there."

Ellen was sitting in the manager's office when Debra walked in.

"Keep your seat, Ellen," she said as she reached into her briefcase to pull out two sheets of paper.

"Just look what these two stores have done just 14 months after opening," Debra said, showing the documents to Ellen."

The Raleigh and Durham stores are already doing better than the older stores. I think carrying more inventory, offering better discounts, and having a great training program have served us well."

"Well, Deb, are you ready for some more good news?"

"Why does it bother me when you look at me and say that with such a big grin on your face?" Debra teased.

"You know what I'm going to say, Deb."

"Yep," Debra said. "Where are the next two stores going?"

"We're going into the beautiful state of Virginia," Ellen said. "The first one will be in Martinsville, and the other one is set for Roanoke."

"Why Virginia?" Deb asked. "Why not Charlotte?"

"Charlotte has enough drugstores," Ellen explained. "Pharmacies in Martinsville lack drive-through windows, and

Roanoke is a pretty good-sized town with a lot of potential business there. Both towns have a lot of small communities."

"When do we get started?" Debra asked.

"We had chosen the locations, and Eric is there now making all the arrangements," Ellen said. "There building codes are a bit different in Virginia, and thankfully Eric already had a contractor's license in the state. You should get with Bob and check out the tax code and all that other legal issues we might face. I'd like to get started as soon as possible."

"Well, Ellen, that's nothing different," Debra said.

"These two stores may be my last ones," Ellen confided. "I'm ready to slow down and start enjoying life with Little Logan. He's going to be 13 soon, and I need to spend more time with him. He'll be off to college before I know it."

"You know you can stop working now," Debra said. "You have more money than you'll ever be able to spend."

"It was never about the money, Deb," Ellen said.

"I know, and I must say you seem happier now than you have been in a long time," Debra said. "You no longer seem distressed."

"I guess you could say I'm at more peace with myself now, Deb," Ellen said. "It's about time. I am 31 and have a lot of life left ahead of me."

"It's about time," Debra said with a smile. "I'm going to drive back and have lunch with Bob. I can't wait to see the look on his face when I tell him about the new stores. He's going to love that, especially when I tell him that they're going to be in Virginia."

They both laughed out loud.

Chapter 28

Logan's first year as Virginia Tech's head coach was difficult. The Hokies posted 15 wins against 16 losses. Logan felt like his coaches did the best they could, but they just didn't have enough talent on the field. He knew they needed better players, which meant they needed to do a better job with recruiting.

Logan called for a meeting with all three coaches. They all gathered at Logan's office.

"Gentleman, we have two more years to turn this program around," Logan said. "Next year has to be a better season for us, or we're all going to be looking for jobs. I realize the recruiting policies around here are challenging but we've got to work with it the best we can. I'm open for any suggestions, so if anyone has any new ideas, please step up."

"Each of the coaches could to more recruiting," Randall Cook suggested. "We can all go out to high schools. I know it will take up more of our time to be out of town. But we've got to make some type of change in our recruiting program. Tommy just isn't giving us what we need."

"There may be one other way, Billy," Coach Walker said.

"What are you suggesting, Jim?" Logan asked.

"Let's start us a baseball camp right here at the college," Coach Walker said.

"Go on," Logan said, curious about the recommendation.

"When I was at Wake Forest, we sent out letters to high school coaches, asking them for the names of any player they wanted us to come out and scout," the assistant added. "We received a good response from them, and we actually chose a couple of players to come to our school. Most of them worked out real well. It would be a good start, but I think we need to go about it a bit different."

"How is that, Jim?"

"I think we should set up a camp, right here at our college, offering five full days of training," Coach Walker said. "We'll send out letters to all the local coaches, asking them to select their best players, regardless of their grade, and send them to the camp. Who knows, we could find a tenth grader with potential, follow his progress for two years, and be ready to offer him a scholarship before he even hits the radar of other schools."

"We could have the camp when they're out of school," Logan added. "And we also can make arrangements to let them stay in campus dorms. It won't have to cost the kids, or their parents, anything to attend. That may be the best idea I've ever heard, Jim. How many kids do you think we need to make it fly?"

"We'd need at least 30 to attend," Coach Walker said. "Each assistant could coach and observe 10 players. At the end of the camp, we'll meet and choose the five players that we'd like to have back the next year. We can still follow up with the others to see how they're doing each year."

Logan instructed his assistants to work on a letter and paperwork to send to the high school coaches. He asked Jim to make a few calls about lining up dorm rooms.

"Let's get moving on this as soon as possible," Logan commanded

The following season was a good one, with 26 wins and 10 losses. The coaches also identified five students from the first camp to monitor. All in all, Logan was pleased with the progress his staff had made.

The mood of the meeting for the end of the 1975 season was lighter than the one that took place a year before. Logan thanked each coach for their efforts and talked positively of the program's future.

"I think the program we have set up is definitely going to pay off for the next two to three years," he said as he gave a nod to Jim. "Don't forget to send those letters out. We'll set up next year's camp for the last week of June. It's going to be a bicentennial year. 1976! I have a feeling that 1976 is going to be a great year for all of us. Merry Christmas! Go home and spend time with your families, and have a happy New Year. I'll see you all back here after the first of the year."

Logan excused the coaches. He was getting ready to leave when his secretary walked into his office.

"Sir, you're still here," she said.

"Is there a problem?" Logan asked.

"You have a phone call from Dr. Stillman at Walter Reed Hospital," the secretary said. "HE would like to talk with you."

Logan sat down at his desk and picked up his phone.

"How are you this afternoon, Dr. Stillman?"

"I'm fine, Billy," the doctor responded. "How are you?"

"I couldn't be better," Logan declared. "We just wrapped up a great season."

"I heard about it, Billy," Dr. Stillman said. "I'm proud of you."

"What's on your mind, Doc?"

"I have some good news for you, but I need you to come to the office first," Dr. Stillman said. "It's time for your checkup. Do you think you can come in early? I'm planning on going home to Massachusetts, for about three weeks over the holidays, to spend a little time with friends and relatives."

"When would you like for me to come, Doc?

"As soon as you can," Dr. Stillman said. "I'll be here through the end of the week."

"What if I just come up tomorrow morning?"

"That would be great, Billy. I'm looking forward to seeing you again."

Logan got to the hospital early the next morning. As he pulled into the parking lot, he couldn't help but think about Terry and how she had to sneak him in and sneak out of the hospital during the early days of their courtship. A mischievous smile came over his face.

Dr. Stillman greeted Logan as he entered the doctor's office.

"Come on in, Billy," he said as he put his hand on Logan's shoulder and guided him to a recliner. "Sit down over here.

The chair didn't look very comfortable, a belief that was confirmed when Logan took a seat. Dr. Stillman adjusted the chair and turned a bright light on less than a foot from Logan's face. He raised the patch off of Logan's eye.

"I see you have been continuing to use your drops," the doctor observed as he probed Logan's eye.

"Yep, I never leave home without it," Logan said.

"I have good news," Dr. Stillman said with a slight grin. "I recently met Dr. Jenkins, an ophthalmologist who works at the Eye Research Center at San Diego Mercy Hospital. He is the best microscopic surgeon in the country, and he's willing to come to Walter Reed and examine five of my patients. I told him about you and what I had done to your eye, and he's eager to look at your eye. He thinks he has a decent chance to repair it."

"That's great, Dr. Stillman," Logan said. "Thank you so much for thinking about me."

"He's only planning on staying one week or so," Dr. Stillman said. "He is planning to visit the last week of June. I know your baseball season will be over then, so it may be a good time for you."

"Anytime will be a good time, Doc," Logan said. "This is an opportunity that only comes by once in a lifetime."

"That's great, Billy!" Dr. Stillman exclaimed. "I will call you about a week before the operation to give you a day and time."

"It sounds great to me, Dr. Stillman. I really do appreciate it."

After leaving Dr. Stillman's office, Logan drove over to Johns Hopkins in hopes of catching Coach Thorne in his office. The coach was hard at work in his office when Logan knocked on his door.

"How are you coach?"

"Not as good as you, Billy," Coach Thorne said. "You had one hell of a season last year."

"Yes, we did," Logan said modestly. "I'm proud of the coaches and my boys."

"For a second-year coach, you did outstanding," the coach beamed. "I'm proud of you."

"Thanks coach, without you I would have never been there."

Logan and Coach Thorne spent an hour catching up. After looking up at the clock, Logan realized he should be leaving.

"I've got to go coach," Logan said. "I wish you the best for next year."

"You, too, Billy," Coach Thorne said. "Stop by any time you're in the area."

Logan was walking down the hall, headed toward the winding staircase, when he heard a familiar voice behind him. It was Mr. Warner, who walked briskly over to Logan with a big grin on his face.

"It is so good to see you, Billy," Mr. Warner said. "I think about you just about every day, and I've been keeping up with you and the baseball team you have down in Blacksburg. We're so proud of you, and I know Terry would be, too."

Logan felt like someone had punched him in the stomach when he heard Terry's name. He felt his face getting red.

"You are doing exactly what Terry wanted you to do," Mr. Warner said.

"I can't say that I have moved completely on, Mr. Warner," Logan admitted. "I think about her every morning when I get up. During every game, I can't help myself from looking over into the bleachers, where I know she would be sitting."

"I know it's hard, but you have to remember that Terry wanted you to move on." Mr. Warner said. "She wanted you to find your new life. She only wanted happiness for you. She knew that if she told you about her condition, you would have put your life on hold to take care of her. That wasn't what she wanted.

"Terry's mother and I would like to apologize to you. We knew she was dying, and I worked in the lab day and night trying to find some type of medicine to help her. She had to take a shot every day to slow the cancer's advance. It was something she hated to do, and we had to push her every day to do it."

"Was that what was in those little brown boxes?" Logan asked.

"Yes, it was," Mr. Warner confirmed. "We couldn't let anybody know because that medicine had not been approved. I guess you could say I experimented on my own daughter, but I was desperate. She was my only child and I loved her so much. And I don't regret doing what I did.

"But we now know that you were the best medicine for her, Billy. The last years of her life, she was happier and showed more enthusiasm for living than she ever had before. Thank you for giving her that. We should have told you sooner but neither of us had the heart to do it. We put Terry's wishes above your need to know, and we're sorry for that."

"You don't owe me an apology," Logan said. "Terry gave me the encouragement and strength I needed to make something of myself. I couldn't have done it without her. I may never find out where I came from, but at least I have a life! I thank God every day for sending Terry to me when I needed someone the most, and I will always be grateful for having her for the time that I did."

"Thank you, Billy, it means a lot to hear you say that."

Logan reached out to shake Mr. Warner's hand. Instead, Mr. Warner, with watery eyes, put both arms around Billy and gave him a squeeze.

"You move on now, Billy," Mr. Warner said. "Make us all proud with what you do with the rest your life."

Logan thanked Mr. Warner again and made his way down the winding staircase and back to his Thunderbird. He felt calm on the drive back to Blacksburg, reflecting on what Mr. Warner had told him about Terry and what she wanted for him. He became even more determined to do his best and to move on with his life. He knew that it would please Terry.

*****

Logan woke up on Christmas morning and peered out the window of his bedroom. It looked like it had snowed about a foot that night. Accepting the fact that he was snowed in, Logan looked around to see no Christmas tree or presents. In many regards, it was like any another day, save only for the religious meaning for the holiday.

Each assistant had invited Logan to spend the holidays with them, though he had politely declined. So there he was, alone, eating two slices of toast with a cup of coffee. Logan walked over to his front window, again looking out at the gray morning outside. The wind was whipping the powdery snow sideways down the street, creating small snowdrifts against the big oak trees in his front yard.

Logan resolved to spend the day on the couch, watching the Christmas parade and football games. As he stretched out on the sofa to watch the parade, he saw all the parents holding their kids' hands, all bundled up, and he couldn't help but wonder what his family was doing on Christmas.

Logan closed his eyes, and he felt a warm hand touching the side of his face. He slowly opened his eyes, not knowing what to expect, to find himself staring into his face of his angel. Her long golden hair flowed down over her shoulders, framing a smile filled with teeth as white as the snow coming down outside. I have missed you, she said in a captivating voice. Logan stretched out his hand to try and touch her. All of a sudden, he sat up on the sofa, glancing around the room. He took a deep breath. This time the dream didn't scare him. Rather, he wished he had been able to spend more time with her.

Logan could still feel the warmth of her hand on his cheek, and he could not get the image of her beautiful face out of his head. He marveled at her words. It had been nearly a year since his last dream about her, and he realized that he had missed her, too.

*****

By March, Logan's confidence had reached new heights. Everyone was back at work, and he was optimistic that the 1976 team would outshine the squad he had the year before. So much effort, and many late nights, had gone into this year, he thought.

Logan was also looking forward to the baseball camp and the operation that he was going to have on his eye. Hope swelled that he might be able to get his full eyesight back.

The season surpassed expectations, with 33 wins and just nine losses. Logan was proud of his coaches and players, and he was getting a lot of recognition from the school's administration. People across the state started following the team's progress.

Logan was buoyant during his coaches meeting. They were making preparations for the baseball camp.

"How many participants do we have so far, Jim," Logan said.

"About 80% of the applicants are in," Coach Walker said. "We should have the rest of them committed by the middle of next week. In all, we should easily have 30 students attending."

"That's great, Jim," Logan said. "Just let me know if there's anything else I can do."

"All you need to do is be there, observe, and give us your opinions, Coach," the assistant said.

"I'm looking forward to it," Logan said with a gigantic smile.

Chapter 29

Ellen had spent most of the morning inspecting the new Roanoke store, checking the inventory and evaluating the staging for various products. Content with the arrangements, Ellen was on her way to Martinsville to meet Debra, who was overseeing the same tasks at the other location. Debra met Ellen at the front of the store.

"Your mother has called here looking for you," Debra said. "She told me that you need to go by the high school and talk to Logan's coach. It's not an emergency, but there's something he wants to talk to you about."

"I wonder what Little Logan has gotten into," Ellen said.

"You know that boy does no wrong," Debra said.

"He's a good boy, Deb, but believe me he's no angel."

Ellen looked at her watch. She had just enough time to make it back to the school.

"Why don't you take off now," Debra suggested. "Everything is going fine here. I'll call you if there's a problem."

"Okay, Deb, you've talked me into it."

By the time Ellen arrived at the high school, there were very few cars left in the parking lot. She pulled up to the front entrance. As she walked through the large gray steel doors, she noticed that Carol Johnson, the school's receptionist, was leaving,

"How are you, Carol?"

"I'm fine," the receptionist said. "The coach is in his office. He said to tell you to come on back when you got here."

As she walked to his office, Ellen couldn't help but remember that this was the coach that had to tell Logan there were no scholarships available for him. The coach knew Logan was hurt, and he apologized that he had been unable to help him, even though he felt like Logan deserved one.

Coach Dooley had only arrived at the high school a year before she and Logan had graduated. He had come from Wake Forest University, where he had played college baseball. Logan liked him very much, and thought he was a good coach.

The door was wide open when Ellen arrived. The coach had his back to her as he scribbled on the blackboard. Sensing her presence, he turned around.

Coach Dooley was a big, muscular man with a neck that was as wide as his face. His shoulders were even wider, making his head appear much smaller in comparison. He walked over and gave Ellen a gentle hug.

"How are you, Ellen?"

"I'm doing fine, Coach Dooley," she replied. "How are you?"

"Just thinking about next season, he said before offering her a seat.

"Is Little Logan in trouble?"

"Lord knows that boy has no idea what trouble is," Coach Dooley said.

"Well, you asked me to come in for some reason."

"Yes, I did," the coach said as he picked a piece of paper up off of his desk. "Are you familiar with Virginia Tech in Blacksburg?"

"A little bit," Ellen said. "I remember Logan expressed some interest in that school before he graduated. But that's about all I know about it."

"I have a friend of mine who is an assistant coach up there," the coach said. "We went to Wake Forest together. He told me that Virginia Tech is revamping its program under this new coach. Since Billy Martin took over, the team has had two outstanding seasons. They have also created a new program where high school coaches get to select one player to attend a free one-week camp for one week. They get to stay on campus, and they will be coached by the school's staff."

Coach Dooley pulled out an application to show Ellen.

"They're doing this so they can get a jump on recruiting the best high school players. They're looking for kids with real potential so they can follow their progress. My friend, Jim Walker, sent me this application.

He wants me to select my best player to come to the camp."

"What has this got to do with Little Logan?" Ellen asked.

"Well I want Logan to participate in this program," the coach said.

"He will only be 13 this September," Ellen said.

"I know he'll be the youngest player there," Coach Dooley said. "As you know I coached your husband during his last year. He worked hard and had so much talent. He was good, but Little Logan has the potential to be even better."

Ellen sat silent as the coach continued.

"I've been doing this for a long time, and I have never seen a kid his age do the things that he does on a baseball field," Coach Dooley said. "He has fast hands on the bat, and he flies around the bases. I have never seen a kid play so hard. He deserves to go to this camp."

"Little Logan has never been away from home, Coach Dooley," Ellen said. "I don't know if he would like to do it or not, and to tell you the truth I don't know if I like the idea of sending him away for five days."

"It will be a great opportunity for him, Ellen," the coach said. "This could be his opportunity to go to college."

"Coach, you know we have the means to send him to college," Ellen said. "Let me think about the camp, and I will talk it over with Logan to see what he thinks about it."

"Let me know as soon as possible," Coach Dooley said. "I've got to send this back within a week."

"When is the camp, Coach?"

"It's the last week of June."

"Just give us a couple of days coach and I'll give you a call," Ellen said.

Ellen drove over to her parents' house to discuss the opportunity with them. They thought that it would be good for Little Logan, stressing that it would give him some experience being away from home. At the same time, it would give him a taste of college life.

She also talked it over with Ms. MacKay,

"Can't you see what Little Logan is doing?" Ms. MacKay said.

"What's that?"

"I think he's trying to do something that his daddy couldn't do," Ms. MacKay said. "He wants to get a scholarship."

"Ms. MacKay, you know Logan will have the opportunity to go to any college he wants to."

"That's not the point, Ellen," Ms. MacKay said. "He wants to prove it to himself, and to his dad, that he can do it."

Ellen just looked at Ms. MacKay with a puzzled look on her face. She had never thought about it that way, but it made sense given the talk they had when they were at the beach. Ellen agreed to talk to her son about the camp.

"It's feeding time for the horses," Ms. MacKay said. "I'm sure he'll be coming inside in about 30 minutes. I'll have supper ready by then."

As they were eating dinner, Ellen began to tell Logan about the meeting she had with Coach Dooley. She explained to him the whole conversation. Logan was ecstatic, and there was no doubt in Ellen's mind that he wanted to participate. She had never seen him so happy. Logan jumped up from the table.

"Where are you going, Logan?" Ellen asked.

"I'm going to call grandma and grandpa and tell them about this," he exclaimed.

Ellen looked over at Ms. McKay with a slight smile and just shook her head as Logan ran into the other room.

"Well I guess I'll give the coach a call in the morning," Ellen said.

A few days later, Ellen received a letter from the coaching staff of Virginia Tech. It said that Logan had been accepted to attend the camp. He was instructed to arrive by noon on Sunday, June 20. Pick up was set for five days later. Little Logan was set to report to Coach Walker on the first level floor at the basketball court.

When Little Logan read the letter, he ran upstairs and started packing, even though he still had three days before he had to leave. Ellen was still hesitant about sending him away from home that long. She did not want to be that far away from him just in case something happened.

She called Debra the day before the camp was set to start. She had an idea.

"I thought I would let you know that I'm going to work out of the Roanoke location the week of June 20," she told her friend. "Little Logan is going to a baseball camp in Blacksburg, and I want to stay close to him. I'll be staying at a Holiday Inn between Roanoke and Blacksburg, if you need me for anything. I'll be back a week from today."

"You're not going to bother that boy while he's in camp are you?"

"No, Deb, but I'm going to be close by in case he needs me, or if he wants to come home," Ellen said. "He's never stayed away from home before, so I don't know how he's going to handle it."

"I'll be at the Martinsville store, which isn't that far from Roanoke," Debra said. "If you need me there, just call me."

Move-in day for the camp had arrived. Ellen was impressed by the campus' beauty and how the grass was well well-manicured. She helped her son with his suitcases and they walked up the winding cemented walkway to the double steel doors that entered the hallway. She looked up at the clock, and realized they had 15 minutes to get to the court.

They met a man in the hallway, and Ellen asked him for directions to the basketball court. He grinned and pointed in the opposite direction.

"Okay, I'm walking away from it," Ellen said as the both started laughing.

"We should have put up a sign up to give better directions," the man said as he reached out to shake her hand. "I'm Jim Walker, one of the coaches who will be working with the students."

"Oh, so you're the one that Coach Dooley told me about," Ellen said.

"Indeed," Coach Walker said as he sized up Little Logan. "And you must be Logan MacKay."

"Yes, sir, I am."

"Your coach had a lot of good things to say about you," the coach said. "Welcome to Virginia Tech. Although you're the youngest young man we have here, Logan, your coach was very persuasive and he has a good eye for talent. If he says you belong here, then that's good enough for me."

"Coach, this is the first time Logan has been away from home, and I must say I'm a little worried," Ellen said.

"I understand that, Ms. MacKay," Coach Walker said. "I will see to it that he's taken care of, and I will call you tonight and tell you what dorm room he's in. We also have payphones in the halls, so he can call you every night if he wants to."

"Well he had better do that," Ellen said as she looked at her son with wide eyes and tight lips.

"I'm staying at the Holiday Inn just up the road," she told the coach as she handed him her business card. "If you call there, the front desk will give you my room number. If you need me during the day, you can call me at the number on the card. ."

"Ms. MacKay, I will assure you he'll be just fine," Coach Walker assured. "We will take good care of him, but I will let you know if there is any type of problem."

"Thank you so much, Coach," Ellen said, turning to Little Logan to give him a hug. His face turned red and his arms dangled by his side. She hugged him anyway.

"I will take the suitcases, son," the coach said to Little Logan. "You just follow me."

Ellen watched her son and the coach walk down the hall. She could tell they were talking. After a while, Little Logan looked back and smiled at his mother.

Ellen walked back to her car. She sat there for a moment, taking deep breaths. She didn't realize just how hard it was going to be. In a way, it reminded her of the day Logan's father got on that bus to return to the Army base. Ellen didn't think she would ever have to experience that kind of sinking feeling again. At least it will only be for five days, she thought.

Chapter 30

Logan was sitting in his office finishing up paperwork when he looked up at his clock. It was almost eight in the evening.

"I had better get out there," he said to himself. It was time to go out onto the field to personally inspect all the talented teens who had gathered for his baseball camp. As he approached the field, he could see all the boys running in a line along the outfield wall.

"Warming them up aren't you, Coach Cook?" Logan said.

"Yes sir, I will call them in now."

Coach Cook started lining the players up, and Little Logan ended up on the end of the first line. He was only shoulders high to the player beside him.

"Boys, this is head coach Billy Martin of the Hokies baseball team," Coach Cook announced. "He is responsible for this program, and Billy would like to say a few words before we get started."

Logan cleared his throat.

"The main thing I would like for you boys to do this week is just have a good time and play ball," he said. "We have the best coaches around, and they're going to help you, in any way they can, to become better baseball players. Just remember that having fun is what this game is all about. With that, I will let the coaches take over. I'm sure I will get a chance to talk to each of you before the week is out."

As if on cue, Coach Cook instructed the boys to split up and go to their pre-assigned dugouts. Like scattered ants, the kids dashed with each trying to get to their dugout first.

"Coach Cook," Logan said.

"Yes sir."

"Who is that little fella on the end down there?"

"You might want to talk to Coach Walker," Coach Cook told Logan. "He would know, he asked him to be here."

Logan motioned for Coach Walker to come over.

"Yes sir, Billy," Coach Walker said.

"Who is that young man on the end?" Logan said. "He can't be more than 13 years old."

"You're right coach," Coach Cook said. "He'll turn 13 in a few months."

"Isn't he a bit young to be in this camp, Jim?"

"Yes sir, he is too young, but a friend of mine, Coach Dooley in North Carolina, called me and insisted that I let this young man try out," Coach Walker said. "I was assured that the kid would surprise us with his hustle and playing ability."

"If it's good enough for you, Jim, then it's good enough for me," Logan said. "What's his name?"

"Logan McKay, sir."

That name sounded oddly familiar and Logan kept repeating to himself as though doing so would help jog his memory.

Logan went back to his office to complete his paperwork, but the kid's name continued to cycle through his mind. Logan decided to walk back out to the field. Coach Walker was running batting practice, instructing each boy to take a turn in the cage. Coach Stackhouse would serve up ten pitches to see what kind of skills each boy had at the plate.

Logan walked up beside Coach Walker, who was standing outside the cage observing the practice with his arms folded.

"How are they doing, Jim?"

"Some are good, and others need to be worked with," Coach Walker said.

"Next batter," Coach Cook shouted out, and Little Logan took his place to the right of the plate.

"This is going to be interesting," Coach Walker said.

The first pitch was right down the middle, and Little Logan smacked it over the third baseman's head into the outfield. The next pitch was a bit low, but Logan managed to pull it over the second baseman's head.

The third pitch was high and tight, forcing the kid to take a step back.

The next pitch was right on the money, and Logan pulled it even more to force over the head of the first baseman, where it dropped neatly to the left of the foul line.

It became clear to the coaches that Little Logan was swinging his bat the speed necessary to control where the ball would land.

Logan had a flashback, and he could envision himself hitting the ball the exact same way. Coach Walker looked over at Logan. "I swear I believe he's placing those hits," he said.

"Yep, that is exactly what he's doing, Jim," Logan said.

Little Logan repeated the process over the next two pitches. Seeing enough, Coach Walker told Coach Stackhouse to hold off on the next pitch.

"Come here a minute, MacKay," Coach Walker yelled out to the boy. The kid stepped to the side and walked to the back of the cage to join the coaches.

"Are you placing that ball, son?" Coach Walker asked.

"Yes, sir," Little Logan responded.

"How far can you hit it, MacKay?"

"I can't hit it over the fence, but I can place the ball where they can't get to it," the boy said. "And I can beat out the throw to first base."

"I see," Logan said as he looked over at the boy. He smiled. "Would you mind trying to hit two or three as far as you can? I'd like to see what kind of power you have."

"Yes, sir, I will do that."

Little Logan stepped back into the batter's box.

Coach Stackhouse's first pitch was right down the middle. Little Logan pulled the bat back and twisted his body. With a flick of his hands and hips he whipped the bat around. The sound of the bat hitting the ball was twice as loud as any of his previous hits. The ball wafted high into left field, forcing the outfielder to run back to catch it.

On the next pitch, Logan did the same thing, though he elected to guide the ball to centerfield. The third pitch was directed to right field, and the fielder had to run back to the fence to make the play.

"Where in the hell is he getting that power from?" Coach Walker said.

"His body and wrist," Logan said.

"Come here son," Coach Walker shouted, summoning Little Logan over to the dugout.

"When will you be 13," Logan asked.

"September 16," Little Logan readily replied.

"Okay, you can go take a break now," Coach Walker said. "We'll talk later."

Little Logan reached up and took his helmet off, and his white hair fell down over his ears. "I'm sorry, sir, that I can't hit it over the fence," he said.

Logan was stunned. He stood speechless beside Coach Walker with his mouth agape as he looked into the kid's blue eyes. He felt himself getting a little weak in his knee.

"Don't you worry about that, buddy," Coach Walker said. "Not everyone can hit it over the fence. You did a great job."

Logan was still standing there with his mouth open, breathing heavily.

"You okay, Billy?"

Logan's own blue eyes were wide as he took deep breaths in an effort to calm down.

"Damn, Billy, if I didn't know better I'd swear he was your boy," Coach Walker said. "He sure looks a lot like you."

Logan went back to his office, but he could not get that young man's face out of his mind. His swing also seemed too familiar.

That afternoon, Logan started down the hall to leave when he noticed Little Logan using the payphone. Logan decided to wait around to talk to the kid.

Logan called out the boy once he had finished his call. "You got a minute?" Logan asked.

"Yes, sir," Little Logan said as he trotted down the hallway.

"I was really impressed with you today, MacKay," Logan said.

"Thank you, sir," Little Logan said. "I try to give it my best."

"Where are you from, son?"

"I'm from Eden, North Carolina, sir."

"I have never heard of that town," Logan said. "What's your coach's name?"

"Coach Dooley, sir."

"What are your parents' names?"

"My dad's name is Logan MacKay, and my mother's name is Ellen."

"Did your dad teach you to play ball like that?"

"No sir," Little Logan said. "My dad is in the Army, so I learned own my own, with some help from my coaches."

"I bet your dad's proud of you," Logan said.

"I hope so, sir," the boy said. "I'm working hard to make him proud."

"Well you're doing a good job MacKay," Logan said. "Keep it up."

"I will, sir."

Logan just stood there watching as Little Logan started walking back up the hall. He was having a hard time getting over the resemblance, reassuring himself with the kid's assertion that his father was in the military and that he was from a town Logan had never heard of.

By the camp's third day, the coaches had selected 18 players to split into two teams. They were set to play a short four-inning game.

Little Logan was playing first base, with one out and a runner on second. The batter slapped a ground ball toward first base. Little Logan scooped it up, stepped on his bag and side-armed a hard throw to third to catch the runner and end the inning. The throw alone was a thing of beauty, tossed low enough that the third baseman didn't have to move his glove an inch to catch the ball.

"Hold it! Hold it!" Coach Walker yelled out as all the players on the field started running toward the dugout. Everyone stopped.

"I want to see that throw again," the coach barked, directing the kid that was running to third, to go back to second base. Little Logan and his assigned teammate remained at their bases.

"The rest of you can go in, but I just want to see this play again," Coach Walker said as he picked up a bat. He told the kid at second to bolt for third as he smacked another ground ball toward Little Logan.

As he did the time before, Little Logan ran up the ball, scooped it up, and flung the ball to third, gunning the runner down. Another tag, another easy out.

Coach Walker jovially punched Logan on the arm.

"That boy knows exactly what he's doing and how he's going to do it," Logan said. "I thought his first throw could have been all luck, but he did the same thing the second time. That boy plays way beyond his years."

"Coach Dooley was right," Coach Walker said. "He's one hell of a little player. If he grows another foot and puts on about 35 pounds, there'll be no stopping him."

"That boy knows how to play the game," Logan agreed with a wink. "I'm going back now to my office. When you get a chance, ask the boy to come up. I want to talk to him about his ambitions of playing baseball. Just maybe he'll want to play for us."

Little Logan knocked on the coach's office door about 30 minutes later, anxious to find out why he was asked to come up and discuss. The coach was sitting at his desk, and Little Logan realized that the thumb on his left hand was missing, along with half of his index finger. He tried not to stare.

"You wanted to see me sir?"

Logan stood up and, as a force of habit put in his left hand in his pocket. "Come on in MacKay and close the door behind you," he told the kid.

"I just want to tell you MacKay that you're playing ball at a higher level than some of the players I have on my college team," Logan said. "I just want to tell you that I'm highly impressed and that I'm going to see to it that you get an invitation to come back up to this camp every year until you finish high school. Hopefully you'll consider Virginia Tech as the place you would like to come to and play ball."

"Thank you, sir, I'd like to do that," Little Logan said. "I will talk it over with my mother."

"What about your dad, MacKay?"

"Well yes, I'll do that when I see him," Little Logan said quietly.

"That's good," Logan said. "You talk it over with them."

"I will, sir," Little Logan said as he stood up and stuck his hand out. As Logan took hold of the kid's hand to shake it, he felt something that he did not understand. And as Little Logan started walking toward the door, Logan marveled that the kid even walked like he did. How can this be? Logan was still thinking about the similarities when the phone rang.

"Billy, this is Dr. Stillman."

"How are you, Doc?"

"I'm fine," the doctor replied. "I just want to tell you that we're going to have a room ready for you here tomorrow afternoon. The next day, I will go over everything with you. Dr. Jenkins is set to operate on you on Saturday morning.

He's is going to put the team together, which I can discuss with you in more detail on Friday."

Chapter 31

Logan met with the coaches and the boys early the next morning to give one more pep talk before heading to Washington.

"I would just like to say that it was a pleasure watching you play ball," he told the kids as they gathered in the home team's dugout. "I'm hoping we were able to provide you help where it was needed. I've got to go to Walter Reed Hospital to have some surgery on my eye. I'd like to say thank you all for coming, and I hope to see some of you back here next year."

Logan knew as he got into his Thunderbird that the camp was in good hands.

Late that afternoon, Logan walked into Dr. Stillman's office.

"Hey, Billy, how are you?"

"I'm doing fine, Doc."

Dr. Stillman instructed Logan to take a seat as he walked across the office and pulled down a large screen. The doctor turned off the lights and fired up a projector. He then placed a small slide into the projector to reveal a detailed picture of an eye, broken down into relevant segments such as the cornea, pupil and iris.

"Here is what we are planning to do during surgery, Billy," Dr. Stillman said, pulling out a wand to point to each part as he described them. "Dr. Jenkins is planning on doing a cornea transplant, where he will remove the cornea and replace it with a new one. The cornea let's light come into your eyes. It then goes through the pupil and the iris."

Dr. Stillman paused.

"I just hope the optic nerve isn't damaged because it can't be repaired," he explained. "That nerve is like a fiber-optic cable. It has more than a million nerve fibers that can't be replaced. If that nerve is fine, then I feel good about our chances of success.

"I have also been wondering if there's a link between your eye injury and memory loss. Perhaps correcting your eye could help restore some of your memory, too. Obviously, that's just speculation, Billy, so don't count on that. For now, we're just going to concentrate on getting your eyesight back. After surgery, we're going to keep your eye bandaged for a few days because we want to make sure to avoid any infection. We'll know after we remove the bandage if the surgery was a success or not."

"Well let's do it, Doc," Logan said. "I'm ready."

"Come on, I'll walk you back to your room," Dr. Stillman said as he flipped the lights back on.

"I hope it's not the same room I had before when I was here, Doc," Logan said. "There are just too many memories in that room that don't want to think about right now."

"I understand, Billy," the doctor said. "This room is right beside the operating room."

*****

Ellen pulled up in front of Virginia Tech. It was late on Friday afternoon and it had started raining. She was hoping Little Logan was ready to leave because she loathed driving when it was rainy and dark. As she opened the door to go inside, she ran into Little Logan and Coach Walker, who were in the middle of a conversation.

"Hey mom," Little Logan said with a wave.

"Give your mom a hug boy," Ellen said. "I haven't seen you all week."

Logan put his arms around his mother's waist as she pulled him closer.

"I have missed you buddy," she said.

"I missed you too, mom."

Ellen turned to shake Coach Walker's hand.

"You have a very special son here, Ms. MacKay," the coach said.

"He's special to me, too, Coach," Ellen said as she gave her boy another hug.

"He is also a special athlete," Coach Walker said. "I have a hard time believing what that boy can do on the baseball field. Coach Dooley was right, he is special. I'm so glad he came to this camp. Coach Martin has given him a special invitation to come back every year until he graduates from high school, and we're hoping that you will let him participate."

"That will be up to him," Ellen said. "It would be fine with me if he wants to come back."

Ellen looked over at Little Logan.

"We've got to get a move on, son," she said. "It's beginning to rain and the clouds are getting darker."

The rain began to beat down harder on the car as they pulled onto the interstate. Ellen reached over and turned the radio down. She could see lightning in the distance, and she realized that the storm was going to get worse before it got better. Ellen tried to get her mind off of what she knew would be coming her way, while doing all she could to stay focused on the highway.

"How was baseball camp, honey?"

"It was great mom!" Logan gushed. "I made a lot of new friends, and the coaches were great, too. They worked with all of us."

"Well that's good," Ellen said. "I'm glad you enjoyed it."

"The coaches were really good to us," Little Logan continued to rave. "Coach Walker took a lot of time with us. And I got to meet Coach Martin. He's really a nice man."

Ellen smiled as she stared through the windshield as heavy rain pelted the road.

Logan just sat and listened to the radio, and watched the rain come down. The relentless rain became too treacherous for Ellen, and the windshield wipers could not keep up with the force of the downpour. She decided to pull over in hopes of letting the storm pass.

"I bet that Coach Martin was a good ballplayer before his accident," Little Logan said.

"Is that right, honey?"

"His left thumb was missing, along with half of a finger," the boy explained. "I don't think he could hold a glove now with that hand."

Ellen didn't say a word. She just stared at the highway.

"And he had a patch over his eye," Little Logan recalled. "Coach Martin must not be able to see the ball all that well right now, especially when he's batting, but he said he was going to the hospital to have surgery on it. I hope it is successful."

"I do, too, honey," Ellen said. "Make sure your door is locked Logan. This rain is coming down harder."

Ellen finally put the car back in drive and continued her trek back home. It took them nearly four hours, and the rain had stopped falling by the time Ellen had pulled into her driveway. It was almost 10 o'clock.

"Okay buddy, we made it." Ellen said as she parked the car. "Let's get your suitcases out. After I eat a bite, Logan, I'm going to bed."

"I think I will, too, mom."

Ellen slept in the next morning, and she planned to stay home the entire day to catch up with Little Logan. As she stepped out of the shower, she could hear her son and Ms. MacKay talking in the kitchen.

Ellen got dressed and sat down at her makeup table. All of a sudden she stopped and stared blankly at the mirror as her conversation with Logan during the drive home reverberated in her mind. She called her son up to her room.

"Honey, when we were driving home last night you were talking about Coach Martin," Ellen said.

"Yes, mom," Little Logan said. "His name is Billy Martin. That's what it said on the name plate sitting on his desk."

"Can you tell me again what you said about him yesterday?"

"I said he was a nice man," the boy said.

"And what else?"

"I said he must have been a good baseball player before his accident."

"Why would you say that, Logan?"

"Well, he had a thumb and half a finger missing on his left hand," Logan said. "That would make it really hard for him to use a glove."

"Didn't you say something about an eyepatch?" Ellen queried.

"Yes, mom, over his right eye," Little Logan said. "Coach Martin told us that he was going to the hospital to have surgery on it. That's why he had to leave camp early."

Ellen suddenly remembered what General Gates had told her about Logan's possible injuries. The general surmised that Logan may have had a damaged left hand, where a bullet shattered the bridge of his gun, along with possible damage to his eye, based on the discovery of the bloodied scope.

What the coach's name? Billy Martin. That was Logan's favorite baseball player. Ellen recalled the poster that was in his room, with the player's name written in large bold letters.

"What color hair did Coach Martin have, Logan?"

"Silvery blonde, mom," Logan said. "It looks a lot like mine."

Ellen set straight up, feeling as though she had been struck by a bolt of lightning. The hair on her arms stood up. She tried to stand up but she could not move.

"What hospital was he going to?"

"He said some Army hospital name," the boy replied.

"Was it Walter Reed?"

"Yep, that was the name of it, mom," Little Logan said. "How did you know that?"

Ellen just sat there and looked at him for a minute. She was speechless. Instinctively, she grabbed her pocketbook and started out the door.

"Where are you going, mom?"

"I will be back later this afternoon," she hollered back as she raced down the stairs. After a quick good-bye to Ms. MacKay, Ellen jumped into her car and started driving toward the Greensboro airport. She bought a ticket to the earliest flight to Baltimore. After landing, she hailed a cab, handed the driver a wad of cash, and instructed him to get her to Walter Reed.

*****

The driver barely had time to stop before Ellen darted out of the car and dashed up the hospital's steps. She quickly made her way up to the front desk.

Ellen just looked at the receptionist, unsure what to say as her mind went totally blank. With some prodding from the receptionist, Ellen found her tongue.

"I'm looking for Billy Martin," Ellen stammered. "I think he may be my husband."

"I'm sorry, ma'am," the receptionist said. "The Billy Martin in our records isn't married."

"I think he is my husband," Ellen asserted. "I've got to see him to be sure of it."

"Ma'am, Mr. Martin just got out of surgery three hours ago," the receptionist said. "He's still in the recovery room, and is likely sedated."

"I have see him," Ellen demanded. "Where is the recovery room?"

"I cannot tell you that, ma'am."

"You can either tell me or I'm going to start looking," Ellen insisted.

The receptionist asked Ellen to be patient as she picked up the phone and called Dr. Stillman. She asked the doctor to come to the front desk. "We have a situation here," the receptionist nervously explained.

"Just hold on for a minute, ma'am," she told Ellen. "Dr. Stillman is on his way. He is Billy's doctor and has been for a long time."

Ellen started to calm down, wondering if she had been jumping to misplaced conclusions. "Lord knows I have done it so many times before," she said softly to herself. "Maybe this is another one of those dead ends. I hope I didn't just make a fool of myself again."

Ellen grabbed two tissues from a box on the front desk and started wiping off the perspiration that had collected on her forehead and cheeks.

She heard a voice behind her that caused her to turn around.

"Can I help you, ma'am," Dr. Stillman said, introducing himself.

Ellen took a deep breath and wiped her mouth with the tissues.

"Dr. Stillman, my name is Ellen MacKay," she said. "I think Billy Martin is my husband Logan MacKay."

"Ms. MacKay, Billy is wrapped up from his nose to the top of his head," the doctor said. "And his face is so swollen right now that you probably couldn't recognize him, even if he is your husband."

"I have a way of recognizing my husband,' she said. "If you'll let me go in there for a minute, I can tell you for sure."

Dr. Stillman could tell that Ellen was extremely upset. Her hands were trembling as she clutched the tissues in her hand. Tears were starting to accumulate and work their way down her face.

"Just a minute," Dr. Stillman acquiesced.

"Thank you sir. I have waited 12 years for this moment."

Dr. Stillman laid his hand on Ellen's shoulder as he took her back to another wing of the hospital. He opened the door to the recovery room.

Ellen walked over to the foot of the bed, looking at the man. His face was covered in gauze and she could tell from the puffiness that his head was swollen. She silently walked over to the right side of the bed.

The blinds were closed and the lights were shut off. The only light in the room was coming from behind a bathroom door that was slightly ajar.

Ellen pulled a chair up to the bottom end of the bed. She was shaking so much, and she was worried that her legs would give way.

Dr. Stillman watched as Ellen started pulling the sheets out from the edge of the mattress to expose the patient's left leg.

Chapter 32

Ellen leaned over to take a closer look. There, on the side of his left calve, was the shamrock birthmark. Ellen couldn't speak but a soothing feeling cascaded over her body as she looked up at Dr. Stillman.

"This man is my husband," she said in a firm, yet calm, voice. "His name is Logan MacKay."

Dr. Stillman wasn't sure how to respond. He was sure, however, that Ellen had found her husband. Finally, after more than a decade, John Doe's real name had been revealed.

"Young lady, you stay right here," he told Ellen. "You don't have to go anywhere. Just take your time and I will be back in just a few minutes.

Dr. Stillman made a hasty exit, returning a few minutes later with Dr. Elkins.

"Ms. MacKay, this is Dr. Elkins," Dr. Stillman said. "He has been Billy's, I mean Logan's, physician counselor ever since he was brought in to Walter Reed. He would like to say a few things to you, if you don't mind coming with us for a moment."

"I don't want to leave him," she stubbornly replied. "Not now."

"Ms. MacKay, I know how you feel, but it's imperative that we talk before he wakes up," Dr. Elkins said as he stood by the recovery room door. "Please come with me just for a few minutes."

Ellen stood up and took a few steps toward the door before looking back at her bandaged up husband. She knew it was him as her hopes and dreams finally gave way to reality.

Dr. Elkins led her back to his office. They sat down and Dr. Elkins took hold of her trembling hands.

"Ms. MacKay, I need you to calm down," he said in an effort to get her attention. "You have to listen to me and understand what I'm going to tell you."

Ellen just nodded as she looked in Dr. Elkins' eyes.

"I have been treating Logan for nearly 11 years," he said.

"That man is like a son to me and his welfare is very concerning to me," Dr. Elkins continued. "Believe me when I say that I want the best for him. Here is our problem. When Logan arrived here, he didn't remember his name or anything else about his past. The only thing he knew that he was in a hospital and been treated for injuries to his hand and eye. We couldn't find any information on him. All we knew was that he had been picked up in the jungles of North Vietnam by two Montagnards. They called in a helicopter to pick up him.

"The soldiers in the helicopter were shocked at his appearance. He was a mess and must have been alone in the

jungle for years, judging by his appearance. The
Montagnards took care of him the best they knew how. They
gave him opium when he was in pain, which I'm sure
happened frequently. I'm sure that affected his mind in some
way. When he wakes up, he may not know who you are, or
why you are here.

"I know you will want to call your friends and relatives, but
for his sake I hope you hold off on doing that. I want to see
if he regains his sight, and the last thing he needs right now
is drama. Please, let's wait until the doctors remove the
bandages and we can assess his physical, and mental,
condition."

"Can I just sit with him until he wakes up?," Ellen pleaded
with a determined look on her face. "I need to be with him."

"Yes, you can sit with him," Dr. Elkins said. "But if you see
him starting to come around, you must come and get
somebody. We're going to have someone with him most of
the time anyway, but let's make sure this is handled
properly."

Ellen seemed to understand. Dr. Elkins escorted her back
down the hall to the recovery room. She sat back down in
the chair that was still beside Logan's bed.

"I'm going to have a nurse come in and check on him, so
remember what I said, Ms. MacKay," Dr. Elkins said in
earnest. "He doesn't need any more drama right now. He'll
have plenty of that soon enough."

Dr. Elkins left Ellen sitting there. She couldn't take her eyes off his face, which was covered in bandages from his nose to his hairline. There was swelling on his cheekbones, but she knew it was him. There was no doubt in her mind. She glanced down at his hand. The thumb and half of an index finger were missing. She reached down and put her fingers between his and held his hand tightly, just like she had done for 12 years as they walked to school. She remembered those days as though they had happened just a day before.

Doctors and nurses came to check on Logan every half hour. That night, around 11 o'clock, a nurse walked in to check on the patient.

"Everybody has left except for us," she told Ellen. "The doctors say they will be back early in the morning to remove the bandages. Otherwise, it is just you and me through the night. I will be right outside, at the nurses' station. If you see any type of movement, just press the red call button."

"I will do that," Ellen said as the nurse left the room.

Three hours passed and, as promised, the nurse continued to make regular visits.

Ellen had not moved since she had taken a seat, and she was getting tired. She pulled her chair closer to Logan's bed and laid her head on his shoulder before dozing off to sleep. All of a sudden, she felt movement as Logan's hand twitched. She started to move her hand, but Logan gripped it tightly.

She looked up at Logan in the dim light coming from the bathroom. He was moving his lips, but she couldn't understand what he was saying. She leaned in closer, putting her ear within an inch of his mouth.

"Hey cotton head," he said in a barely audible whisper.

"Yes, yes, it's me, cotton head," she said as tears started flowing down her face.

A big smile came upon Logan's face as she laid her head back down on his chest. His hospital gown began soaking up her tears.

Logan took his right hand and placed it on her head. "This is my cotton head," he said.

Ellen could not speak. She just tried to get closer to him. Her whole body shook as she cried. "Yes it is," she whispered repeatedly with trembling lips.

"It's going to be okay now, cotton head," Logan said as he put his arms around her shoulders. "How is mom?"

"She's doing fine, Logan," Ellen said. "She's living with me now."

"That's great," Logan said.

"A lot has changed in the last 12 years, Logan," Ellen said.

"I know and I'm so sorry."

Ellen held both of Logan's hands in her own. "There's something else I've got to tell you, but I don't know if I should tell you now or wait until later," she said.

"Tell me now while we're alone," he said. "It won't be this way later."

Ellen hesitated.

"I hope I'm not making a mistake by telling you this now," she said with a heavy sigh. "Here it goes. You have a son named Logan. He's 12 years old."

Logan didn't say anything. He squeezed Ellen's hand and slightly raised his head. She could see his bottom lip was quivering and the bandage around his eyes was beginning to get wet.

"Logan, I'm sorry I don't want to upset you," she said.

"I'm not upset," he said in a stronger whisper. "I couldn't be happier."

"You have met him," Ellen said. "Little Logan was at your baseball camp. He's the reason I am here."

Logan's lip kept trembling as he started to make the connection.

"I knew we had a connection," Logan said. "I could feel it, and he looks a lot like I did at his age. You have raised a wonderful son, Ellen, and I'm so proud of him."

"He really is a good boy, and I know he's looking forward to seeing you."

Ellen and Logan were so drawn to each other that they didn't notice Dr. Stillman and Dr. Elkins walking into the recovery room.

"When the nurse called us at home this morning, she told us you had gotten your memory back," Dr. Elkins said. "Is that right?"

"Yes sir, I have," Logan said. "I remember everything, from my childhood up until the time I got wounded in Vietnam. The next thing I remember, I was in that helicopter on my way to the hospital."

"So you remember this young lady sitting beside of you here?" Dr. Stillman asked.

"Doc, she has been my sweetheart since the first grade," Logan said. "Dr. Elkins, do you remember me telling you about the dreams I was having about an angel? You know, the one that saved my life?"

"Yes, I remember," Dr. Elkins said.

"I would like to introduce you to her," Logan said blindly held up Ellen's hand. "This is my angel and my wife, Ellen."

"I can sure see the resemblance based on what you told me about your dreams," Dr. Elkins said.

Dr. Stillman turned around and turned the lights on. "Well, I can see that both tear ducts are working," he said, pointing to the wet spots on Logan's bandages.

"Ellen, would you mind leaving the room until we're finished with this examination?" Dr. Stillman asked politely.

Ellen stood up to leave.

"No, Dr. Stillman, I want her to stay," Logan begged. "I want her to be the first thing I see, with one eye or two. I want her to be here with me."

"Okay that's fine, Logan, she can stay."

Dr. Stillman ordered Logan to keep both of his eyes closed as he cut and meticulously removed the bandages. Once the gauze was removed, he asked Logan to open his eyes.

"What do you see, Logan?" "I can see light," Logan said as Dr. Elkins moved around to the foot of the bed. "And I can see some dark movement."

"Just lay still for moment, Logan," Dr. Stillman said as he approached Logan to apply some eye drops. "We need to get your eye a bit more adjusted to the lights."

Dr. Stillman wiped off the excess liquid. He urged Logan to close his eyes again before slowly opening them. This time, Logan could see the doctors standing at the foot of the bed.

"I can see both of you okay, but not great," he said before looking over at Ellen.

"And there's my angel," he said with a wide grin on his face.

"Logan, I would like you to stay here for another day," Dr. Stillman said. "If all goes well, you and your wife can leave in the morning. I think your vision will be even better by morning. It's just going to take some time to fully heal. It may take up to a year or more before your sight is back to 100%."

*****

Dr. Elkins entered the recovery room early the next morning holding a sheet of paper.

"Logan, the best I can figure is that your memory loss must have been tied to your eye injury," the doctor said. "My best guess is that the corneal transplant triggered improved blood flow to the part of your brain that was blocking your memory. Dr. Stillman plans to release you today by lunchtime, with an understanding that you will be back on Monday morning for re-examination.

"It's going to take at least a year of follow-up exams and adjustments before you can be close to 100%. And remember no coaching for one year."

"That's fine, Doc," Logan said. "I can do that."

Logan and Ellen tearfully made their way around the hospital, thanking the doctors and nurses that had cared for Logan for all those years. Finally, it was time for him to check out and go home.

It was a beautiful summer day as Ellen and Logan walked down the steps holding hands. The sun peaked out from light clouds and a cool breeze cut across the parking lot.

"This weather is great," Logan said as he took in a deep breath of fresh air.

Ellen turned to Logan. "Where are you parked, honey?"

Logan coyly pointed in the direction of the far end of the parking lot.

"There are going to be a lot of people who will be happy to see you, Logan."

"Do they know I'm coming?"

"I called Debra last night," Ellen said. "She was going to go to our house this morning and explain everything to your mom and Little Logan. By now, they know that I'm bringing you home today. I'm sure they are excited beyond words!"

"I can't wait," Logan said as he suddenly stopped in front of his white Thunderbird.

"Is this one yours, Logan?"

"It sure is."

"You always wanted a '55 Thunderbird, Logan," Ellen said. "Even when we were kids, you always said you wanted a car like that someday."

"Well I've got one now," Logan said as he opened the door for Ellen to get in.

"I love it," she said, as they backed out of the parking space and pulled off to the main exit.

Logan noticed the bright green grass and the tall oak trees as he pulled out of the parking lot onto the drive out from the hospital, and he couldn't help but admire the beautiful landscaping.

Just before he got to the matching rock columns that flanked the way out to the highway, he looked to his left.

There on a slight hill in the distance, in the shade under a huge oak tree, was Sarge sitting in his wheelchair. Terry stood behind Sarge, and both flashed smiles at Logan. He stopped his car for a moment to gaze at them, and Sarge gave him a quick salute as Terry threw out an exuberant wave.

Logan saluted Sarge back, and waved at Terry.

"Who are they, Logan?" Ellen asked.

Logan quickly turned to look at his wife with a surprised look on his face.

"Can you see them, Ellen?"

"Yes, yes I can," she said, puzzled at his question. "It looks like a soldier in a wheelchair with a pretty young nurse standing behind him. Do you know them?"

Logan looked at Ellen with a big grin on his face.

"Yes, they are two close friends I got to know in the hospital, Ellen," he said.

"I will always have those two in my thoughts," he mused as he slowly pulled through the two rock columns and onto the highway, with Ellen clinging closely by his side.

The End

Acknowledgments

To my granddaughters, Avery and Sydney Wilson, for keeping me on my toes and inspiring me to be the best papa that a grandfather I can be. I love you with all my heart.

To my daughters, Heather Wilson and Malia Barrett, for all of your assistance with the research that was required for this novel. Thank you so much. I love you.

And to my son-in-law, Brad Wilson, for his assistance with researching and publishing this novel. Thank you, Brad, for your support. Love you man.

To Rudy Barrett, my son-in-law, who designed and created my webpage, and who was there for any technical advice that I needed. Thank you, Rudy, for all of your help and support. Love you man.

I would also like to give my thanks, to my brothers and sister, JB, Roger, and Linda, for the research they contributed to this novel, along with the moral support they have given me, not only for this novel, but throughout life. Thank you. Love you all.

A special thank you to Roger Axsom, for the use of the title of one of his songs he wrote years ago "A Whisper A Way".

To Penny Wilson, thank you for taking the time to proof read this novel, you helped me in a pinch and I appreciate that tremendously, love you girl.

Paul Davis, from Greensboro, N.C., is the editor of this novel. Paul has made this novel what it is today. Thank you, Paul, for doing such a great job, and for becoming a friend along the way.

I would like to thank Dawn Mitchell, G4G interactive Inc. for doing such a great job on the book cover, it looks great.

Made in the USA
Charleston, SC
16 November 2015